Sweetwater Sisters

A contemporary women's fiction novel

about overcoming trauma together

By Tiffany Nicole Terry (TNT)

TNTauthor.com

ISBN: 979-8-9946562-0-4

ACKNOWLEDGMENTS

I want to thank my sister for her fashion brand help, my early readers, my cover designer, Les, and my editor, Malory at The Missing Ink.

WARNINGS AND RATINGS

No animals or children are harmed in this book. Aside from cursing, it is a mostly clean book. Romance is behind closed doors, but sexual acts are discussed. There's a wake, talk of death, prayer, and the use of Tarot cards.

There's an exorbitant amount of whiskey drinking.

I would rate this book as a PG 16, depending on your teenager's reading maturity.

DEDICATIONS

For my sister.

I moved to Seattle after college, and my sister moved to New York City to go to college. During this time, I was inspired to write a story about two sisters who were completely different: they dressed differently, listened to different music, had different perspectives on life, dated different types of men, and even moved to opposite ends of the country.

When we were stressed out, we used to talk about opening a café and bar that offered everything from yoga to psychic readings. I still dream of having a dog park/bar someday where I can lounge, write, and let my dogs play.

This story is not based on our lives, only inspired by our differences. I am admittedly not the best at being a sister or a friend, my life consumed by work, house remodels, my husband, my children, dogs, and writing, but I know she forgives me for that, and our love is unconditional.

1 SAVANNAH

Summer in Seattle

Savannah's cell phone woke her up playing "Every Day Should be a Holiday" by The Dandy Warhols. Her eyes opened, looking up at the water-stained apartment ceiling that she swore sank lower and lower every night. She closed one eye and then the other, back and forth. Either her depth perception was jacked, she thought, or that ceiling would eventually fall in and smother her in her sleep.

She looked to the space beside her, turning her neck to confirm that her boyfriend was not tucked into the bedding of their full-sized mattress. It wasn't a surprise to find herself alone. In fact, if she woke up and found him sleeping peacefully beside her, that would be the surprise.

An involuntary grumble escaped from her chest as she heaved herself up and over to turn off her musical alarm. At twenty-two, it shouldn't be so hard pulling yourself up from the mattress on the floor, she thought, but every day felt heavier, like gravity was growing vindictive. Of course, it could just be that she was drinking a little more and more every night. She was sure that wasn't good for her body. Didn't they say that alcohol ages you? But she was still young. She had time to heal the damage she'd worry about later. Hopefully, many years later.

Savannah walked naked to the bathroom, threw a robe around her shoulders, and started to get ready for her first job of the day as a service bartender. Savannah really needed the hours since Jaxon seemed to spend more and more gig money on celebrating successful shows. Of course, she wasn't sure how successful a band was if they couldn't come up with rent money after a month of shows. She filled their bathroom sink with warm water, splashed it up onto her face to wash off the night's oil, then dunked her shoulder-length, dyed black hair into the white basin as best she could to flatten and restyle it for the day. When she first moved to Seattle from Nebraska, her hair had been long and dirty blond. Needing to completely rid herself of her small-town, plain Jane identity, she'd requested a pixie cut from a local salon and had it dyed a purply-black. No piercings or tattoos, though. *Well, not yet. Baby steps*, she thought. Defining an identity was expensive, and they were just barely getting by. To save money, she'd resorted to cutting her own hair herself and using $9 box dyes from the corner store.

Keys jingled in the hallway, and there was a familiar creak of the ancient, heavy wood door swinging open on sagging hinges. Savannah's eyes shot over to her phone, even though she knew what time it was. Her boyfriend was coming home from a late-night show that had ended around 2 a.m. He'd gone out drinking with his band, per usual, and stayed out until who knows when, passing out who knows where, to show up back home at noon.

"Savvy, you home?" Jaxon called out. His buttery voice was smooth, soft, and musical, and sent a mix of excitement and irritation, followed quickly by disappointment flooding her body. This wasn't a man about to come in, cover her in kisses, and carry her to the bedroom. No. She had shit to do.

Their apartment was small, just a studio with a kitchen that opened to the living area, one bathroom, and one "bedroom" separated only by a few freestanding dividers.

"I'm here," Savannah said, barely above a whisper, knowing he was literally an arm's length away from where he stood in the doorway.

"Mmmm," he purred, coming up behind her in the bathroom like a cat ready to cuddle up under her chin.

"I gotta get going, Jax," Savannah said, trying not to sound annoyed. Not hearing her, he started to pull off his sweaty black T-shirt. Her eyes traced the lines of his sinewy torso. He wasn't muscly, but he was lean and toned. Lord knows neither one of them could afford to overeat, so their thinness probably wasn't healthy. He worked out on the stage every night by jumping, shaking, and holding onto the guitar with fierce control. Savannah's exercise came from all the walking around the city, since neither of them had cars. They walked, bussed, and borrowed from friends if they really needed to go somewhere. His band would borrow vans from various friends and family to hit gigs up in Canada or down to Portland or even into California.

They hadn't ventured much further than that, but Savannah knew it was only a matter of time. Jaxon's band had one radio hit potential, and KEXP was starting to take notice. Her gut was telling her that Subpop Records would be reaching out soon to sign them. And then they would tour. Savannah knew she wouldn't be able to afford to go with them if they did start touring, and she didn't want to think about what that would look like for their already-strained relationship.

"We had a killer gig tonight," Jaxon said, taking her place at the sink to wash his own face.

"That's great, babe," Savannah said, heading to their closet to get dressed for her shift. June was pretty decent in Seattle, cooling down overnight but warming up during the day. She had to wear something that would last all day, since she'd be going from Reserve Café to The Drowned Note later that night. Light jackets seemed to work perfectly.

Back in her hometown, Savannah's parents owned a café and bar, so working in those establishments felt familiar and right. She knew she should choose a more professional and grown-up path like her older sister had, but she didn't feel ready.

Savannah's sister Sierra had moved to New York City right after college, taking a job in the fashion industry. Every day, Sierra dressed like a million dollars, walking tall and proud down the city streets like a supermodel. In contrast, Savannah chose a low-cut black V-neck shirt, a ripped pair of skinny jeans, and a black jacket with silver buckles. Jax was still talking from the bathroom, but Savannah's mind was drifting back to her hometown, back to a fight she once had with her sister over clothing. Sierra had been so mad at her for borrowing a shirt. It wasn't that Savannah had borrowed the shirt; the issue had been that she hadn't asked permission first and ended up spilling a drink on it at a party where she'd been with a bunch of high school friends.

There had been some spiked Kool-Aid mix, *red* Kool-Aid mix, and not only did clothing get ruined, but her best friend's carpet had gotten her grounded when her parents returned. That's when Savannah learned that if she was ever brave enough to throw a party, nothing with colored dyes would be allowed in the house. Nothing says your kids had a party like red Kool-Aid stains on the carpet.

Savannah's big sister had *not* been understanding about the stained shirt—not that she blamed her. Savannah looked up to Sierra, but the tall, popular sister had ignored the younger, shy one in high school, and then, when Savannah finally joined Sierra in college, it was like she didn't exist. Savannah also didn't last, flunking out and deciding to move with a guitar player she'd met up to the musical mecca of Seattle.

Jaxon walked out of the bathroom just as Savannah was crossing toward the front door. He had pulled down his shaggy blond hair from its bun, the waves cascading over his bare shoulders. He reached out and grabbed Savannah's hips, pulling her into him. He was only a little taller, so his belt buckle hit right at her belly button.

"You gotta run off so fast, Savvy?" he asked, teasing her with one of his many nicknames. There was a heat in his eyes and a coy smile on his lips as he looked down her V-neck shirt. She smiled and lovingly pushed him away.

"Shift starts in fifteen minutes, so yeah," Savannah said, trying to be sweet without sending him any mixed signals.

"I only need five minutes, tops," he promised, starting to pull her black jacket down from her shoulders.

Jaxon was always interested in sex, but never came home with enough time to provide her with any. Some days, it felt like their relationship had started with sex, and now, without time for it, there wasn't much of a relationship left. It wasn't like they had date nights or morning snuggles. They were on opposite shifts and opposite wavelengths.

"Five minutes is exactly how fast they'll evict us when I can't make rent this month, *Jaxxy*." She knew that the nicknames did not go both ways. What he felt was cutesy when he applied them to her did not apply when she gave him a nickname. Besides, Savannah might have thrown just a tiny bit of snark into the name to drive her urgency to leave to a point.

"Too right," he remarked, his eyes leaving her and floating over to his phone on the kitchen counter. "You gone all day?"

Savannah grabbed her shoulder bag from a hook near the door, readying herself to leave. "Yeah," she answered. "It's Friday, so I'm going from Reserve to the Drowned Note to open it for tonight's shows. You playing at Sound Den again tonight?"

He didn't answer her, so she paused with her hand on the vintage bronze doorknob and looked over at him. He was smiling at something on his phone, not listening to her at all.

"What?" he finally asked, looking over at Savannah.

"I'll be back around 3," she said, her voice lower, softer as if that would get his attention better.

"All right, babe. I'll let you know where we're hanging out after Sound Den.

Cool?" His eyes were back on his phone before Savannah even had a chance to answer.

"Cool," she said, walking out into the hallway, closing the door behind her. But it wasn't ever cool. Every night she came home from her shift around 3 a.m. alone, went to bed alone, and never received a text about where her boyfriend and his friends were hanging out, even if he'd promised her a hundred times that he'd text her. She didn't know if it was purposeful or if he just got too drunk and distracted to remember her. Of course, she didn't try reaching out to him either. She had, in the beginning, but after two years of the same routine, decided she preferred being home alone and sleeping.

Savannah walked out of the basement-level apartment, up a flight of stairs, and out onto a busy sidewalk. The afternoon sun was high in the sky, blinding her momentarily. Luckily, they weren't far from the bus stop, but she'd lost track of time and had no idea if she'd catch the next one in a few minutes or fifteen minutes. Being late wasn't a habit of hers, per se, but nobody had ever accused her of being punctual. Luckily, nobody was waiting for her to show up so they could finish their own shift, which bought her a little leniency. Her coworkers also knew she had multiple jobs and tended to work late into the night. But still, Savannah's schedule was up at noon, ready in forty minutes, catch a bus before 1 p.m., and try to make it to her first job by 1:15.

Savannah quickly walked past the usual shops, dodging pedestrians and leashed dogs, and people squatting by lamp posts, asking for change. She saw the bus approaching her stop and picked up the pace to a light jog. She grabbed a seat with relief, cringing at the smell of pee that one just never got used to. There was plenty of room on the bus, since all the corporate people were already tucked away in their cubicles downtown. The good thing about her schedule is that she always had a seat on the bus. The bad thing was that the buses didn't run at 3 a.m. Walking home late or finding cabs meant her pocket always concealed a knife.

Her cell phone vibrated in her crossbody bag just as she was climbing down the metal bus steps and onto the sidewalk. She rolled her eyes as she dug into her bag. Savannah's mother, Deborah, was the only one who still cold-called her without a text first.

"Hey, Mom," Savannah answered.

"Oh, honey, I'm glad I caught you. Did I wake you up?" Deborah's Nebraska accent was thick but charming, like musical lyrics in a country song.

"No, I'm on my way to work, but I'm kinda running late, so can't talk."

"Oh, that's no bother, I'm just so glad to hear your voice," her mom said. Savannah turned a corner and saw the dark-stained mahogany sign, the name Reserve Café embossed in gold-toned metal hanging up ahead, then picked up her pace. "How are things? Are you doing OK? How's Jaxon? Are you still in that apartment?"

Savannah took a breath. Her mother loved to pepper her with questions, but it was understandable since she hardly kept her mom updated otherwise.

"We're good, Mom. We work, we play, we sleep, we eat. We're getting by." Savannah stopped in front of the Reserve Café windows, hoping they'd see her stuck on the phone and know that at least she'd shown up close to on time.

Deborah was quiet on the other end for a moment. Her mom was never quiet.

"Mom?" Savannah asked.

"Well," she responded, seemingly coming back to herself. "I just want to make sure you are doing well. Are you happy? Are you doing well?"

A bus whizzed by Savannah on one side and a bicyclist on the other. The sky was gray, but it wasn't raining or windy. Her thrift-store jacket was warm enough, and she had jobs that helped her pay the bills. Jaxon's band wasn't super successful yet, but they were getting gigs. They only had the bare necessities, but their apartment was decent and comfortable enough.

"I'm pretty OK, Mom. Don't worry about me. But I gotta go into work now."

"OK, I'm glad to hear that. I love you, Savannah."

"Love you too, Mom. Bye."

Savannah hung up the phone and darted into the Reserve Café. The place was in full swing for the lunch crowd, so she waved to the hostess, then to the bar, signaling she was there and ready to help. The manager, Jerry, was standing at the back.

"Lunch started early today," Jerry commented as she gave him a nod on her way to her locker. Much to her disappointment, he followed her. He was a gentle, soft-spoken man with a rotund belly and a penchant for brightly colored clothing.

"I think we need you to get here a bit earlier, if you can, Savannah," Jerry said. It wasn't a question, and she knew the request had been coming. They wanted her to work more of a split-shift, which would be OK if she didn't also work nights at the Drowned Note. The hours were already wearing her thin, and if she came to work earlier, she would literally never see her own boyfriend anymore.

"I get off my night gig at 3 a.m., Jerry," Savannah said, turning to him as she tied her black apron around her waist. Although she knew she'd get warm running around the bar, she kept her jacket on to maintain a more complete look.

"I get that," Jerry said, "but there must be a way to figure out how to make it work. If you can't be here earlier to help start the lunch rush, I'm going to have to find someone who can. OK?"

"Yes, I understand," Savannah said, staring back at him for an uncomfortable moment. Finally, she shrugged. "OK, yeah, I can be here at 10:45." Savannah felt her eyes start to burn at the edges, thinking about how much less sleep she'd be getting and how tired she already was.

"Great, thank you." Jerry smiled and went back to the floor. She followed him, smoothing down wrinkles in her apron as she walked, moving to the bar to help fill server orders.

Landon and Lara were on opposite ends of the bar, buzzing from one customer to another. Savannah grabbed the stack of requests that had come from server tables and started working on the first order, a simple gin and tonic and a vodka lime. God bless simple drinkers.

"Hey, Sav," Lara said, coming up beside her to make her own customer a drink.

"Heeeeey," Savannah said, carrying out the vowel in a sarcastic here-we-are-again sound. Lara smiled.

"You get into trouble with Jerry?" she asked. "I saw him follow you back." Lara was taller and older than Savannah, with a head full of golden beach waves pinned back. She dressed in florals, lace, and wide-legged linen pants.

"Nah, he just wants me to come in earlier," Savannah said, shrugging.

"Sleep is overrated, right?" Lara asked, winking at Savannah as she replaced one bottle in the bin and pulled up another.

"I hear all the scientists are wrong about how much you actually need," Savannah added sarcastically. Lara smiled warmly.

Savannah moved her drink order to a tray and set it on the pickup side with the ticket so the server would know it was theirs. Then she grabbed the next ticket and went to grab glasses. Lara handed off her drinks and came back beside Savannah to scoop ice into her next order.

"Seriously, though, kid," Lara said, a gentleness to her tone. Lara was in her early thirties and sold paintings online. "The bohemian lifestyle only gets you so far. If you want to live in a van down by the river, that's fine. But don't waste your life chasing some guy as his groupie. Find something you care about and chase that. Find something that gives you purpose."

"Gee, thanks, Mom," Savannah quipped, turning to look for the grenadine. Lara laughed and turned to deliver the drink she'd made to her customer.

As Savannah put the next order of drinks onto the tray, she took a moment to look out at the space. The owners had designed a sophisticated café with rows of booths on one side and tables neatly ordered throughout the middle of the restaurant. It was quaint, simple, with mountain landscapes framed along the walls. The menu was delicious but fast, serving the needs of corporate workers on lunch breaks and tourists alike. Did the owners of this place have some sort of purpose, or were they just trying to run a business to make money?

Savannah's parents had bought a space and converted it into a café and bar in their hometown when she and her sister were in middle school. Even though Savannah chose to work in the business because she knew it intimately, having grown up in the service industry, she still felt resentful about the time her parents had committed to the café that had taken time away from her when she was just a child.

Jerry laughed obnoxiously at something a customer had said. Savannah honestly wanted to tell the manager to fuck off, that she wasn't going to come in earlier, that she needed her sleep, but she couldn't help but think about her father in that position as a manager, as an owner, needing more help. She took a deep breath. What was her purpose, anyway? Jaxon had a purpose. He created music. Lara created art. Photographers took those pictures that hung on the walls. The owners ran a business. And Savannah just made the drinks.

2 SIERRA

Summer in New York City

Pink's "Raise Your Glass" blasted Sierra awake at 7 a.m., and she immediately reached over and shut it off. The alcohol from the night before still pounded in her head. She and her roommates had all gone out after work at 6 p.m., but the happy hour had continued into a late night. Fridays at her office were never super busy, anyway. At least, that's what they told themselves as they ordered shots at midnight on Thursday.

"Whatever, I got this. Get your ass up," Sierra told herself, sitting up and scooting to the edge of her twin bed in her New York City apartment. Her room was small, but at least it was pretty private for sharing the apartment with three other girls. Each of them had an enclosed space for their twin beds, basically the size of the closet Sierra had as a child back home in Nebraska. They shared a bathroom, so there was a strict morning routine they all followed to ensure they had a turn to get ready, get out the door, and head to their jobs on time. Sierra's bathroom slot began at 7:05, and she only had fifteen minutes to shower and do her unpolite business.

The girls had all fashioned themselves makeup and hair stations at the foot of each of their beds in refinished trunks that some craftsman had added legs to in TriBeCa. Sierra loved little functional solutions like that.

She pulled on her pink floral pajama bottoms and top, then left her small room to go take her turn. As she approached the bathroom, she heard the unsettling sound of vomiting. Sierra didn't hesitate in swinging open the door to see Jamie on her knees, bent over the white toilet bowl.

"Jamie, it's 7:05," she stated curtly. Sierra tapped her barefoot on the beige tile floor.

Jamie sat up slightly, pushing her short black hair behind her ears, then grabbed toilet paper to dab at her mouth and nose.

"I can't exactly control it, Sierra," Jamie said.

"Yeah, but we have a schedule, and I need a shower. This," Sierra waved her arm around the small bathroom, indicating Jamie's poor lack of planning how much alcohol she could handle, "isn't my fault, and I need to get ready for work."

"Can't you pee in the shower?" Jamie asked.

"Gross." Sierra's nose curled up involuntarily, looking over at the shower stall. "Tell me you don't do that? Other people live here. Whatever, I can't deal with this right now. Move over."

Sierra reached over Jamie to the shower stall, turning on the knob to start heating up the water. She rearranged her towel so that it would be within reach of the shower, then carefully removed her pajamas to hang them where she could dress back into them when she was done. With her lip curled up in disgust, she maneuvered around Jamie and climbed into the shower, closing the floral curtain behind her.

Sierra had such little patience for people like Jamie. She always seemed to be running late, never had her shit together, and was just sort of floundering through life. It reminded her of her sister, Savannah, who was currently doing God-knows-what with God-knows-who in Seattle. She honestly couldn't believe that Savannah had left Nebraska. That girl couldn't plan her way out of a paper bag. If it hadn't been for that rocker-wannabe boyfriend of hers, she'd probably still be working at their parents' café and bar.

Sierra rinsed the shampoo out of her hair, then loaded up her long, dirty-blond locks with conditioner. Following her routine, Sierra pinned up her conditioned hair and grabbed her loofa and soap to wash. She'd used adhesives to affix clear plastic shelves along the back of the shower wall. There were four, one for each of the girls, so that their soaps, shampoos, and conditioners all stayed separated and didn't pile up in the tight corners.

Jamie purged again, and Sierra closed her eyes and cringed in response to the retching and splattering sounds. This was not how she wanted to start her morning—any morning, really. Since Jamie was still using the toilet, Sierra went ahead and peed in the shower. She had no choice. It was either that or hold it in painfully. What an inconvenience.

She rinsed the conditioner out of her hair, fantasizing about being out of this apartment and married to a successful man, living in a brownstone on the Upper West Side or an expansive apartment in Midtown. She'd be managing a team of product developers at Fytté by then, showing up in designer suits and taking long, glamorous weekends away with her husband. Opening up her eyes to her present reality, she groaned. She was only a stylist at Fytté and had a long way to go before she made any decent career progress. Worst of all, she was currently sharing a bathroom with three other girls, one of whom continued puking mere feet away from her.

Sierra grabbed her towel, a soft, fluffy pink one, and dried off from within the shower stall. She wrapped herself up, carefully stepped around the crumpled Jamie on the floor, snatched her pajamas, and headed to her room in a huff. Their next roommate, Sarah, was heading to take her turn.

"Good luck," Sierra said, rolling her eyes toward the bathroom she'd just vacated. Sarah's sleepy brown eyes shifted to follow her gaze, looking curious.

Sierra ducked back into her small room and chose an outfit from the portable metal rack. It was a stylish black and gray pin-striped suit with a light pink collared silk button-up shirt. She laid the outfit out neatly on her precisely made sage-green-covered bed, then opened the trunk to set up for her hair and makeup. After about thirty minutes, she was ready with perfectly understated natural makeup, blond hair dried and lightly wavy, and dressed like a girl working toward her next promotion. Sierra left the apartment, not seeing anybody else, and headed down the eight flights of stairs. They had one elevator, but it was small, slow, and smelly. On mornings like this, she preferred to whiz down the flights to get out to the street as quickly as possible.

The stairs ended in the lobby, a gray carpeted space with a wall of mailboxes and double glass doors. Sierra went outside and looked around the area first, for safety. In New York City, you never knew what you could be walking out into. She turned and headed into the heart of Manhattan, feeling good that despite the drama with Jamie, she was right on time. The early June morning was a perfect mid-sixties, but the sunshine above promised a hot day. She stopped at a cart for an ancient grain kolache and a black coffee. She walked many blocks to her office building and took the elevator to the Fytté offices on the twentieth floor.

The doors opened to a glamorous lobby, white marble floors, a large wooden desk with two receptionists taking calls, chandeliers, and mannequins staged with the latest Fytté styles. As part of her role, she had started styling the mannequins at the entrance. It was a huge honor, and one that filled her with pride the moment she stepped into their lobby every morning and when she said a silent goodnight to the mannequins at the end of every evening. Sierra loved the smells of the clothing, the sounds of people walking and chattering, meeting and planning.

She stood higher, pulling her shoulders back, then marched to the row of desks on the open floor behind the receptionist's desk. Her own desk was small, simple, with a top that could rise and tilt at an angle for drawing. Sierra wasn't really a designer, but she could start ideas, pull images together, then piece them together for the actual designers.

She set down her breakfast and coffee, then looked to see who else had arrived before sitting down. Nobody looked at her. Everyone walked past, heading to their offices or sat at the desks around her one-by-one without a word. Sierra didn't know what their problem was. All she wanted to do was be one of those women who supported other women. She wasn't interested in competing, but after two years at Fytté, she still hadn't made any good friends.

Her cell phone rang, startling her. She checked and saw it was her mom.

"Good morning, Mama," Sierra said in a polite but hushed tone.

"Hi, sweetie, am I catching you at a good time?" Deborah asked, her country accent charming. Her mother had grown up on a dairy farm in Nebraska, but had moved to the nearest town to marry a man who had a dream to open a community café and bar. Sierra and her sister had grown up helping their parents, cleaning up after customers, and doing their homework before the dinner crowd came in at that café.

"I just got to the office, but I have a few minutes before I start my day," Sierra answered. "How are you? How's Daddy?"

"Oh, good," her mama said with a sigh. Sierra heard the relief in her mother's voice at being able to get a moment of her daughter's time. "We're just fine over here, deary. Daddy just got a new shipment of some small batch barbeque sauce. He's excited, but it just tastes like regular ol' barbecue sauce to me. He always was one with the better taster."

"I'm sure it's amazing," Sierra said, keeping her voice low so nobody in the office could hear her conversation. Sierra also worked hard at keeping her Nebraska accent from sneaking into conversations. Since moving to New York, she'd tried to have a more non-regional accent. Hearing her mother's voice in her head made it difficult to avoid reverting back. "Daddy knows his sauces."

"That he does," Mama chuckled. "What are you up to out there?"

Sierra paused a moment. She had her life in order. Even staying out late last night, she'd woken up on schedule, adjusted to the puking disruption, and she'd made it to the office on time. Sierra looked at her Outlook calendar on her screen, showing the day's meetings.

"I've got a meeting starting in about ten minutes with my manager to go over the schedule for the day. I'm styling for a magazine shoot right after that, then running numbers…" Sierra trailed off. "Just work stuff, Mama. But I'm doing great. I'm getting it all done. You know me."

Deborah was quiet on the other end of the line for a moment.

"Mama?" Sierra asked, checking that they were still connected.

"I'm just always so impressed with you, Sierra," she said, finally. "You always seem to have everything under control. You've been planning most of it out since you were five. Now, I think it's all fantastic with you out there in New York City working for a big fashion brand." Deborah paused again as if she were thinking out her words carefully. "It's like I got two daughters on opposite ends of a spectrum. You're on opposite ends of America for Christ's sake. I just wish we could get us all together soon, maybe for the holidays this year, at least."

Sierra took a deep breath and straightened her pens and notepads on her desk for the tenth time during their call.

"I hear you, Mama. I'm just not sure I can get time off during the holidays. I'm pretty low in the pecking order, and all the bigwigs will want time with family. Fytté will have big events throughout the holidays that I'll need to help support. Big sales and new releases for the holidays."

"So, you're not as in control of your life as you thought?" Mama's soft tone had lost its levity. It was direct, nearly accusatory. Sierra felt her skin prickle, but didn't want to start her day off with a fight. If Sierra were being honest, she loved Christmas in New York City. She wanted to work the fashion shows. She wanted to network and build relationships with people who could help her grow her career. Sipping whiskey with her parents in an old café filled with townsfolk was not on her Christmas wish list.

"Mama, we didn't all start the same way as you and Daddy," Sierra said, trying to keep a friendly tone to her voice. "You both knew what you wanted to do, and you did it. You made sacrifices throughout the years, and that's what I'm doing now. I can't just come running home to visit when I feel like it, just like you couldn't just enjoy a family vacation with your daughters without shutting down the café."

"Well, maybe that's what I'm missing now," Deborah's voice was raised, and Sierra leaned back into her gray office chair. She hadn't meant to upset her mama. The woman was a saint. They spoke almost daily, but this call was starting to feel much more serious than Sierra was used to. She heard her mother take a deep breath.

"I'm sorry we didn't take you on big trips," her mama said. "I'm really proud of you chasing your dreams as fiercely as you have. I could never imagine living in New York City. I just see how your sister has underplanned everything, and you have overplanned everything. I think the best place to be is somewhere in the middle. I want to make sure you're enjoying the life you've so rigidly structured. I know you, Sierra."

Sierra closed her eyes and pictured her sister, Savannah, drifting aimlessly from man to bar to job to apartment. Mama was right about both of them. Sierra didn't feel safe unless she was controlling every aspect of life around her. It's what made her so damn good at her job. She anticipated every issue; she was ready for every meeting in ways her manager wasn't, and her mind calculated and designed five years in advance. She was almost surprised that she hadn't predicted her roommate's hangover because people just did not surprise her anymore, either.

"Thanks for looking out for me, Mama," Sierra said. "I'm alright. I'm making time for a little fun. But I gotta go now."

"OK, baby. I love you."

"Love you too, Mama."

3 SAVANNAH

Summer in Seattle

Savannah left the café and headed to the Drowned Note for her second job. It was only thirteen blocks away with a few corners. She passed the line at the front of the venue and went to the side door, knocking four rapid knocks to cue the man inside that it was staff. The door swung open, and Savannah nodded her greeting while passing the burly guy, going down a long dark hallway, and gleefully checking in at the bar.

"Hey kiddo," Mack said, winking. Savannah was pretty sure Mack did not know anybody's name, so she was grateful for the iPad he slid over to her so she could sign into her shift. She imagined a crime scene detective asking Mack about who was present at an event. He'd answer *the bartenders, the band, kiddo, kid, bud, buddy, big guy, shy girl, sexy girl, and legs*. She smiled and slid the device back to him.

"Alright, let's have a good night," he said. A manager and a bartender, Mack was dark-skinned with a head full of long dreads, smelled of weed, and had only worn the same exact outfit of natural fibers the entire year she'd worked here. She loved everything about his careless, loving, positive nature. She'd once seen him break up a fight before it started by smiling at the men and offering them free drinks if they'd toast each other. Pure peace, that man. She loved working for him.

Savannah turned around and scanned the empty theater. She took a deep breath. This was her church. Music venues were the one place she truly felt like herself. Being empathetic, she soaked in the sounds and the emotions of the place like a sponge, and that energy was always positive. The place smelled like bleach and booze before a concert. But when the people came in, when the band set up and sound checked, when the lights went down, and the first chords were struck, she felt enveloped in pure religion. Gospel.

She watched the servers, bartenders, bouncer, and assistant manager slowly enter, lock up their things in the back room, then emerge and start prepping their stations. The Drowned Note was a medium-sized venue, and Savannah had been able to see an assortment of bands of various genres. She wished she could buy their CDs and merch, but with her financial strains, she hadn't been able to collect as much as she'd wanted. All she really wanted to do was support these artists, but here she was working, not even having to pay for a ticket.

Most nights, the crowd was so thick and thirsty that she barely had a second to look up from behind the bar to watch the band. She took orders, sang along, smiled in reply to all the flirtations she received, but mainly just listened to the orders and to the music.

Savannah joined Mack behind the bar closest to the entry. There were two other small bars along the edges of the venue, but Savannah had only worked the main one. Once the doors opened, a steady stream of patrons funneled inside. She loved to see how much they matched their band style. The hipsters came for emo, straw hats came out for country or country rock, and the urban crowd came dressed in oversized, baggy pants for rap. She considered her own hairstyle for a moment, and how she'd chopped it off and dyed it in order to seem different and independent. However, on nights when the indie alt-rock bands played, she saw dozens of other girls with her exact short cut. Maybe there really is no such thing as individuality, she chuckled to herself, stacking clean glasses from the dishwasher.

The night went smoothly. Savannah maneuvered fast and friendly from customer to concoction to customer. The boys flirted, but nobody went too far. The girls were kind, which wasn't always the case. Some nights, a girl would throw daggers at Savannah simply because the girl's boyfriend flirted with her. Some men got grabby or propositioned her right there at the bar. Savannah rolled her eyes, remembering those nights. *What girl is ever swooned by a grabby, aggressively inappropriate drunk buffoon?* she thought, shaking her head as she scooped ice into a glass.

The opening band had come all the way from Dallas, and she adored them instantly. They were twin brothers with big hair playing a mix of original and cover electronic rock songs. The sounds reverberated in the cavernous space and dove straight into her chest. Their name, Nite, seemed to perfectly embody their musical energy. The light beams washed over her in funky patterns, and as she poured a whiskey drink, she was transported back to when her dad had played New Order and The Cure on their café's jukebox.

Growing up at a café and bar had been lively and strange, but there had also been dancing, singing, laughing, karaoke nights, and a mix of regulars and strangers. She saw her daddy, Dennis, in her memory, pouring himself a whiskey.

"Getting high on your own supply, Daddy," their mom, Deborah, would ask, always calling her husband Daddy.

"You know it, baby," he'd reply, shaking his butt to the music. "It's five o'clock somewhere."

"It's well past five o'clock here, ya ding bat," their mom had said.

"Exactly." Then he'd take the first sip with his eyes closed, and Savannah and Sierra would lock gazes, their grins growing wider. It would be closing time soon. Daddy's drinks always meant the night was winding down. Savannah and her sister would switch into cleaning mode, wiping down tables, gathering dishes, following their routine so they could go finish homework in the upstairs office, sneaking a couple of Cokes on their way.

A buzz in her pocket jolted her back into the present moment.

"Ugh, Mom, I'm working," she mumbled to herself, choosing not to pull the phone from her pocket. At twenty-two, nobody called Savannah except for her mother, so it was a fairly good guess.

She smiled up at a customer, a young man in his twenties who ordered a Jack and Coke. Savannah poured his drink, took his card, and slid it across the reader. She handed the man back his card. Her cell phone buzzed again from her pocket.

An uneasy feeling started to tingle up her spine. *No*, she thought, *I'm just feeding off the moody music.*

It buzzed again.

Savannah waved to get Mack's attention, and then she made the ASL symbol for bathroom, placing her thumb between her index and middle fingers, then shaking it slightly. He nodded and shifted his gaze to ensure her station was covered in her absence.

She quickly ducked out of the bar, pushed through a throng of people, then went to a hallway that led to the restrooms. For bars, their restrooms weren't terrible. Of course, there was a long line already at the women's. She passed by them and headed to a back-office door. She punched a code into the doorknob and slipped dimly lit closet-sized room, closing the door behind her.

Savannah leaned against the door and pulled out her phone. A number she didn't recognize from a Nebraska area code lit up her screen with multiple missed calls. Savannah bit her lip nervously. If the call was bad news, did she want to call the number back? She could just go back to the bar, pour a shot, work the rest of the night, and then deal with whatever this was later.

Her heart pounded in her chest. She knew she didn't want to return this call, but she knew she wouldn't be able to do anything else until she knew what this was.

"Please be spam, please be spam," she repeated as she hit the call button.

"This is Caleb Porter." The man's voice was deep but gentle, and almost…sad?

"Um… hi, I missed a call from this number," Savannah said, trying not to whisper or stutter.

There was a pause, and then, "I've been trying to reach the daughters of Dennis and Deborah Sweetwater."

A fire like Savannah had never experienced burned her cheeks and neck from the inside out, moving behind her eyes, to her ears, and up into her brain, eating her into a stupor.

She couldn't talk. She couldn't breathe. Her heart thundered somewhere in her ears, but it felt a thousand miles away. The stone floor moved below her feet.

"Is this Sierra or Savannah?" the man asked again, his tone even, his words slow.

"Savannah," she whispered, using the last bit of air from her lungs.

"Savannah," the man repeated. "I'm Caleb Porter with the Lincoln Fire Department. I was called to an accident tonight on the county line road, coming back to the city. I found both of your parents unresponsive. We did all we could to save them. Deborah had you both saved as 'daughters' in her phone, so I wanted to attempt to call you as soon as I could and have been trying both numbers. Are you able to come to Bryan Medical tonight?"

Bryan Medical. Medical. Deborah. County line. Accident. Fire Department. Words just kept flying into her ears and out, not tracking, not sticking, not making any sense.

Unresponsive.

"Dead?" Her voice choked out the word like she was burning in acid.

"Yes, ma'am," the man confirmed. "Your parents are deceased. I'm so sorry."

Savannah didn't look for a chair; she just slid her back down the wall until she was on the floor. *Dead.*

"Are you able to come to the hospital?" he asked, persistent but still calm as her world was crumbling like she imagined Seattle would in an earthquake.

"No," she whispered, still in shock. "I'm in Seattle."

"OK," he said, methodically moving through a script he'd probably used many times before. "How about your sister? I've been trying to reach her also."

"Sierra is in New York City," Savannah said, her words slow like they were trudging through mud.

"Well shoot," said the fireman. "If you could try to reach her, she's not answering my calls. Do you have local family? I know it's late. Listen, you have my number. Call me tomorrow after you and your sister have talked, and I'll help you coordinate from here until you can both get here, OK?"

The man's voice was kind, gentle, planning and pragmatic. It reminded her of her sister. Sierra was always better at handling business, drama, situations, life… everything. She needed to tell her sister. Sierra would handle it.

"OK," Savannah responded. Her body had slowly slid down the door, and she was now lying on the floor with her hand holding her phone to her ear, her eyes staring out dead-eyed across the tiny office. She fixed her gaze on a box. *What was in that box?* she wondered.

"Thanks. Call me tomorrow. And again, I'm sorry."

He disconnected the call, but she kept the phone to her ear like a conch shell. Would she hear the echoes of her parents' voices?

The door thudded against her back.

"Shit, what the hell?" came the voice of the assistant manager, Meridith.

"Sorry," Savannah muttered as she scooted her body along the floor.

"Savannah? What the hell? What are you doing?" Meridith's voice was high-pitched and shrill, but quickly regrouped. She'd never had an issue with Savannah, and Savannah wasn't one to cause trouble, so her tone turned from frustration to worry.

Meridith crouched down, bending over her to place a hand on her forehead. Meridith had a grown son, so the motherly gene ran deep. The woman's red hair cascaded down over Savannah like a forest on fire.

"What's wrong?" Her question was direct and emotionless, pressing to get to the honest answer quickly, not out of a lack of empathy. She had raised a son, after all.

The words circled in Savannah's heart and mind, but she couldn't bring herself to say them out loud. It wasn't real. It wasn't right. It wasn't natural. She was only 22. She was a child. She couldn't do this life without her parents. Right now, she was in a choose-your-own-adventure chapter book, but her safety net, her home, was still there with her parents in Nebraska. What was home if her parents were no longer in it?

"Mom," Savannah said in a gut-wrenching gasp bursting from her chest like a drowning person coming up for air.

Meridith needed nothing else. She wrapped her surprisingly strong arms around Savannah and pulled her up into her chest. Savannah's tears began to flow, heavy sobs pushing them to the surface, everything uncontrolled and raw.

"It's OK, sweetie, I've got you," Meridith whispered, just as her own mother had for years. After a few minutes of sobbing, Meridith asked, "What happened?"

Savannah didn't want to say it. She didn't want to put the words out into the universe. She didn't want to acknowledge that this was a reality that she and her sister would now have to face. But it was true. The words kept repeating over and over in her chest, blinding her vision, burning on her tongue.

"My parents," Savannah started, breathing in heavy heaves of air, sobbing and blubbering like a child. "They're dead." And then nothing existed but her cries and attempts to breathe through them.

4 SIERRA

Summer in New York City

It was four o'clock on a Friday afternoon in New York City. The sun was out, and so were all the thin legs in short skirts. Summer was upon them, and that meant long days and outdoor weekends drinking on patios. Sierra stole glances out at the sunshine while she waited for her boss to leave the office for the weekend.

Her roommates' group text was flying as the girls tried to decide on which new places to explore as soon as they finished their days. Of course, they'd all meet back at the apartment, head to the gym, then, after showering (nice to have that backup plan instead of all fighting over the one in their apartment), they'd stroll through the park on their way to dinner. They'd go to two different places for drinks before choosing a club where they could get lost in waves of people and sound.

Sierra smiled, thinking about how lucky she was to be living and working in NYC. She was living the dream she'd had since dressing up in her mother's shoes and makeup at five years old. Her sister would swim in her oversized hand-me-downs, not caring about the brand or whether or not she even matched. But Sierra was thoughtful, purposeful, saving her money up for a single trendy top that she'd wear for a full year before passing it down to Savannah.

Sierra sat up straight at her desk and smoothed down her A.L.C. tailored blazer proudly. The chic charcoal pantsuit with a pop of pink underneath was enough to make her feel like a successful executive, even if she wasn't one yet. She was dressing for a life she didn't have, but Sierra knew that was the first step to making it happen. She had accomplished every goal she had ever set for herself. Of course, working at her parents' café at a young age helped her do two key things. First, save the money she made from cleaning tables and serving customers. And second, get out of Lincoln, Nebraska.

She loved her parents, and she appreciated the life they had chosen for themselves. But Sierra didn't connect with the fields, the farms, the country folk, and the lifestyle. Growing up in Lincoln, she'd seen a lot of non-country folk, sure, but even in the quaint downtown area where their café was, even with the clientele that ranged from cowboy to college kid, she never fit in. She didn't want their life in that little place to become her life, too.

The café and bar lifestyle fit her sister, Savannah, more. Sierra was honestly surprised that Savannah wasn't still there, loitering by the jukebox, sipping whiskey with their dad. But some musician had rolled into town and swept Savannah so much off her feet, she landed in Seattle. Still working in cafés and bars, though.

Sierra rolled her eyes, thinking about Savannah's life choices. The girl was smart but lacked motivation. When Sierra had been studying, working, volunteering, and planning for college, Savannah had been skateboarding and daydreaming.

Sierra turned to check her text thread, but quickly dropped the phone into her lap. Her boss was moving behind her glass office walls. Sierra was grateful for the see-through office. *Fashionable* and *functional, at least for me*, she thought to herself, sitting up a little straighter and moving her computer mouse to check her inbox.

Margot Lancaster, Executive Product Developer and fashion icon, walked with so much ease in her six-inch Louboutin heels that Sierra would have sworn the woman's feet to be made of plastic… or steel. Margot floated in her direction, and Sierra put a controlled smile on her lips. It was respectful, thoughtful, not overtly kiss-ass or fake.

"Sierra, dear," Margot said, addressing her kindly but without returning the smile. "Can you rearrange some of my early Monday meetings? William and I are taking a short trip this weekend and may not be back until late Sunday. I want to make sure I am well-rested before the day begins."

"Absolutely," Sierra said with confidence. "I'll take care of that right now."

A small smile cracked the edge of Margot's bright red lips. "Appreciate you." Then the glamorous woman turned and elegantly strolled to the elevator as if on wheels. Sierra fantasized about herself walking with that level of refined class when she became a wealthy fashion icon and executive. Then she shook her head and took to task rearranging Margot's calendar.

As soon as she finished, Sierra began shutting down her workstation, checked the update on the text thread, and headed out of the office toward the apartment.

Friday afternoon followed their schedule right into Friday evening's dinner plans. The four roommates, the only three friends in New York that Sierra had made, all piled into taxis, walked across broken concrete, and stepped over dog poo in their nicest heels and shortest skirts. As the night got cooler, they pulled their jackets around themselves tighter.

And then they arrived at their final destination for the night, Club Win. Located on the Lower East Side, Club Win was so new that people only knew about it by word-of-mouth, which is exactly how people liked to keep things in New York City.

The four girls smiled and chattered loudly as they approached the line, shivering but excited. They knew they wouldn't be waiting long. In their early twenties, curvy, beautiful, with short skirts, they would be pulled from the line. Sure enough, a man who was about half the size of the bouncer walked down the long line, scrutinizing the patrons who were trying not to look desperate to be chosen. The four girls did what they always did. They stopped talking and posed, hands on hips, biting their lips, eyes sharp and sultry.

"You," the man said, jerking his head up at them. They tried not to look excited, but their lipstick-donned lips all snuck up into bigger smiles as they followed him to the door. The bouncer with muscles so big they needed their own zip code checked their IDs… barely, and let them in.

The four roommates walked in wide-eyed, not knowing what to expect. There was a narrow hallway lit by flush sconces along the walls on both sides. They followed the hall to a coat check table. A lovely young lady took their coats in trade for cash tips and tickets. Then they continued to follow the sconces up a staircase, the music getting louder and louder with every step. The staircase was wide enough where Sierra and Claire led the way with Jamie and Sarah right behind them. They reached the actual entrance to the club behind two heavy black velvet curtains. Two more bouncers pulled the curtains open for the women.

It took half a second for Sierra to spot the bar and then lead the young women in that direction. Claire, the fourth roommate with naturally red, curly hair, was right on Sierra's tail. Claire was the daughter of a prominent real estate agency owner and had become a realtor herself. Since she'd grown up in New York, had attended prestigious schools, and knew all the hot areas, she was connected to every new renovation, restaurant, and club. If you *think* you heard about a new hotspot in such-and-such area, she already had the name, address, opening date, and ratings.

Sierra had a loose blue Trina Turk top that flowed around her torso as she walked. Her black shorts were tight leather. Both girls walked fast and confidently despite their high heels. They landed at the bar together, looking back to see the shyer girls, Jamie and Sarah, lagging behind. Those two would dress up, but their heels were clunkier, their outfits more casual than nightlife glamorous. Oddly enough, more men seemed to gravitate toward Sarah. She had a softness to her. Her hair was warm, wavy brown, matching her brown eyes. She dressed reservedly but always with a push-up bra and a low-cut blouse. Maybe that was her secret, Sierra realized as she and Claire ordered everybody's regulars plus a round of shots, of course.

Jamie and Sarah showed up beside them, and Claire and Sierra handed over all the drinks. The four girls slammed the shots first, depositing the empties onto the bar top before easing themselves out into the club crowd.

The DJ mixed the current song into Jennifer Lopez's "On the Floor," and the girls squealed in joy as they started to dance together.

Jamie shook her short black hair back and forth while she danced. She was the one with the most layers on, and Sierra wondered if she would eventually get too hot in her black pants and baggy sweater. It was loose and low-cut, looking expensive, but Sierra knew Jamie had picked it up at a thrift store. Even though she didn't make as much money as Sierra, Jamie had really great fashion sense. The two girls had met in fashion school in New York, became friends, and eventually, roommates. They had met Sarah, who was literally talking to her mother on the phone about having to find an apartment while she was at the grocery store. Sierra and Jamie had followed Sarah around the store until she'd ended her call and then popped up like a couple of Looney Tunes, offering their own extra room.

Claire, with her curly red hair, green eyes, and freckled face, just showed up outside their door one day.

"Hi, I'm Claire Donovan, Realtor," she said confidently with eyes bright and full of fire. "I hear you have an extra room."

Sierra and Jamie had looked the young woman up and down. She was in designer clothing, her curly hair hanging perfectly in ringlets, makeup magazine worthy.

"This is not a fancy place," Sierra said, assuming the woman had misheard what was going on inside this building. Or maybe there were better apartments than theirs, and her expectations were misplaced. Claire just blinked and smacked her gum.

"I know," Claire had said. "The rooms are small. There's only one bathroom. I come from money, but I'm not made of it. I'm saving up for something specific, and I'm willing to make a little sacrifice. Besides… I need friends. Different friends. New friends."

Then she'd moved in, and there were four.

The night flew by in waves of colored smoke, pop bangers, equal parts handsome and hideous men, and drinks. Lots and lots of drinks. From time to time, the girls would check their phones, but for the most part, the people who contacted them regularly were already there, drinking and dancing together. They would go on dates, but none of the girls had serious relationships and weren't interested in anything serious. Claire was trying to avoid her parents and the friends she'd grown up with, like they were parasites, but she always redirected the conversations when old friends or parents came up. Sarah regularly went to temple and to dinner with her parents, siblings, and extended family. She was just quiet and seemed content with her life and her job in publishing.

Jamie, like Sierra, wasn't from New York. She had come all the way from Oregon, and, like Sierra, did not travel back home often. Sierra was pretty sure that Jamie was a lesbian, but they didn't talk about it. She didn't want to pressure Jamie or make it seem like it was a big deal. But Sierra knew that when Jamie did finally announce it, she would have her full support. It was the 2000s after all. No need to be weird about these things.

Sierra pulled her phone out to check the time. It was 1:45 a.m., and she had… twenty-eight missed calls. Some from an unknown Nebraska, number, and many from her sister in Seattle. Were there voice messages? Did she even know how to check voice messages?

"Shit, shit, shit, shit, shit, shit, shit, shit."

Claire's sharp green eyes lasered over to Sierra's brown ones. "What?" she mouthed in the room so loud it would be impossible to hear each other. Sierra turned her phone screen toward Claire. Her eyes flicked to the screen, then back up at Sierra. Jamie and Sarah had stopped dancing, and they all turned in toward Sierra's phone screen. Claire grabbed Sierra's hand, holding the phone, and like a conga line, the girls headed to the bathroom.

There was a pre-entrance room to the stalls, like a foyer with full-length mirrors and vintage cream couches. Gold chandeliers lit the small room.

Thankfully, there was one empty couch. Women came and went to check things, but very rarely just stayed in the bathroom foyer.

Claire directed Sierra to the couch, gently pushing her down by the shoulder, then she stood and crossed her arms, waiting and ready for anything.

Jamie shrank into herself, standing beside Claire, and Sarah dropped into the space beside Sierra.

Sierra sat straight up and looked first for texts, then voice messages. Nothing. This was going to have to be a call back to her sister. Then the phone buzzed, Savannah Sweetwater's name with a picture of her that Sierra had taken before she'd left Lincoln for the fashion school in New York.

She answered the phone on speaker. All her roommates were invested now, and it made more sense than trying to repeat it all later.

"Savannah?"

"Oh my God," Savannah mumbled in response, and then it was just sobs. Crying loudly with bits of words interspersed between breaths. It was like listening to Morse code. "Mama…don't…how…Daddy…fire…what…"

Just then, the phone popped up another call coming in. It was the same unknown one from earlier. Sierra hesitated, looking up at her friends. Something had clearly happened in Lincoln. Claire's eyes were wide. Jamie's hand was covering her mouth. Sierra knew that Savannah would keep balling and speaking incoherently. She needed to know what happened. She put Savannah on hold and answered the incoming call.

"This is Sierra," she said, switching into professional mode.

"Sierra Sweetwater?" a man's voice asked, gently, slowly.

"Yes," Sierra confirmed.

"My name is Caleb Porter, and I'm with the—"

"What happened?" Sierra asked, cutting him off.

"Right. Sorry. Your parents passed away tonight in a car accident."

"No!" Jamie screamed through the fingers pressed against her lips.

"Oh, Sierra," Sarah said, the words rushing out as she placed a hand on Sierra's shoulder.

Claire's lips tightened, but she said nothing.

"You're with friends?" Caleb asked. "That's good. I also called your sister, but she said you are both—"

"Out of town, yes." Sierra closed her eyes. She couldn't believe she cut this man off for a second time. This stranger, a first responder, who probably saw her parents in the most horrific situation of their lives, who maybe tried to save their lives, putting out the flames that engulfed them, had made multiple attempts to reach her and her sister in their darkest hour.

"It's almost 2 a.m. here," Sierra said into the speakerphone, taking a calming breath. "You can text me more details tomorrow. I will start making arrangements to come home tomorrow."

"Yes, of course," Caleb responded. "I will keep in touch. And please, call me anytime. I'm happy to help in any way I can."

The screen was blank. It was just a number, but Caleb's voice was kind.

"You've done a lot tonight, Caleb. You have helped, and I thank you for everything you do. I will reach out if I need more information. Thank you." Sierra disconnected the call before he could respond. The girls immediately closed in on her, talking all at once, and then Claire said louder than them, "Your sister!"

"Oh shit," Sierra said, pulling her phone back up to her face to reactivate the on-hold call with Savannah.

"Savan—" but the wailing and sobbing were still there, right where she'd left it. Her little sister was hysterical. With only two years between them, sometimes throughout their lives, Sierra had felt like it was more like a 25-year difference. She squeezed her eyes tightly together and switched into the older sister-tone.

"Savannah," she said firmly. "I need you to take a deep breath."

The girl on the other line continued sobbing.

"Breathe," Sierra repeated calmly. Steadily. "Deep breath in." She heard her sister from over two thousand miles away, finally take a heavy breath.

"Savannah, where are you?"

"At… work…" she said between shorter sobs.

"Can you get back home? Can you get a ride? Can your boyfriend come get you?" Sierra peppered questions, trying to make sure her trainwreck of a sister could keep herself safe in this situation. Ever since they'd been children, Sierra had been the child to bite through the pain of falling off her bike, but her sister would bawl if the cat scratched her as if she'd been attacked by a mountain lion. It drove her crazy.

The sobbing lessened on the phone as Savannah considered her sister's words. 11 p.m. in Seattle meant her night shift at the music venue was just starting. This wasn't a woman who could face a tragedy and then get up and go pour shots for customers. She needed to go back home. But this also wasn't a woman who could get herself safely home while in hysterics.

"Can you stay in the office until closing, until someone can take you home?" Sierra's voice was strong, firm, loud. She heard her sister murmur on the other end as if saying yes or considering. "Savannah?" she pressed.

"Yes. I can stay here." Savannah's words were breathless, strained, but she sounded genuine.

"You can use a ride-hailing app, but make sure a coworker walks you to the ride if none of them can give you a ride, OK?"

Claire took a step forward, and Sierra looked up. Claire was shaking her head, knowingly. "Just stay on the phone with her. Let's go get our coats and head back. We'll catch a car, and you stay connected until she gets home."

Sierra's nostrils flared, trying to hold herself together. For a moment, she'd forgotten that she wasn't sitting there alone, talking to her distraught sister on the other side of the country. She nodded, and Claire took over, leading the way through the club to the coat check. She took Sierra's ticket, got her coat, and helped her into it while she held the phone, still on speaker with Savannah crying on the other end.

The girls were silent on their way home. Claire was the only one who spoke when necessary to steer them as a collective or address someone in their way. They all listened to Savannah sniffling, crying, and heading back to her own apartment.

An hour later, Sierra fell asleep listening to her sister's keys jingling into her Seattle apartment's lock.

"I'm home," Savannah said, letting her sister know that she'd arrived safely.

"No," Sierra muttered as she drifted off. "We're not."

5 SAVANNAH

Summer in Seattle

She woke up around 5 AM on a wet pillow, the fabric sticking to her face. For one blissful moment, she was confused about the feeling until she remembered. She wasn't just Savannah in Seattle on any other early morning. Her parents were both dead. Tears welled up again, although she shouldn't have an ounce of water left in her body at this point.

She went between trying to sleep and crying for a few more hours before she called her manager at the Reserve Café. She texted Mack at the Drowned Note, even though she knew she didn't have to. Since she'd felt so out of it last night from the time Meridith had cradled her in her arms, she faintly remembered the woman telling her she'd let Mack know what happened. She'd put Savannah into a car, paid for by the bar, and sent her back home to her apartment before her shift had ended. Sierra had been on the phone with her the entire time.

It was strange, after all that, to wake up alone again. She knew that her boyfriend had no idea what had happened and was just out partying with his bandmates and friends. Savannah had tried to call him after getting to the apartment, but he hadn't answered. Texting him or leaving a voice message hadn't felt right.

A spark of jealousy jolted up her spine, and then she pushed the feeling aside, as she had for years. She couldn't be with Jaxon on his way up, enjoying the live music without working a bar, taking terrible cell phone videos from the crowd, but she could still support him. Savannah couldn't help but see the wide eyes, the big, red-lipped smiles of the women in Jaxon's crowds every night. They haunted her dreams.

She turned onto her stomach and screamed into her pillow, trying to drive the images away. Here she was in the most traumatic event of her life, and she saw women throwing themselves at her boyfriend. Savannah rubbed the tears from her eyes and tried to focus. She pulled her phone up and scrolled to Jaxon.

Please, she started to text, but her mind froze. *What am I asking him? Am I telling him my parents died over text? Am I asking him to come home? His show is over. He shouldn't need to stay out. He's just out for fun—like every night. It's not like he's drinking with music producers.*

Why did she feel guilty disrupting him from his fun night out with the guys? She wanted to scream again, but swallowed it back down.

Hey, she texted. *My parents…* her fingers shook as she typed the words, *I just got a call that my parents died.*

She threw her phone across the room and broke down into howls of sobs again.

It took fifteen minutes for her to recover enough to climb out of bed and find her phone. When she unlocked the screen, her text was still there, waiting to be sent.

There was nothing more to say, she realized. Nothing more to add. No request for him to come back to their apartment. She hit the send button and then plugged it into the charger. She peed and then went back to hide in the sheets.

Jaxon was probably at a bar five minutes down the street. Downtown Seattle wasn't much to travel across. You grab a cab, a friend's car, or even walk it in fifteen minutes. Savannah fell asleep and woke up to his keys in the door several hours later.

She woke up but stayed quiet. She knew it was after noon because the sun streamed in through their thin curtains. Savannah kept her eyes closed and waited. She wasn't sure why. She'd been distraught, crying all night, tossing and turning, then finally falling asleep. Some small part of her romantic, feminine mind expected her boyfriend to swoop in and support her throughout this traumatic life event. She knew it was what her dad would have done for her mom.

Savannah loved her parents. She'd had friends over the years expressing different feelings like hatred, spite, animosity, and even fear toward their own parents. There were friends who couldn't keep up with the unrealistic expectations their parents had placed on them. She had friends who felt like they were never good enough. Some felt pressured into marrying, pressured into becoming doctors, pressured into choosing one political party over another, or a certain religion. But Savannah couldn't relate.

Her parents had always just worked and parented the best they could. They were loving, kind, friendly, pillars of their community without altering their values. They shook hands with the richest members of Lincoln, sent their daughters to the college, and fed the homeless. They hadn't yelled at her or judged her for running off to Seattle with a musician she'd just met. Her parents were amazing… *had been* amazing, she reminded herself, her eyes burning again, nose running onto her sheets.

"Savannah?" Jaxon's voice was gentle but came from the edge of the bed, so far away.

"Yeah," she whispered in response.

"What's going on?" he asked as if he hadn't seen her text. As if there was something wrong with her.

She squeezed her eyes tighter, trying to collect everything about her emotions before rolling over to face him. It took all her energy to roll over.

He stood at the edge of their bed wearing his country rock uniform: cowboy hat, black tattered shirt, leather jacket, black skinny jeans ending in boots he'd bought at a thrift store on Broadway. His hair was pulled into a messy bun. He played with it down, for effect, but the heat and sweat always caused him to pull it up.

"My parents," Savannah started with all the confidence in the world. She was going to get the words out. She was going to tell him how she felt, how they had been the best parents in the world. How it wasn't fair. This wasn't right. And then she melted into hysterics again.

He climbed into the bed and took her head into his lap, the same way that Meridith had, but without that parental love, that energy that can heal all wounds through sheer force of empathy.

"Baby, I'm so sorry," he said, stroking her short black locks back from her face. "What happened?"

"It was a car crash back home," she said in a whisper, straining through her tears.

"Was it their fault?"

Savannah jerked up so fast it made her dizzy. "Why would you ask that?"

"Didn't you say they work at a bar?"

"They aren't drunk drivers, Jaxon," she nearly spat the words at him, snot mixing with salty tears covering her face. She tried to rub it all off with her arm, but glared at him. What kind of question…

"I'm sorry, OK?" he said. "It's just such a random thing to happen, and I wondered what happened."

Savannah couldn't look at him. She turned her face toward the interior of their small apartment as if searching for an answer. Her memory clicked in, and the firefighter's words on the phone came back to her.

"A deer ran across the front of their car. It was dark. Rainy. They didn't see it." She could hear the curtness in her own words, but she didn't care. He had turned her grief momentarily into hot anger.

"How could a deer possibly cause a wreck that would kill them?" Jaxon asked. Savannah's head snapped back faster than a slingshot.

"Deer can weigh up to 200 pounds!" she yelled. "If a deer hits you at sixty-miles-per-hour, you die."

Savannah and Jaxon just stared at one another across the bed. He looked lost, confused, and completely unprepared. Here was this man who had started a band, could play multiple instruments, but mostly guitar—something Savannah just hadn't been able to master—sang deeply beautiful songs, emotional songs, and yet he looked completely confused in this real moment of true tragedy.

"And they did," Jaxon said, filling the silence.

"What?" Savannah's heart was beating in her chest, her mind whirling with emotional turmoil.

Jaxon reached his hand out and placed it on her leg. She looked down as if she'd never felt Jaxon touch her before.

"Your parents died," he said, slowly, like he was telling her this news for the first time. Her brown eyes jerked up to meet his. The anger within her chest bubbled like water in a pot on a stovetop, but she didn't know why. She wanted to yell at this man that she knew that already. But before she could unleash the emotions, he spoke again.

"Are you going to go back home?" Jaxon asked.

Savannah looked toward the window in their apartment. *Shit*, she thought. *I have to go home. I can't just stay here and cry. There are things to do. Oh my god, what am I supposed to do?* She immediately pictured Sierra handling it already. Her sister would have the answer, and she needed to call her. Instead, she looked at Jaxon to answer his question.

"I have to," she said. Her hand shot out to grab the hand he had on her knee. "Will you come with me?"

Jaxon's nostrils flared, and his eyes went wide. He leaned back and pulled his fingers slowly out of her grip.

"Ohhhh, babe," he said. "Savvy, you know we have shows for the next six weeks scheduled, and there's the festival in Portland. I can't leave the band right now."

The air in Savannah's lungs turned to stone. Although she had cried all night and throughout the morning, she felt a new well building up behind her eyes. She felt instantly sorry for herself as if she were the loneliest woman in Seattle. She pulled her hand back and crossed her arms, turning to look through the window. Then she turned and made a quick inventory of their apartment. She didn't know why, as it seemed more like something Sierra would do.

If the apartment were on fire, what would I grab? she wondered.

"Savvy?" Jaxon nudged her bare leg softly, as if trying to wake her from a trance. Maybe she was in a trance. Tears and snot flowed from her, but she was trying to think beyond the next few hours. She had to fly home, she knew. She had to book a flight… shit, an *expensive* flight… and pack a bag. She had to call her managers and let them know she'd be gone for… how long?

Savannah closed her eyes tightly, shutting off the flow of tears for a few seconds. Her sister would know what to do. She'd know how to manage an estate, the café and bar, the house, the funeral, everything.

"I'm OK," she said, finally, opening her eyes to meet Jaxon's—although he seemed like he had something more important to do than to be concerned about her. "I have to book a flight back to Nebraska."

Jaxon's eyes shifted to his phone, and he started to scoot off the bed, standing up like a lean dream in his tight jeans. The bed had barely dented underneath his weight. She felt another instant loss as her body called out for his physical comfort, his touch, his hands, his lips, anything. But he just walked away, staring at his phone.

"Let me know when you're coming back," he said before disappearing into the small bathroom.

Savannah's eyes narrowed, and the momentary flash of desire vanished. Something clicked like hitting play on a movie, and she started to process through the steps of booking a flight, packing a bag, texting managers, texting her sister her flight information, and for some reason she couldn't explain, taking inventory of her apartment as if this could be the last time she ever saw it. She had no idea how long she would be in Nebraska. It wasn't just going there for a funeral; there would be a lot of work to do and things to take care of with her parents' property and business.

The bathroom door was shut, but she heard Jaxon texting away on his phone, chuckling lightly to himself. Here she was experiencing the most traumatic thing that had ever happened to her, and he was taking a shit, giggling. *Is this what being in the* Twilight Zone *is like?* she wondered.

No. It's grief. Savannah was experiencing something that nobody else, aside from her sister, Sierra, would understand. Every sound Jaxon made sent shivers up her spine, an anxious tingling of anger and the fear of something she couldn't quite explain.

She pulled a suitcase out of a closet. She didn't have much. Clothing, shoes, mementos. She could pack up her entire life and leave. Sure, the furniture was there, but she wasn't in love with it. There were a few framed pictures she'd gotten from thrift stores around town, but nothing priceless. If the apartment were burning down, she could just walk out with her wallet, phone, and be fine. She had enough cash in the bank to buy a new wardrobe from the thrift store.

Why am I thinking like this? she wondered. She was coming back; she just didn't know when. She didn't know how long all of this would take, so she needed to pack as much as she could, which just so happened to be everything she owned.

"Whoa, babe, you taking the big bag?" Jaxon asked, coming out of the bathroom and into their bedroom just as she was zipping everything up into a floral duffel bag. All she needed was her bathroom toiletries, and she'd be done.

"Yes," was all she said, searching for one-way tickets now on her phone.

"You think you're going to be gone that long?" he asked again, sidling up to her. The song lyrics, 'you only love me when I'm leaving' drifted into her mind, but she ignored them and him and kept searching for the next flight out of SeaTac that she could reasonably get to in time. Prices were crazy high, but she still had room on her credit card.

Savannah wasn't sure if he knew he was being ignored or if he cared, but he eventually climbed into the bed where he'd rest before his next show. She briefly considered not saying goodbye. It sounded poetic, just taking her bags and drifting out into the daylight, flying away from him for some undefined amount of time.

Fear clenched her gut as she booked her tickets. What if Jaxon didn't care whether or not she came back to Seattle? What if he didn't care whether or not she said goodbye? Was this it? If she left this man alone, trying to afford the apartment on his own, women throwing themselves at him nightly, friends with couches for him to crash on, would he just be freer to live his dream life? She looked up toward the bedroom. It was just a partitioned space in a studio apartment, not a room at all, and yet, Jaxon seemed like he was off in his own little world. She set her bag onto the floor and then turned to face him, sweat trickling between her breasts beneath her shirt in the un-air-conditioned apartment.

"I'm coming back, you know," Savannah told him. He was lying across the bed in just his boxers, looking at his phone, but settling down. He glanced up, that wry smile gliding across his face.

"I didn't doubt it, Savvy," he said. "Come here." He clicked his screen off and slid the phone underneath his pillow, patting the space beside him with his other hand. Savannah slid into the bed, snuggling into him, breathing him in. He smelled like sweat, leather, and cigarette smoke. They wrapped up in each other, and Savannah let him take her clothes off, knowing it wouldn't be too long before she'd be heading out to catch her flight home.

6 SIERRA

Summer in New York City

Sierra woke up to Claire standing over her.

"What time is it?" she wondered out loud.

"9:02," Claire answered, precisely. "I've booked you a flight to Lincoln at 1:13. You'll be home by 6:22 this evening."

Confusion flooded through her mind like a cloud. "You did what?" Sierra asked. Claire knew numbers. Loved numbers. Loved being precise—but had the woman actually gone out of her way to book a flight for Sierra?

"I booked your flight," Claire confirmed. "I'd pack your bags for you if I could, but that would probably cross a line. Time to get up."

Sierra heard Claire start to rummage through her tiny room, maybe looking for a bag, and she sat up wearily. She wasn't sure how long she'd stayed on the phone with her sister, but Sierra knew she hadn't slept enough for this.

Then the memory of the night before came back and struck her like a lucid dream. Her sister on the phone, balling. The first responder's deeply gentle voice. Her parents... She sucked in a breath and shot straight up out of the bed.

"I got it, Claire," Sierra said, probably too harshly, but her eyes were burning, and her stomach ached. "Could you get me some water?" she asked, trying to sound kind while giving Claire a distraction.

"Absolutely," the woman said, bounding off on her mission, red curls bouncing with her exit.

Sierra took a breath and pushed the realization that her parents had died behind a door in her head, shut, and locked it. Once the memory of pain was compartmentalized, she opened her eyes and surveyed her room, putting her mental list together. She needed to thank Claire for booking the flight. Then she needed to pack a week's worth of clothing, at least. She needed her toiletries, makeup, and hair products. She needed to call work and take bereavement leave.

Home. Nebraska. There would be a funeral to arrange. She stood in front of her rolling wardrobe, the beige fabric already unzipped and hanging open. She slid one article over and then another, surveying her collection. Staud maxi dress, Anine Bing jacket, Favorite Daughter pantsuit, processing options one-by-one as if on a conveyor belt of designer depression.

Sierra grabbed a handful of black articles and tossed them onto her unmade bed. At least she could take something nice with her for her sister to wear to the funeral. Savannah had never been into fashion and was used to wearing Sierra's hand-me-downs. If the clothes didn't come from Sierra, they came from strangers via thrift stores. Granted, her sister did have a good eye for second-hand fashion, but for this occasion, she wasn't sure Savannah would have a black outfit worthy of wearing next to anything Sierra would wear.

"Water," Claire said, handing Sierra a plastic cup filled to the brim. She took the glass and chugged it; her body parched from alcohol dehydration and tears.

"Thank you, Claire," Sierra said. "For booking the flight, for taking care of me last night and today. I'm just…"

"Lost?" Claire asked, finishing her sentence.

"Yeah," Sierra answered, nodding slowly as her eyes drifted down to her pile of black clothing.

"I got you. Sit," Claire commanded, motioning to her bed. Sierra, reluctant to relinquish full control, still sat down due to her exhaustion. Claire cycled through lists of basics out loud: bra, panties, socks, daytime clothing, comfortable plane outfit, shoes to wear, shoes to pack. As Claire organized options into neat piles on the bed, Sierra went to the restroom to pee and grab her toiletries.

When she finished in the bathroom, she headed back toward her room with a toiletry bag, makeup bag, and a hairbrush. She'd be staying at her parents' house, her house, so she knew she wouldn't have to bring styling tools. Her mom had everything.

A wave of emotion washed over her as she realized she'd be going to an empty house. Her parents wouldn't be there. Sierra froze just as Sarah came out of her bedroom.

"Sierra? You alright?" Sarah asked, moving toward her.

Sierra's eyes filled with tears, and her nose burned. She turned to Sarah, whose thick brown hair was messy from sleep.

"I'm going home today," she said. "Claire got my flight, and we're packing."

Sarah was standing beside her now, stretching her hand out to touch Sierra's arm. Sierra bit back her tears. "But are you okay?" Sarah pressed.

The tears fell, and their tiny apartment got even smaller. Sarah pulled Sierra into an embrace; the makeup bags squeezed between them.

"They're not going to be there," Sierra said, finally giving in to the emotion and the tears. She sobbed so loudly that both Claire and Jamie came out to join the empathy hug. It only lasted a few moments, and Sierra regained control of her emotions, wiping her face and shooing them away so she could focus on packing.

Feeling grateful for her friends, Sierra waved goodbye to them later that morning and climbed into the back of a cab. She swept away all emotion and was now dutifully focused on all the tasks at hand. The checklist she created on her phone was getting longer with each minute as new things came to mind.

Thankfully, she was able to fall asleep on the plane, her head resting comfortably in a neck pillow. She awoke hours later just in time to see the patchwork farms turn into neatly organized neighborhoods just on the other side of the Lincoln airport.

The cozy airport was a relief after the hustle of New York. She loved city life, craving the noise and people, but the country music piping through the halls, the university advertisements lining the walls of the terminal, the baggage claim already handing out bags, and the short walk to the cabs was better than landing in larger airports, where landing only meant traveling more on trains to reach home. She was home. No more waiting.

Sierra let the cab driver rattle on about the weather and local politics while she checked her messages. Her roommates had all been active in their group text, where she let them know she'd landed and was on her way home. Savannah would join her at the house in a few hours, and then their parents' CPA, who happened to be the executor of their estate, would meet them there.

Tears began to well in her eyes just thinking about how Millie would swarm them with hugs and sympathy. Sierra sucked a breath in through her nose, trying to quiet the emotions building.

Pulling into her old neighborhood felt surreal, like moving through a ghost town in the middle of the desert. Everything was the same, but nothing made sense. Something was missing.

"Here we are, ma'am," the driver said. Sierra paid him with a phone app, and then he helped put her suitcase onto the curb.

The house she and her sister had grown up in was an old Craftsman two-story house painted blue with white shutters. It was shrouded in overgrown evergreen trees. Even though it meant that grass could never survive in the yard, her mother couldn't resist planting trees around the property. Most of them had come from Christmas parties they held at the café over the years. The rest of the neighborhood houses had maybe four trees each, but their house was hidden by a forest of at least twenty of varying heights, all smooshed together.

Sierra took a deep breath and walked up the front, broken concrete pathway toward the porch steps, rolling her suitcase behind her, a bag and purse slung over her shoulder. She dropped it all in front of the door and fished out her keys.

Sure, there'd been hundreds if not thousands of times she'd put the key into the lock and opened the door, but this was different. She walked into an eerie silence with the weight of emptiness pressing down on her like a heavy blanket.

The front door opened to a small foyer, a staircase on the left, and a hallway on the right that went back past the living room and into the kitchen. Her parents' bedroom was toward the back of the house. She dropped her things in the foyer and walked down the hall, flipping lights on along the way. The kitchen was as she remembered: small, a flood of warm maple brown colors, clean, and devoid of food since her parents mostly cooked and ate at the café.

She sat down at an old, heavy wood table, her memory flooding with rushed footfalls and laughter as her younger self got ready for elementary school. Her parents hadn't opened the café and bar until after Savannah and Sierra were both in middle school, so the girls had taken responsibility for themselves, making cereal, getting dressed, and then biking off to their school. Once she could drive, she would take herself and Savannah. The mornings had been quieter then, and almost as empty as the house was now.

Sierra turned her head toward her parents' bedroom, where she knew she'd find the most proof of their existence. There would be clothes on the bed, shoes on the floor, toothbrushes on the countertop. She closed her eyes, knowing that she wasn't ready to go in there. Not wanting to sit still, she went back to get her belongings and carried them upstairs. Although humid, the weather was currently similar to New York, drifting around the mid-seventies but threatening to bring the heat soon. She'd still worn a heavy hoodie for the airplane, but now pulled it off and carried it upstairs with her bags.

The house was simple. Up the stairs to the left was a bedroom directly above her parents'. It's the room that Sierra had grown up in. Down the hall was her sister's room, and they had shared a bathroom in between.

Her room was just as she'd left it when she'd moved to New York after her first two years of college. Her bed was a standard size, covered in white sheets and an oversized blue comforter. She was sure that her mother probably washed the bedding to keep the dust off at least once every few months, just in case her daughters came back to visit. It wasn't that Sierra hadn't visited since she'd moved away from home; the visits had just not happened as frequently as maybe they should have.

You couldn't have known, she told herself, tucking the guilt away.

Her phone pinged a message from her sister, letting her know she had landed and was on her way to the house. She sucked in an anxious breath and closed her eyes, mentally preparing herself to not only hold her own emotions, but her sister's as well. Sierra and her sister could not possibly be more different. Where Sierra was calm and calculating, Savannah was high-strung and emotional. Aside from having to take care of the funeral plans, the house, and the café, Sierra knew that taking care of her sister's emotional needs would fall onto her shoulders as the eldest sister.

Just down the hall, the younger sister's room had always been completely trashed. Clothing on the bed, bedding on the floor, makeup on the wall and desk, scraps of paper that never made it into the bin. If Savannah got a new poster, she just haphazardly hung it up over two other ones, creating a hodgepodge of layers akin to the lining of a puppy pen.

When Sierra had gone off to New York, Savannah was still living at home but in college at UNL on her third or fourth major. It hadn't mattered because Sierra and their parents always expected Savannah to continue working with them at the café, maybe even living at home until she got married. Sierra wasn't much for small talk, but her sister, who seemed introverted, somehow managed to turn on the charm with strangers at the café. It was as if she came alive a little bit in that old building. Sierra didn't mind being there or mind the patrons, but for as long as she could remember, she felt a desire to leave the café, leave this house, and leave Lincoln behind. She had pursued her dreams and accomplished so much since leaving home that she couldn't imagine what would have happened if she'd stayed.

And now, she was back, preparing to review her parents' last wishes, sell their prized possessions, and someday move beyond the tragic loss.

She squeezed her eyes tight, holding back tears. Walking back down the stairs, it took everything she had not to look at the photos on the walls. Sierra had to keep it together. She had to take care of the funeral arrangements and whatever came next. Although she might feel resentful of her responsibilities, she felt the need to be strong for her little sister.

Sierra found some coffee in the kitchen and put on a pot while she waited for her sister. She took down three coffee mugs, just in case Millie also wanted a cup. Sierra was always prepared for every scenario. She planned. She was methodical and organized. When Millie outlined all the steps for her to follow, she would be ready, pen and paper in hand, to take notes and then execute. She could handle this, she told herself as she went to the junk drawer to dig out a pen and paper.

Sierra was just pouring herself a cup of coffee when she heard the door open.

"Sierra?" Savannah called through the house. Her sister's voice was still childlike to her ears, a soft baby whisper. Feminine and musical. She liked to consider her own voice stronger and more authoritative.

"I'm here," Sierra answered, setting down the cup and making her way through the hallway to the foyer. She watched her little sister, a skinny, short waif with chopped black hair, set down an oversized duffel bag that looked to be made from a quilt.

"Hey," Savannah said, both sisters now a few feet apart in their childhood home. Their arms shot out, and the girls, sharing what twenty-somethings should never have to experience, embraced each other. Savannah crumpled into Sierra's arms, drenching her shoulder with thick, wet sobs, mumbling incoherent cries. Sierra patted her sister's back without saying a word or shedding tears of her own. She was the pillar that held them both up in the entryway.

7 SIERRA

Summer in LINCOLN

Sierra finally got Savannah into the kitchen, at the table, and sipping on a cup of coffee. Sierra drank black coffee, but Savannah had required two tablespoons of sugar. *Two.* Absurd.

Just as her sister seemed to be settling down, the doorbell rang.

"That'll be Millie," Sierra said, getting up from the table.

"Millie? Oh my God, Millie!" Savannah squealed and then began crying again.

Sierra answered the door to one of their family's oldest friends, Mildred (Millie) Carter of Carter & Carter Tax & Accounting Services. When Sierra's parents had opened Sweetwater Café and Bar, they'd hired Millie to manage their books. Sierra's mom loved tending to customers and cleaning up; her dad had loved coming up with new food and drink ideas, but neither of them had cared much for the accounting end of running their business. They found Millie, and it was true love. Millie, her husband, and Sierra's parents had become best friends, spending their nights together at the bar, joking and drinking. From time to time, even dancing.

"Oh, my baby," Millie exclaimed as soon as Sierra had opened the door. "Oh, my baby girl, I'm so sorry, come here." The woman swept into the foyer and wrapped her arms around Sierra fiercely. Millie was short and round, soft like a pillow, and draped in a flowery, brightly-colored tunic. The girls had grown up in a diverse area of Lincoln, but Millie was the first person of color who had treated Sierra like any other girl, and not just a white girl. Millie was the first person who showed Sierra that family came in all colors. The woman's sympathy made Sierra's eyes sting with tears. Seeing her, being held by her, made Sierra feel like a kid again. She nearly cracked but forced herself to close her eyes tightly, holding in her emotions.

"Where's that sister of yours?" Millie asked, leaning back out of the hug, sniffling, and wiping her tears. "She here yet?"

"In the kitchen," Sierra said. She closed the door, and Millie headed down the hallway. Sierra followed Millie but stopped at the threshold. Her shock and exasperation at seeing Savannah huddled over the table in tears was almost too much for Sierra to bear. Millie flew to Savannah's side and loudly consoled her, trying to calm and comfort her. Sierra took a deep breath, regained control of herself, then walked into the kitchen, carrying Millie's briefcase for her. Millie pulled a chair beside Savannah's, who was now leaning over into the woman's lap, bawling loudly.

"Oh, baby, you always were the sensitive one," Millie said, smoothing down Savannah's wild dyed-black hair with her hand. "Hush now, child. Hush now."

Sierra sat down and put Millie's briefcase onto the table, hoping they could hurry up and move through this process. Millie looked up over the devastated Savannah. "Is that coffee?" she whispered. Sierra jumped up to pour the woman a cup.

"Bless you," Millie said instead of thanks, and then used the puffy sleeve of her dress to wipe tears and snot off her face.

After a few moments of the women sipping coffee, Savannah finally sat up and blew her nose on a kitchen napkin, dropping the used item to the floor.

"I'm ready to start, Millie," Sierra said, pushing the briefcase across the table.

"Let's get to it, then." Millie opened the black bag and pulled a manila folder out. She carefully, and maybe too slowly, opened the folder and pulled out a stack of papers.

"Have you started funeral planning yet?" Millie asked.

"I haven't," Sierra said. "We just got in today. We haven't gone to see them yet."

The firefighter who had called them had texted details about the funeral home their parents had been moved to. She knew they were waiting for her call and had planned on doing it right after speaking with Millie. She wasn't exactly sure about her parents' wishes and hoped that it was documented within the paperwork. Her parents were a bit quirky, like Savannah. They could have wanted to be shot from cannons into the sea on a Tuesday at midnight for all she knew.

Millie sat up straighter in her chair, as if remembering something when her eyes scanned over the documents. A tingle crawled up Sierra's spine, and she sat up straighter, too.

"Your parents had different wishes, depending on whether one of them died before the other," Millie explained. "I'm scanning down to the section on what happens when they both pass at the same time, which is where we are." She cleared her throat.

"We, Dennis and Deborah Sweetwater, should we pass at the same time, wish to leave our home and our business, Sweetwater Café and Bar, to our children, Sierra Lynn Sweetwater and Savannah Eve Sweetwater."

Millie sat up even straighter as if bracing herself against the back of the hard wooden chair and cleared her throat again. Her dark brown eyes, now dry and studious, paused on the papers before looking up at each of the two young women. Sierra was growing concerned now.

"However," Millie continued, her eyes back on the papers, *"our wish is that our café and our house stay in the family. We are concerned that if the girls sell the properties, they will return to their far corners of the country, and this family will truly fall apart. Everything we have worked so hard for, put so much love into, including our children's relationships, will fall apart."*

"What?" Savannah whispered, leaning forward onto her forearms, a look of confusion crinkling her face.

A tear slid down Millie's dark brown cheek, and she wiped it away and sniffed. Sierra gripped the edge of the kitchen table so tight that her knuckles were turning white. Shock and fury started to flood her body. Millie cleared her throat again and continued.

"In order for Sierra and Savannah to receive their inheritance, they must both continue to run the Sweetwater Café and Bar for one full year. They may live in the family home or in the apartment above the café. After a year, if they still do not want to keep the family home or café, they may sell the assets and divide the proceeds equally. Our wish is for this year to bring the girls back together and that they will hopefully decide to keep the home and café in the family."

Sierra pushed her chair back from the table and stood up so violently that Millie and Savannah both jumped.

"Are you fucking kidding me?" Sierra yelled toward Millie, but really, yelling at her parents from within their Will.

Sierra stormed into the middle of the kitchen and started opening and closing cabinets, looking for a bottle of whiskey, vodka, anything. She needed a shot. Finally, she found a half-finished bottle of Jack tucked back behind a box of cereal. Living alone with grown children, and they still hid the alcohol. *Not at the café*, though, she told herself, unscrewing the bottle. All that alcohol had been out and available 24/7. She rolled her eyes and took a swig from the bottle.

"Sierra?" Millie asked, her voice calm and gentle like approaching a feral cat.

Sierra turned sharply, swallowing the brown liquid. "This is bullshit, Millie, and you know it. What parents die and then force their kids to move back home to take over their meaningless little lives? I have a life." Sierra pointed at her chest with her free hand; the other hand gripped the bottle. "My life is in New York City, Millie." Sierra pointed off into the distance. "That's where I have a job, a career path in a competitive market, I have an apartment with roommates, friends who depend on me to be there and pay my share. New York has been my dream since I was a child. That's where I'm supposed to be. Not in this small-ass town in Middle America. This is not my home!" Sierra was yelling now, and she paused to take another swig from the neck of the square bottle. The heat in her throat felt good, connecting a physical burn to the emotional pain and confusion she was feeling.

Savannah was shaking her head slowly from side to side, looking completely confused.

Savannah, of course, Sierra thought as her brain clicked into problem-solving mode. She moved back to the table and stood behind her chair. She put the bottle onto the table and looked from Millie to Savannah.

"Why can't it just be Savannah who works the café?" Sierra asked. "Savannah does the same type of work up in Seattle. She can stay here and run things for a year so I can go back to my job in New York."

"I have a life in Seattle too, you know," Savannah said, feigning vigor in her voice.

Sierra raised an eyebrow. "Really? You're working your dream job with roommates who depend on you?"

"My life doesn't have to look like yours for it to be valuable, *Sierra*," Savannah said, spitting out her sister's name. "I have a boyfriend, two jobs, and an apartment. Jaxon could lose the apartment without me."

"Is that guy ever going to be famous?" Sierra asked. "Is he ever going to be more than just a mooch off you? Who cares if he fails and loses the apartment?"

"I care!" Now, Savannah was yelling. She angrily reached for the bottle and took a drink, staring daggers across the table at her older sister.

"OK, girls, let's calm down and maybe not get too heavy into that bottle just now," Millie said, her motherly energy attempting to spread over them like a warm blanket during a storm.

Millie put her hands palm down onto the papers. "I know your parents meant well in making this request. First, they never actually thought, *nobody* thought that they'd pass this young. After Savannah moved clear out to Seattle, the one they thought would stay, they noticed how you both lost contact with them and with each other."

"We text," Savannah said.

"We didn't lose contact," Sierra said.

Millie took a deep breath and cleared her throat again. "That's good, girls. I think your parents want you both to be closer to each other now that they are gone. They feel this may be more important in the long run than jobs and apartments. Could you put some of that on hold for a little bit?"

Sierra stared down at Millie, her fingers gripping the back of her chair. She was pissed, but she didn't know what to do with the anger. She couldn't yell at her parents. She couldn't tear up the Will and walk away. For a moment, she considered dousing it with whiskey and setting it on fire.

"What happens if we do not acquiesce to their request?" Sierra asked, fingers itching to grab the bottle back from Savannah.

"You'll lose the house and café, I'm afraid." Millie looked genuinely concerned for the girls, but not nearly as upset as they were. Of course, she'd probably known about this for years.

"But how can they do that?" Sierra pressed. "We grew up in this house. We worked in that café. We should be next in line to inherit these properties and the proceeds from the sale of these properties."

"Yes, but their Will says otherwise, and the judge at probate will follow the instructions as laid out in the Will," Millie said, her voice calm and empathetic.

"And the instructions are?" Sierra asked, clenching her teeth.

"The properties will be sold, and the proceeds will be donated in their name to the University of Nebraska."

The words hit Sierra hard. Her parents worked so hard to be able to put the girls into school there. Sierra only did two years before transferring to a fashion school in New York City. Her parents were devastated. They had both dreamed of having UNL grads. Although Savannah had also started, she had run off to Seattle with Jaxon before finishing. The red and cream UNL gear was all over their parents' café and bar. They showed all the college football games. They gave discounts to college students. Neither one of her parents had been able to go to college, so they'd been so proud when their daughters had been accepted. They told everyone who spent more than two minutes buying coffee or beer, and anyone wearing UNL colors, that their daughters were going to school there. But neither girl ever became a UNL grad.

"Millie," Sierra said, leaning over the back of her chair and bending down to look the older woman in the eye. "You can lie for us. For me. I'll go back home, to New York, but I'll come back more often to visit with Savannah."

"Why do *you* get to go back to *your* life?" Savannah asked, her tone hurt and maybe a little frightened about the prospect.

"Because your life is the same whether you're here or not," Sierra answered sharply. "You work at a café there, you can work at a café here. Maybe even save some money. Maybe you keep running the café and give up on that bohemian groupie lifestyle."

"I'm not a groupie! Jaxon is my boyfriend." Even though Savannah said the words loudly, Sierra wasn't convinced that she believed them herself. Savannah had always been the girl to go along with the flow. She didn't make waves. She looked at musicians with dreamy eyes like they could save the whole world, when really, maybe they could make great music, but they rarely made great boyfriends.

"A boyfriend would understand," Sierra said, ironically, then turned back to Millie, looking for a response. Millie was shaking her head.

"I'm sorry, girls," she said. "I can't lie for you or cover for you. A Will is a legally binding document. I can't get you out of this. You two have to decide if you are going to stay here and keep running the business or if you are handing it all over to the University."

All three women stayed silent for a few moments. Sierra's and Savannah's eyes drifted to the bottle between them. It was the one thing they had in common.

"I hate this for you both, I do," Millie said. "These are your copies, so I'll leave them with you."

Sierra and Savannah stayed quiet. Millie slowly pushed herself back from the table and grabbed her briefcase. She stood up and looked at both the young women, who did not return her gaze.

"I'm glad to see you, despite the circumstances. You both talk things out and call me tomorrow to let me know what you've decided. The code to get into the back of the café is the same if you need to make a visit. It's been closed since the accident. It'll be up to you whether it's reopened again. Zadie's been working there." Millie's somber tone perked up a bit at the mention of her daughter. "She'll be excited to see you. Well, sad, but she always liked you both. She's always looked up to you. Anyway, I'll see you at the funeral once you get that all arranged. Let me know if you need any help."

With that, Millie left the kitchen. Sierra listened to her close the front door behind her before reaching for the bottle. She grabbed it and began to walk away from the table.

"Where are you going?" Savannah asked.

"To get us glasses," Sierra answered.

8 SAVANNAH

Summer in LINCOLN

Savannah took the whiskey glass her sister handed her. They didn't toast. There was nothing to toast to. Sierra took her spot back at the table and held her glass for a few seconds, staring at the table before taking a sip.

Savannah also caught herself staring into space, so she turned her attention to the whiskey glass. It was part of a collection they'd had her entire life. Perfectly weighted with a thicker base and an etched diamond pattern around the outside. She ran her fingers across the ridges before taking hold of it and lifting it to her lips. *Why did whiskey have the power to calm down nearly every situation?* she wondered. She closed her eyes, savoring that magical salve, forgetting reality for a moment. With her eyes closed, she could see her mother in the corner of the kitchen, opening the pantry doors, then walking across the kitchen tile in fluffy red socks with giant cream Ns embroidered on the tops. And then another memory popped into her mind of her dad dancing to the jukebox at the café. She opened her eyes.

"I want to go to Sweetwater," Savannah said.

Sierra looked up from her drink as if she'd forgotten her sister was even there. "The café? Now? Why?"

"We need to make a decision, right? And besides, look at this place. We need to go get some food, and sooner than later, more whiskey." She raised her eyebrows toward the nearly empty bottle her sister had left on the kitchen counter.

Sierra's gaze followed hers to the bottle. "Too right. There's no food in this place."

"Figures," Savannah said. Both girls cracked the slightest of smiles, remembering the years after their parents had started running the business. The girls had milk and cereal, lunch money, and got themselves to school, but snacks and dinners were at Sweetwater Café and Bar. Their parents were always there. On busy weekends, their parents would sleep in the apartment above the café, leaving the middle-school-aged girls home alone. Savannah had been so scared she'd slept with a knife under her pillow and tried to find ways to booby-trap her bedroom door. Then a thought that had never occurred to her sprang to mind.

"Hey, were you scared those nights it was just us in the house?" Savannah asked.

Sierra furrowed her brow. "When our parents slept at the café?"

"Yeah."

Sierra looked off as if into a memory. "Yeah, I was. I was afraid I'd have to fight someone off and save us from something. I hardly slept those nights."

Savannah nodded. "Me too."

The girls were quiet for a few more moments, taking sips of their drinks.

"We need a car to drive to the café," Sierra said pragmatically.

Both girls locked eyes as if wondering the same thing. What car had they driven to the wedding? What car had the deer totaled? What car had they died in?

"Not the truck," Sierra said, reading Savannah's mind.

"No way," Savannah agreed. "That truck could survive a tornado. It's a tank."

"It's a legend," Sierra added.

They both shot up out of their chairs and went to the door that opened into the two-car garage. Savannah felt nervous as her sister flipped on the light. There, on the far side, was their father's 1990 Ford F-150 in Nebraska red with a cream stripe across its width.

Savannah felt such a strange rush of conflicting emotions at seeing her father's truck. She was relieved that it had not been damaged, and then angry that they hadn't been driving it instead. Surely, it would have gone just a little slower than their mother's more modern coupe. Maybe they would have missed the deer completely. But if a deer had hit that truck, her parents would be injured, but they'd still be alive. Unable to control the wave of emotions, she started crying again.

Sierra turned toward her sister, and even though there were sparkles of tears in her eyes, she said, "Get it together. I'll get the keys."

Her chest tightened at her sister's words, but the tears kept falling. Much to her chagrin, Savannah never could quite get things together. She felt so deeply, and they had just lost her parents. Savannah knew how strong her sister was, but sometimes, the woman felt downright cold. Maybe Savannah was the emotional one, but in her eyes, it was better than the alternative.

Sierra drove the truck a few miles deeper into downtown Lincoln, with Savannah staring out of the passenger side window. It was an older part where the buildings, including the café, had a beautiful red brick exterior.

Pulling up to the café sent another mix of nostalgia, nerves, resentment, anger, and regret flowing beneath Savannah's skin. Why hadn't she come back sooner to visit?

It was a beautiful two-story building on a corner. Patio tables and chairs were on the sidewalk in front of wide windows, a cascade of warm yellow lights swinging in the breeze. Savannah was glad someone had left the patio lights on. SWEETWATER CAFÉ AND BAR letters were plastered boldly high above the double doors that they kept propped open when the weather was good.

Sierra pulled the truck around to the back of the building, following a narrow alley where the trash was picked up. She pulled right up to the door, slightly blocking the alley, and parked, turning off the engine.

"Let's go," Sierra said. Her sister was always barking orders, but Savannah was so used to it that she had no energy to fight. Besides, what would she say, no?

The girls went to the keypad and punched in the combination of both of their birthdays, Sierra's first. Opening the door, the only light was what the patio lights provided through the front windows. Sierra walked in first, and Savannah closed and locked the door behind them before following her sister down the hallway and into the main dining area.

The old wood flooring, the patio light passing through the windows and sheer draperies, the empty tables and chairs, and the smoothness of the clean bar top made the place seem ghostly and romantic. *I bet Jaxon could write a song about the energy in this room*, Savannah thought to herself.

"OK, we're here, so now what?" Sierra asked, spinning around in the middle of the room, missing the beauty of it all.

"You don't feel it?" Savannah asked.

"Feel what?"

Savannah closed her eyes and took a deep breath. The room spun to life around her with memories. The college kid who puked by the dartboards. The woman who ended things with her husband in the corner booth then bought shots for the whole bar after he stormed out. Hundreds of couples who held hands at tables, who danced together, like her parents would from time to time. The morning regulars who came for a simple coffee, and her mother's smile. She could see her mother with her thick, curly blond hair tied back in a practical bun, her weathered, sun-kissed skin full of freckles and devoid of makeup. Her mother laughed from behind the bar, cleaning up after a late rush as her father danced to a song in the middle of the floor with patrons watching and laughing along.

She let the breath out and opened her eyes. Sierra was looking at her like she'd just traveled to Mars and back. "This place is full of memories," Savannah tried to explain, knowing that it would be lost on her sensible sister. Sierra was always squarely planted in reality, where Savannah… well, what was reality without a touch of fantasy anyway?

Sierra crossed her arms. "You belong here," she said. "I do not."

"I don't belong here anymore than you do," Savannah said defensively, snapping out of her daydream.

"You work at a café during the day and at a bar at night," Sierra clarified. "You grew up here, worked here, and now do the same damn work in a different city. And you didn't get a degree, so what the hell else are you going to do?"

"You think you are so damn special for some reason? Why don't you get over yourself!" Savannah finally snapped, anxiety and anger crashing in. Her sister was the only person she ever knew who could take her to the breaking point. Savannah had always been a happy-go-lucky, easy-going, going with the flow, while looking on the bright side of life kind of girl, but Sierra seemed to push her buttons to the point where she'd raise her voice. Of course, Sierra always responded with an eyeroll, seeing Savannah's reaction as a continuation of her emotional deficits.

Savannah growled in frustration and headed off toward the bar. "Since I belong in a bar, I guess I should pour us some fucking drinks." She half mumbled the words to herself, grabbing a bottle of Jameson with one hand and two glasses with the other. The shots at her parents' house had been straight up, but she wanted ice. She slid the lid to the ice machine back and scooped two spoonsful into each glass. These glasses were sleek but with an indentation on each side for better grips. Her father picked these out specifically, thinking they'd be dropped less often, and he'd been right.

Sierra strolled closer to the bar, and Savannah thrust a glass out to her. "Here," she said curtly. It felt weird for Savannah to be so rude from behind a bar. Throughout most of her adulthood, she'd been able to laugh off obnoxious or inappropriate patrons, brush them off kindly, or throw a facial expression at a male coworker or bouncer to take care of someone for her. To be rude while handing a glass over felt unnatural, except that this was her bossy older sister. It had never felt weird being rude to Sierra because she absolutely deserved it. Sierra accepted the glass without expression, completely unfazed by Savannah's outburst.

They both sipped their drinks from opposite sides of the bar, standing in the silence of their memories within their parents' space. Savannah's annoyance abated quickly, as it often did, as she relaxed back into the quiet of the spacious room. The jukebox caught her eye, and she walked over to it, placing her hands on the machine that had been upgraded to digital sometime after she'd moved away. People could now play music from an app on their phones. Their parents still collected a small percentage of the proceeds.

Savannah pulled out her phone and snapped the QR code, created a quick account, and then chose a song. The familiar intro of "The Weight" started to fill the hollow corners of the bar. Savannah heard Sierra huff into her glass.

"You and Dad always did like the old rock," Sierra said.

Savannah's lips curled into a smile. "And Mom loved Bette Midler and Celine Dion. Dad hated that music." Both girls laughed, remembering the friendly banter their parents would have about music.

"We can't let this place go, Sierra," Savannah said, turning from the jukebox. "This is more than just our parents' café and bar. Our name is on the sign outside, for Christ's sake. This place is ours as much as theirs. This place is a part of the community. And I know it's a lot to ask for us to stay here and run it, but I get it. Mom and Dad wanted us to be like we were as children. We did move as far apart as we could get within the continental U.S., and we've lost touch. I know this is harder for you than for me. You love your job, and you're right; I'm doing the same kind of work, just in another city."

Thinking about Seattle gave Savannah pause. Being absorbed in the pain, memories, and emotions of the café nearly made her forget about the other painful issue—leaving Jaxon. She pictured him shirtless, standing in front of their apartment window, looking back at her lying across their bed the first week they'd moved in. There was so much hope, optimism. And so much sex…

She wondered if they could handle a year apart. A year would feel like forever, maybe even like abandonment to him. If she didn't go back to Seattle for a while, either he would end things, moving onto a new girl and new apartment quickly, or it could make him realize just how lucky he was to have her. The thought of Jaxon leaving her sent an anxious fear through her body, but the thought of saying goodbye to the café took the air from her lungs. One definitely cut her more deeply than the other.

Savannah decided then and there that if Jaxon moved on, then it wasn't meant to be. There was a small chance, even a hope, that maybe not seeing her for a few months would knock some sense into the man-child and drive him to take the next step with her, whatever that might be. She imagined Jaxon on his knees, singing to her, begging her not to leave him, and telling her that he'll do anything for her. *Yes*, she thought with a small smile, *that could be nice.*

Still looking around the bar, she shifted her thoughts back to the present. "I don't want to lose this place, Sierra. I don't want to lose our house, either."

Savannah tentatively walked back toward the bar. Sierra had moved over to sit on a barstool, so Savannah took the one next to her, grabbing the glass she'd left on the counter. She took a sip and then said, "Listen, I know this is a huge burden on both of us. It's a lot. But I'm not ready to say goodbye to all of this for good. Are you?"

Sierra looked to the jukebox, around the room, took a sip of her drink, and then back into Savannah's brown eyes. Dirty blonde hair and brown eyes, pointy noses and full lips. Everybody could clearly see the two were sisters, except that Savannah had chopped her hair off and dyed it black in a fit of rebellion as soon as she'd arrived in Seattle with her rocker boyfriend. She'd wanted to shake off the evidence of her Middle America roots. As their eyes met, Savannah missed her long blonde hair for the first time in years.

"I don't think so, no." Sierra's words were short, quiet, but firm. Savannah felt a little lighter, as if they were closer to a decision.

"But what will you do?" Savannah asked.

Sierra put her business face on and was clearly calculating, building plans on top of plans as she always had.

"OK," Sierra said, placing her palms onto the shiny bar top. "I'll ask my friends to sublet out my bedroom and send them money to pack up and ship me the rest of my things. I'll ask for a medical leave of absence from work. They can't question it or fire me for it. I'll help you out here for a year, and then when a year is over, we'll sell this and the house and go our separate ways." Sierra paused, blinked rapidly, and then shrugged. "Again," she added.

Savannah's nostrils flared, and her eyebrows climbed up her forehead. That wasn't exactly what she'd expected, and the thought of selling her childhood memories of her parents and her life stabbed her like a knife. Would the sisters truly never speak to or see each other again, as their parents had worried? Savannah tried to think logically, like her sister would.

Sierra had a great career opportunity in New York City. The girls had already lived apart for years, and even though they hardly texted, they had both come together in a tragedy. No matter how far apart, they would still be sisters.

Savannah loved the café, but without her parents, without her sister, was it really something she wanted to take care of all by herself? The situation they were in wasn't ideal, but it was one year to either convince her sister to stay or learn how to say goodbye to the café, to her childhood home, and to her parents for good. Maybe both girls were destined to leave this place behind, even if it hurt. Maybe their parents' dying was the additional push for the sisters to truly say goodbye to Nebraska, to their pasts, and to each other forever. Maybe they didn't belong here.

"OK," Savannah said, nodding her head slowly. Her nostrils and eyebrows returned to their regular positions as Sierra turned to face her on the barstool. "We stay for a year."

"We stay for a year," Sierra confirmed.

Savannah swallowed down the feeling of excitement doused in doubt.

9 SAVANNAH

Savannah stayed at the bar, sipping on whiskey while Sierra went to work. She watched her sister leave the room through a door into the kitchen, knowing she was heading toward their father's office. In the office, she'd find the numbers for the few employees that she would call back to their regular shifts. She'd find the inventory reports and make sure they were stocked up. She'd work into the late hours taking care of business to ensure the girls could restart the café as if it had never come to a sudden halt.

A smile spread across Savannah's face, realizing that her older sister would be trapped back in this small town with her for an entire year. It was a sick little victory, sure, knowing that her sister would be miserable, but Savannah was glad to see her knocked down a peg. This was something completely out of her sister's control for once in her fucking life.

Sierra had always been the best dressed, best grades, best of literally anything and everything. She was a golden child, a star. Savannah would accidentally pour orange juice into her cereal bowl and have to start her morning over again. Savannah's teachers would call her parents on the regular to tell them about how she daydreamed and was incapable of focusing on one simple task for more than two minutes. Eventually, her parents just stopped answering the calls.

"Are you passing?" her dad would ask.

"Yeah, I think so," Savannah would shrug.

"Alright, that's fine for now. Just try a little harder, sweetie." And then he would wrap her into a tight bear hug, tussle her hair, and return to whatever task he was on at the café.

She'd really been lucky. She knew her parents loved her; she just didn't get a lot of one-on-one attention. Savannah knew they were busy and that all the work they did was for their kids. Nobody was more shocked than Savannah when she actually got into college.

She looked around the café, reacquainting herself with the space. She'd done her homework at this bar. She'd cleaned the tables and bathrooms. She'd learned how to make simple drinks like lattes, Americanos, and iced tea. Then, after she'd gotten a license, she progressed to making bar drinks. The café served alcohol all day, but the orders usually picked up around four in the afternoon, during happy hour, and went until midnight, when they closed. On special nights, like when Nebraska won a game, they'd stay open until 2 a.m. She wondered if her sister would agree to keeping the tradition.

Everything was the same. She knew where the light switches were, the cleaning supplies, the fridge, and the pantry. They could reopen the next day, and she would just pick up right where she'd left off two years ago. Some anxiety eased in her chest. *A year would fly by*, she told herself.

A couple of hours later, Sierra returned to the bar where Savannah had stayed, texting with Jaxon about his upcoming shows and some band drama while scrolling through her phone. She wasn't ready to tell Jaxon what was happening. Luckily, he hadn't asked when she was coming back.

A wry thought came to mind. What if she didn't tell him that she was staying in Lincoln for a full year until he asked her? No, she realized that would be passive-aggressive.

"OK, I got ahold of the staff," Sierra said, refilling her own glass. "They are all coming back to work tomorrow—except for one who found another job. I think we're good, regardless. They know how to get in, so if we want to sleep in and come in later, we can. Zadie and Mario will open for us."

"This place still opens at 6 a.m., I'm guessing?" Savannah asked. Her sister added an ice cube to her whiskey and swirled it for a second.

"Yep," Sierra confirmed. Neither one of them had ever been early birds by choice. They loved staying up late with their dad at the bar, not opening the coffee shop with their mom.

Sierra took a sip of her drink and turned toward Savannah. "I feel like I need the rest tomorrow. It's already pretty late. But with Zadie and Mario opening for us, maybe we can come in at 8 instead."

Savannah perked up, finishing off her glass and holding it out to her sister for a refill. "I'll sign up for that."

Sierra grabbed the bottle and refilled her sister's glass with whiskey, then added two ice cubes.

"I guess we're back," Sierra said, clinking her glass to her sister's.

"We're back," Savannah agreed. They finished their drinks and headed to the house to unpack and sleep.

The next morning, the girls did sleep in. Their bodies were confused with time changes, stress, sorrow, and whiskey. Savannah awoke with a start. She dressed quickly and then ran down the hall to Sierra's room, rapping quickly against the door.

"Oh, my gawd, what?" Sierra mumbled, sounding as if she were half asleep. Savannah opened the door and walked in, finding her sister still in bed.

"What about the funeral?" Savannah asked in a panic.

"I'll schedule it sometime this week. They've been cremated, and so it's more of a celebration of life. I hired someone to create a video from all our online photos. I've started working on a flower order. It'll be at the café, and Zadie and her mother will get the word out. It's all mostly handled."

Then Sierra put the pillow over her head and mumbled for her sister to go away. Savannah was more surprised that she hadn't already guessed her sister would have handled all the details. And so quickly. She really had a knack for taking care of business, Savannah realized, feeling a little bit ashamed. While she was sipping on whiskey at the bar, drifting from one memory to the next, her sister had literally taken care of every last thing.

Feeling a bit guilty, she started to get ready to go to the café. It would be strange, walking into a place that she now owned after a two-year hiatus. She finished in the bathroom and headed downstairs, just as Sierra was leaving her room. *Good timing*, Savannah thought. It was good that they both didn't want the bathroom at the same time.

After they'd both got ready, they took their daddy's F-150 back to the café, parking along the street this time and paying the meter.

In the daylight, the Sweetwater Café and Bar looked less romantic and ominous. It was cool and active, with people sitting at the patio tables and streaming in and out of the place.

"Is it always this busy?" Sierra asked.

"I was just wondering the same thing," Savannah admitted.

A group of college girls on the patio stopped laughing and looked at the sisters. A couple with a golden retriever on the other side also stopped talking and turned to watch the Sweetwater sisters walk into their parents' café and bar.

Chills climbed up Savannah's bare arms. She was in a light cotton flowing shirt over jean shorts, but it wasn't the warm June breeze giving her prickly skin.

They passed through the old, heavy wood doors, the sun behind them making it hard to see through the glass on the top of the doors. Savannah was momentarily blinded when she walked in and wasn't prepared to be immediately engulfed in a hug. As her vision adjusted, she realized it was little Zadie, who wasn't that little anymore. Millie's daughter had spent her young years listening to music and ordering sodas. Savannah would try different mixes with flavors they used with coffee drinks, dropping cherry and vanilla flavors into Zadie's colas. Now Zadie was as tall as Savannah, a grown woman instead of a little girl.

Before she knew it, Zadie wasn't alone. More and more arms, bodies, heads of hair, all joining in the hug, moving into the sisters like a magnetic blob of colors and fragrances. Savannah lost it, and she felt someone grab her hand and squeeze. She sobbed into the mob of empathy, feeling as if her own parents were there, hugging her, pouring their love into her soul.

After what felt like many minutes, the people released and stepped back. Through blurry eyes, Savannah saw old teachers, high school friends with their husbands and kids, the man who delivered their coffee beans, the woman who greeted everyone at church, a grocery store clerk, a bagger, and so many regulars she'd served over the years. They were all still here as if the years Savannah had been in Seattle hadn't even happened. Aside from a little aging and height on the kids, everyone was the same.

Zadie was the last to let go, leaning back but still keeping her hands lightly on Savannah's arms.

"How you doin'?" Zadie asked in that charming accent that Savannah hadn't realized how much she'd missed until that moment.

She wiped away her snot and tears, then looked into Zadie's beautiful black eyes that seemed to reflect a starless night. "You're so grown," Savannah said, sniffling, not answering the question. Honestly, she wasn't sure how she was doing. Two days ago, she was working two jobs and hoping her boyfriend would fall in love with her all over again. Now, surrounded by people who only existed in her memories, in a place she loved and resented so deeply, living in a new world where her parents didn't exist. She had no idea how she was or even who she was. "I'm glad to see you. You're still working here?"

"Duh," Zadie answered with a wink. "I'm still in school. If I want to be in finance, I need a place like this where I can study behind the counter without the owner getting mad and tossing my laptop in the trash. Your parents… they loved me like their own daughter. This place is like my second home. They encouraged me to study when it was dead instead of scrubbing the coffee machines."

Zadie's words choked out into a whisper as more tears wet her own eyes.

Savannah pulled her back into another hug, one just between them, without the swarm of regulars.

When the two girls parted, Savannah noticed that her sister had left the entryway. Sierra was behind the bar talking to Mario, a man of Mexican heritage in his mid-forties who had worked for her parents as the cook and bartender for years. He was about as tall as Savannah and Sierra and about as wide as both of them put together. Mario was a kind soul with a sarcastic twinkle in his eyes, always ready to tease somebody about something. Savannah had always liked the man. His wife, Edith, frequented the café after her shift at the bank and on all bank holidays and weekends. She had silky brown hair and brown eyes, wearing her curves like Marilyn Monroe, walking like a star about to receive a reward. Edith's schedule was actually a huge benefit because she would step in to help during the busiest days and times. After clocking out, she'd stay late and drink with Mario and her parents.

Savannah caught herself… Edith *used to* stay late and drink with her parents. She looked around the busy room. The regulars, neighbors, and friends all returned to their tables and chairs or barstools. Savannah wondered what would change and what would stay the same with her parents gone and Sierra running things now.

Her sister could be a bit of a bossy micro-manager, but she wondered if that would extend to this place. Savannah hoped not. She watched Zadie walk back behind the counter to take orders, just like the old days, but taller. Her curly black hair was pulled back into a tight bun, making her look like a ballerina.

Savannah sighed and headed toward the office. She wasn't sure what to do. Did she need to cook, clean, make drinks? She saw a young boy taking dishes to the kitchen and, through the open door, saw another boy washing at the big metal sink. Mario had resumed cooking. Savannah froze at the kitchen door as it swung back shut. Changing her mind, she turned back toward Zadie.

"Can I help you?" Savannah asked.

"Absolutely!" Zadie said, handing Savannah a slip. "Special drink orders?"

"I think I can still do that."

There was soda, water, and tea available to everyone as self-serve, along with two coffee pots. For everything else, someone had to make them. Depending on the complexity, it could slow down the line.

Savannah was pouring hot water over an espresso when her phone vibrated in her pocket. "Shit," she said, nearly dropping the hot water. She popped a lid onto the cup, handed it over to Zadie, then pulled out her phone just in time.

"Hello," Savannah answered.

"Hey, Savvy, how's it going down there, country girl?" Jaxon's smooth voice reverberated in her heart through the phone. She rolled her eyes.

"I'm no country girl," she said.

"Spend too much time down there, and you may revert to your roots," he added. "But really, all good? When's the funeral? When are you coming back?"

She narrowed her eyes into a squint. He didn't sound particularly interested in a caring boyfriend kind of way. "Funeral is going to be this week. I may not come back right away, though."

"Are you kidding?" Jaxon's tone turned on a dime. "Rent is gonna come due, and I gotta head outta town for a show. This is really bad timing, Sav."

Her mouth dropped open. She stepped into the kitchen and walked until she thought she'd be out of earshot of everyone.

"Real sorry my parents couldn't have died at a more convenient time for you," she said in a harsh whisper.

"Now come on, you know that's not what I meant. I'm just stressed out." Jaxon put that charming tone back into his smooth voice, but Savannah wasn't having it.

"I get that you've never had to deal with the death of parents, but this is all new to me, and there's a lot to take care of here," Savannah said, speaking slower as her anger burned. "I don't know when I'll be back."

"What do you need to take care of there, Sav, aside from the funeral?" Jaxon asked, flippantly.

"My parents' café, their home, my dad's truck," Savannah listed.

"Can't your sister take care of all of that? Isn't she the responsible one?"

Savannah's anger boiled over. "Are you saying I'm not responsible?"

"I'm just saying, let her be the older sister and take care of all this shit for you and come back home."

"I am home!" Savannah yelled into the phone and then disconnected the call, shoving the phone into her front pocket.

Did he not think she was capable of taking care of things? Did he think that her sister was better and more equipped to handle this type, any type of complicated situation?

Savannah looked up and met Mario's eyes. He was standing over eggs on the cooktop.

"You good, kiddo?" he asked, gently.

Savannah shrugged. She didn't know. Could she handle this? Would this be a year of failures with Jaxon begging her to come back to Seattle daily? If he broke up with her and lost the apartment, would it be her fault? If she went back to Seattle and they lost their inheritance to the University, would her sister ever forgive her?

Had she made a mistake agreeing to run this place for a year? Savannah felt so confused and scared, her chest ached, and she wondered if it was too early to start drinking.

10 SIERRA

The tiny office in the Sweetwater Café and Bar would have been more spacious if it weren't for the dozens of boxes stacked all around it. Sierra shook her head as she observed the disorganized chaos that her father had left behind. Clearing a path to the desk was going to have to be the very first thing she did. Thinking the boxes must be important, she'd opened them to find nothing more than kitchen supplies. There were bulk rolls of paper towels and toilet paper, spray bottles wrapped tight in cellophane, and things her dad must have just bought at a bulk discount before he needed them. It was typical of her father to over-plan and yet underperform. His mind worked faster than his actions. She smiled to herself, rolling her eyes and shaking her head, remembering how he'd plan big vacations that they missed due to getting caught up in café schedules.

Sierra left the office and went to the storage closet. As she expected, it was full to the ceiling with barely any room to walk in. She had a big project to tackle, reorganizing her father's chaos, and, honestly, she was glad. This was something that obviously needed her attention, and she didn't have to focus on anything else, like grieving for her parents, but could instead put things in neat, orderly rows. She would clean out the storage closet, find homes for items, donate things they didn't need, and then move supplies out of the office. One organized step at a time.

Sure, she realized she was avoiding the people out in the café by focusing on this project, but it wasn't like she was making it up. This *needed* to be done. Her sister could serve drinks, take orders, and make small talk with the rest of the staff. Savannah was better with silly social conversations, giggling with strangers, and such. Sierra wasn't interested in frivolity. She didn't have time for small talk.

For hours, Sierra lost herself in her work. At some point, Mario brought her a turkey sandwich, remembering what she liked from when she worked there in college. She always liked him and his wife, Edith. Maybe when the year was over, she'd sell the café to them.

No, she thought. *They might not be able to afford it. Would they lose their jobs if she sold Sweetwater to someone else?* Sierra shook the thought away and lifted a box filled with multiple packaged rolls of toilet paper. She'd seen that the spaces underneath the bathroom cabinets were mostly empty, so her plan was to jam-pack them full of as many rolls as possible.

The late afternoon crowd was very thin compared to when they'd arrived earlier, and the evening crowd had not yet started to stream in. Things were quiet except for Zadie and Savannah catching up from behind the counter.

With Sierra's arms wrapped tightly around the awkward box, she left the kitchen and headed down the hall to the bathrooms, running straight into someone she hadn't seen in the dimly lit hallway. The box fell and split open, tossing neatly packed white rolls in bundles of six in every direction. Sierra landed on her rear with a smack, and then, on instinct, just kept falling backward to soften the overall blow. From her back, looking up at the ceiling, she heard a familiar voice say, "I am so sorry, are you alright? Here, let me help you up."

And then his face came into view, drifting above her like a saint with slightly tousled brown hair and warm hazel eyes. His skin was tan and weathered, like he had spent a lot of time outdoors or in harsh environments. His strong jawline was peppered with brown stubble, and he looked to be in his late twenties. He extended two massive hands, and she found it easy to reach up and take those hands as if she were called to them. Not that she was knocked down a lot, but Sierra wasn't the type to accept any assistance, no matter what the circumstances. To her surprise, she didn't feel angry or annoyed about falling. Sierra wasn't sure how anyone could feel angry looking into that face. He had the face of a… hero?

Sure enough, standing back up on her feet, she realized that he was indeed wearing a firefighter uniform jacket.

"You came around that corner so fast," he said. "Or, I should say that giant box came around that corner so fast, it caught me off guard."

Sierra felt her cheeks get warm, and she quickly looked down at the mess around them. *Avoid eye contact and pick up the toilet paper*, Sierra, she told herself. But he held her attention.

"I'm Caleb," he said. "And you must be one of the Sweetwater sisters."

"Yes, I'm Sierra, the oldest," she confirmed.

"The one in New York City."

Sierra squinted, puzzled. She knew it was a small town, but it still felt uncomfortable when a stranger knew something about her that she hadn't told them herself.

"I called you," he said, clarifying the situation. "I'm the one who…" he stopped as if trying to change his tone before continuing from a flirty meeting to a somber realization. "I found your parents that night and tracked down you and your sister."

"Right," Sierra said, recognition uncomfortably flooding through her. He'd been the one who had left the message. That's why his voice sounded slightly familiar. He'd reached Savannah, and she'd called Sierra, hysterically crying. He was there and had seen their parents dead. Sierra bent down and started to restack the packaged rolls in neat piles along the wall.

"Here, let me help," Caleb said.

"No," she said sharply. "I got it, thank you." There was no way she was letting this handsome fireman, who had tried to save her dying parents on a rainy night, who had tracked their children down in two different states, who had the deepest eyes she'd ever seen, help her carry toilet paper into the bathrooms. Sierra felt like a janitor, dropped so low from her high-rise New York City office, carrying a bundle of paper to wipe asses instead of designer fashion ideas to her manager.

He stood and hovered over her for a second, and she felt even more embarrassed. "Please go get yourself a coffee, or anything really, on the house." She smiled, trying to reassure him that it was more than ok for him to go. *Shoo, handsome fireman, shoo.* She was not interested in making small talk with a rugged stranger, who happened to be the last person to see her parents alive. She would rather dive back into her task of stacking things into an ordered structure. She wanted to maintain that feeling of being in control, and the best way to do that was to get back to restocking and stacking items.

Just then, a fluffy gray boulder smacked into the back of her legs and sent her down to the ground again, this time, landing on her palms.

"Smokey, no, sit, sit. Stay." It was Caleb speaking to a large shepherd mix with thick, smoky-gray fur accented by darker charcoal patches and a hint of white around his muzzle and paws. His head was lowered, and his amber-tinged eyes stared right into Sierra's soul. She hated him immediately.

Caleb touched her shoulder, offering to help her up yet again, but she shrugged him off this time. Eyes locked on the mutt who'd knocked her down, she was less mesmerized. The spell was broken.

"I am so sorry," Caleb said, trying to look her in the eyes while keeping a firm hand on Smokey's collar. "I recently rescued him, so he isn't very well trained.

We're actually working on it today. I heard this place was reopened, so I wanted to come see how you and your sister were doing."

Sierra brushed fur and dirt from her slacks as she stood up. "I was doing better when I was on my feet," she said curtly.

"I'm so sorry, again," Caleb said, his volume low and sincere. "I'm going to retie him up outside and get that coffee. I'll get out of your way, for good this time."

His smile was so disarming that she had to look away, back to the toilet paper rolls, and try to focus on finishing her afternoon project. Organization = good. Handsome, distracting fireman and fluffy dog = bad.

Sierra carried as many packs as she could into the women's bathroom, opened the cabinet drawers under the sink, and started stacking them inside. Zadie showed up beside her with a handful of toilet paper roll packs.

"What was that?" Zadie asked, her dark eyebrows raised.

Sierra rolled her eyes. "Absolutely nothing," she answered.

"It didn't look like nothing." Zadie was young, with a baby-round face, and her optimistic eyes were wide, trying to force an insinuation onto Sierra.

"He ran into me, and then his stupid dog knocked me over, again," Sierra explained. "Obnoxious, end of story."

"OK, well, that end of story looked like the beginning of one to me." Zadie grinned from ear-to-ear, handing over the packs for Sierra to shove into the cabinet. "See what I did there?"

"You haven't changed," Sierra said, rolling her eyes but smiling playfully. And the girl hadn't. Aside from a little height increase, she was still the happy-go-lucky, sunshine in a hurricane she'd always been. Sierra's parents truly had loved this girl like one of their own. Millie had been their best friend. Sierra felt guilty remembering how she'd reacted to Millie reading the Will. She knew she needed to make amends. It wasn't like Millie had written the Will for them.

The sweet girl kept helping Sierra until the job was done, but Sierra's project wasn't quite completed yet. She started to head back to the office, trying not to look to see if Smokey and the fireman were still lurking in the café.

Someone else did catch her eye, and she froze at the swinging door that led into the kitchen. An older woman, plump with long grey hair, dressed in a black gown, sat at a table in the corner. She had a small green lamp on her table that Sierra had never seen before. The woman was rocking and humming to herself, and on the table lay a row of cards next to a deck.

Tarot cards, really? Sierra asked herself. Was that really what was going on in her parents' café? They had just died, and already some charlatan was in here, in their café, their home, taking advantage of who, Savannah? Zadie? Their customers?

Sierra stormed over to the table and put her hands down so hard that the cards in the pile shuffled apart. "Who are you and what are you doing here? You need to leave, now."

The older woman's eyes stayed closed, and her palms were face-up on her lap, wrists layered in chunky bracelets. "I wondered when we might meet, Sierra."

"This isn't a merry meet or whatever crazy nonsense your type says. You don't belong here. We don't buy into this crap."

"Crazy. Crap. Nonsense. Yes, dear, I've heard it all, and I understand." The woman's tone was calm, even-toned, like a stoned hippie in the desert. She slowly opened her eyes and looked up at Sierra. The woman's gray eyes sent an uncomfortable tingle through Sierra's body, so she released her palms from the table and stood back up to cross her arms protectively across her chest.

The woman smiled. "Your parents were friends of mine, and they let me sit, buy coffee, sandwiches, and read cards for people, here. I understand if you want me to leave, now that this place is yours."

"This place isn't mine," Sierra said, feeling odd hearing that it was. Savannah came out of nowhere to stand next to the woman.

"She doesn't have to leave," Savannah said. "This is Laurel." Savannah placed a hand on the woman's shoulder, lovingly, fingers patting Laurel's flowy, black smock. "She is a paying regular, and people love to come see her to talk about their problems, have their fortunes read, cards read, and just for her company. She stays." Savannah smiled down at Laurel, but then lifted her head and glowered at Sierra defiantly.

Sierra glared at her eccentric and irresponsible sister with disdain. She didn't want to fight about this, but she also didn't have the power to talk Savannah out of it right now. Sierra huffed and stormed off to finish her organization project with fervor.

11 SAVANNAH

Savannah heaved out a sigh and then sat down in the chair opposite Laurel. She was a lovely woman with grey hair, grey eyes, pale white skin, rosy cheeks, and wearing a very black silky dress with intricate flowers woven throughout, also black.

"I'm so sorry about my sister," Savannah said, trying to help gather back the cards that had fallen off the top of her deck. "She's never really been open-minded about this stuff and probably assumed you were here because my parents died… well, you know what I mean."

"Assumed that I'm an opportunistic old psychic," Laurel said with a teasing tone. Her voice was deep and melodic, her words spilling out as if from an instrument. "Well, I think I understand your sister better than she does at this time."

"What do you mean?" Savannah asked, genuinely curious for any insight into Sierra's mind and personality. Her older sister had seemed so detached and angry for longer than she could remember. High school, maybe?

"Everybody processes grief differently," Laurel explained. "Spouses, children, siblings, friends. We all move through the stages of grief at our own pace. Your sister has always been comfortable being the oldest, smartest, best, the one in charge, the one who knows better, the one in control of her emotions, the one in control of her life. Nothing throws off a person like that more than an uncontrollable event, like death." Laurel began reshuffling the cards. The skin of her hands was so thin that Savannah could make out the woman's blue veins.

"I don't know much about grief," Savannah admitted. "Just that this... all of this sucks," she motioned her hands around the room, but meant more the loss of her parents, them not being present in the café with her, than her new responsibility of running it and being trapped in Lincoln for a year.

Laurel smiled, her lightly stained pink lips lifting to show a spot of lipstick on her teeth. "The stages of grief are denial, anger, bargaining, depression, and acceptance. You are both still in the denial and anger stage."

"Sierra is always in the anger stage," Savannah jabbed.

"Not always, Savannah," Laurel corrected her. Savannah felt her cheeks flush with guilt. The woman laid down a card in front of her.

"Did you read my parents' cards?" Savannah asked.

"Your mother enjoyed it a few times. There was nothing significant, of course. She lamented the distance she felt from you girls. She missed you terribly, and I assured her that you'd return home. Of course, I didn't foresee the reason why, if that's your next question. There are some things we are not allowed to see in this life. Some things we are not allowed to know."

Laurel turned over the Five of Cups, a hand-painted image of five golden goblets all stacked together, floating in the clouds. "Well, that's an obvious one, I suppose. This is your current loss, your sorrows. There is pain and sadness that you must face alongside your sister. I'm sure this place has brought back many memories. Your pain will not go away anytime soon."

Laurel shuffled while she spoke and then lay down and flipped over another card: The Lovers. The image on the card was that of two naked people, a man and a woman.

"You see how their arms are outstretched, palms facing up?" Laurel asked. Savannah leaned closer and nodded. "These two are both open to receiving love. That's an important piece of the puzzle. The potential for love could be right in front of you, but if you are not open to receiving it, that love will pass you by."

Savannah thought of Jaxon. She saw him suddenly walking through their Seattle apartment with a woman who was not her. Savannah envisioned him touching and kissing on the woman, and she immediately shuttered the thought away, wondering where it had come from. She'd never been jealous about Jaxon, even when she knew that women threw themselves at him nightly. She'd always trusted him.

"Here's the last card," Laurel said, laying down the Ten of Pentacles. "Ah, this is a good card, Savannah. It's a message from your parents as it represents legacy, inheritance, and stability. All will be well. You'll find your purpose."

Tears had blossomed in Savannah's eyes from out of nowhere, and she excused herself in a hurry, heading to the bathroom to have a cry. She wanted to believe that the card was a message from her parents, but she knew there was no message besides what they'd written in their Will. They hadn't expected to die. They hadn't expected to force their kids to work together for a year, not really. By the time Savannah had calmed down, her face was puffy, and her eyes were red. She splashed some water on her face and eyes to cool off, then dried her skin and blew her nose into the wet paper towel.

"What a mess," she told her reflection. "How am I supposed to do this for an entire year if I can't even make it through the first day?"

Savannah left the bathroom and walked back toward the bar. The afternoon sun shone brightly through the front windows of the café, so she couldn't see the customer who was walking in. Within the silhouette, she could make out the shape of a cowboy hat and tried to keep from rolling her eyes. There was one thing she just hadn't ever connected with, and that was the cowboy lifestyle. She knew that farms, ranches, and real cowboys were plentiful here in Lincoln, what with farming and ranching and everyone listening to country music. She didn't hate that music, but she definitely preferred old rock and punk rock. Jaxon had tried to do a hybrid combination of country rock, but his true colors shone through his leather pants. He was a rocker.

Savannah dipped behind the bar to prepare herself to take the customer's order. The closer he came, the further from the sunny front windows, the more his face and features came into view. He was about six feet tall with broad shoulders and shaggy blond hair tucked underneath a dusty cowboy hat. *So, not a poser*, she thought. He looked like he legitimately had just gotten off farm work somewhere.

"I'm gonna go wash up first," he told her, with a thick accent. "But I'd love a little coffee with some Jameson in it, if ya got it."

"Oh, we got it," Savannah said, being friendly. He tipped his hat and headed toward the bathroom. She chuckled to herself and turned to pour a cup of coffee with a shot of whiskey. She wondered if he'd care for any sugar or vanilla flavoring, but doubted it. This was a black coffee drinker through and through, like most cowboys. She did love a good vanilla whiskey mixed into coffee herself, but it was a rare treat.

The man was like a walking cowboy cliché: bow-legged, tall, handsome, and covered in dirt. His sun-worn skin made him look closer to thirty, but she guessed him to be more in his mid-twenties. Taking wide, slow steps in his brown Ariats, he sauntered back toward her with his wallet out. "What's the damage?" he asked. His accent made her smile involuntarily. It was all just too much.

"$5 for the whiskey, coffee on the house this late in the day," she answered. He handed over a warm, wrinkly five-dollar bill.

"I knew that. I was just testing ya." He winked at her and took a sip, sighing audibly and closing his eyes, savoring the whiskey more than the coffee, she assumed. "You must be one of the Sweetwater sisters," he guessed. "I've seen pictures of you smaller."

"You're a regular?" Savannah asked.

"I guess that's what you'd call me."

"I'm Savannah."

He seemed to smile wider. "The baby that moved to Seattle," he said, confirming what he knew about her. It felt a little strange being known by a stranger. She guessed she'd need to get used to people like Laurel and this cowboy knowing her from stories her parents had told them.

"That's me," Savannah said, trying to think of a way out of this conversation. He just looked at her with Earthly-green eyes. More people came into the café just then, and she turned her head. "Welcome in!" she yelled loudly.

"Nice to meet you, Savannah," said the cowboy, nodding at her before heading over to say hello to Laurel. *A fireman, a tarot card reader, and a cowboy walked into a bar*, she thought to herself.

She busied herself with making drinks for the small group of girls who had come into the café. They'd all asked for complicated mixed alcohol drinks, so she didn't have time to notice how much they looked over at the handsome cowboy. Savannah was certain that man was taken anyway, or had a little wife at home with babies, knowing her town.

More and more college kids started to trickle into the bar for a happy hour that turned into a very late night before she knew it. Sierra even came out to help her and Mario keep up with drinks after the kitchen closed. She found it surprising that the place would be so busy on a Sunday and wondered if it was just morbid curiosity that brought the people in, although they wouldn't admit it.

Although Savannah had been working two jobs for a while in Seattle, at the end of that first night back at her parents' café, she'd never felt more tired. She wished she could say that she'd been too busy to think about her parents, but nearly every person or group that ordered something asked how she was doing, how her sister was doing, if they were home to stay, and if they were going to keep running the bar. They shared their condolences, prayers, thoughts, memories, and a continuation of emotional roller coaster journeys as Savannah struggled to keep her eyes dry and mind focused. All she wanted was to get through her day and go to bed.

The lights were dimmed, the last customers were ushered out, and the rest of the tables were cleaned off. Sierra and Savannah said goodbye to Mario and Edith, Zadie, who had returned during the evening to work the late shift, and the two young boys who helped clean and wash dishes as they all left through the back door.

The girls pulled up two barstools and poured themselves whiskeys on ice. Savannah had grabbed a nicer bottle of Basil Hayden, feeling they deserved it. The girls clinked their glasses together wordlessly before taking sips. And then in unison, they both said, "I can't do this."

They both laughed, took more sips, then stared off into the now-empty café.

"I'm going to lose my job if I stay here, Savannah," Sierra said in a quiet voice filled with desperate honesty.

"But we'll lose this if we leave," Savannah said, nodding toward the empty dining area. "We could potentially lose hundreds of thousands of dollars. How much do you think both properties are worth? This might be prime old town real estate with a successful café and bar in a college town. We would be giving up so much money if we just walked away."

"I know, I know, I know," Sierra said, raising her voice. "I get the situation we're in; I just hate it. I never wanted this stupid business. I never wanted to work here. I have a degree in fashion, a career, and I'm pouring fucking drinks at a bar."

"Wow," Savannah said, taking a bigger drink.

"You know what I mean," Sierra defended herself.

"You mean that you're better than me. Better than Mario. Better than Zadie. Better than Mom and Dad."

"First of all, Zadie is going to go out and have a career after she graduates, like I did," Sierra said. "Mario's wife makes enough money that he can work here and be happy. And Mom and Dad owned the place. They weren't just the bartenders and baristas."

"Just the bartenders? Just the baristas? Listen to yourself." Savannah was getting angry. She knew that her sister thought she was better than everyone just because she had a degree and had moved away from their small town, but Savannah felt that all jobs had value. Although Savannah hadn't finished school, didn't really know what she wanted to do with her life, and had followed a boyfriend and his band to Seattle, she never felt like a loser until Sierra opened her big fucking mouth.

"I don't see what the big deal is," Sierra said. "Our parents wanted us to have better lives. That's why they basically abandoned raising us to run this place."

"They didn't abandon us," Savannah said, but even as she said the words, she knew in her heart she also felt abandoned. It was true that their lives drastically changed when her parents started the Sweetwater Café and Bar. When Savannah tried to recall positive memories from her youth, she only saw her parents here, working. She did her school homework or cleaned something. She wanted to remember it as cool and fun, but really, it had been lonely.

Sierra pushed back from the bar, stood up, finished her glass, and then took it into the back kitchen to clean. "They did abandon us, and they are doing it again now."

Savannah didn't have anything to say in her parents' defense. Although she wanted to argue, wanted to defend her parents, their death felt exactly like abandonment.

12 SIERRA

Sierra started her next day's shift at the café by punching twenty early 2000 pop bangers into the jukebox. Even though she could download an app, hitting the numbers with her fingers just felt more satisfying.

A few old ladies sat together at a small round table, fragile hands clasped around warm cups, and they all jerked their heads up in disgust as the first song began to play. Sierra smiled at them and headed to the kitchen as Avril Lavigne's "Here's to Never Growing Up" filled the space. *Just wait until the Flo Rida song starts to play*, she thought to herself.

Savannah was making coffee and taking orders with Zadie, so Sierra assigned herself to the kitchen with Mario. If she was going to be running the café for a year, she needed to know how to manage every aspect, just as her father had. She never cooked, but assumed that with a few lessons from Mario, she could master grilling a sandwich. How hard could it be? Their menu wasn't complicated. Breakfast pastries were delivered early from a local bakery. Then they basically put a selection of eggs, cheese, sausage, and bacon on top of whatever type of bread the customer requested.

For lunch and dinner, the menu consisted of fried appetizers, a charcuterie plate that was very popular during happy hour with glasses of wine, hamburgers, hot dogs, ham or turkey sandwiches, and a vegetarian patty option. Desserts were also brought by the same bakery, but not put out on display until the afternoon. There was a variety of salads, too, which really just altered the toppings and dressings. Once people started drinking, they steered clear of the salads and chose the heavier, greasier foods.

Sierra grabbed a black apron, draped it over her neck, and tied it around the waist of her Agolde skinny jeans. Mario flipped an egg, turned his head toward her, and then cocked it at an odd angle, looking her up and down with a quizzical expression as if she'd just shown up to a swimming competition in ski bibs.

"Whatcha doin'?" Mario asked.

"Helping," she said, trying not to sound snarky.

"Oh, no, chica, no need, I got it."

"Mario, I have to learn how to run this kitchen. What if you're out sick?" Sierra put her hands on her hips.

"I put on a mask," Mario said, turning back to his stovetop. He pulled over a croissant that had been sliced in half and buttered and laid the butter side down onto the cooktop.

"Did Dad help you cook?" Sierra asked.

"Dennis? Oh no, not Dennis. He only cooked for himself when he was hungry." Mario flipped one half of the croissant onto a plate, then scooped up the eggs and laid them on top. With a gloved hand, he grabbed the other half of the croissant and completed the breakfast sandwich.

"Did Mom ever cook?" Sierra asked.

"Nah, Deborah didn't cook. Your mama barely ate. Never knew how a woman who ate so little could be so curvy. Must have been you kids."

Sierra shook her head, confused by his story and by the fact that her parents didn't cook in their own café. She thought she remembered them cooking, but maybe they had only cooked at home when they were very young, before the café. Her heart ached remembering how, as middle schoolers and teenagers, they would put their lunch and dinner orders in just like the customers. Their parents hadn't even cooked for their kids. To Sierra, it was just something else that the café had taken from her childhood. She quickly shifted out of the sadness and channeled her emotions into frustration.

"Well, then what am I supposed to do for a year in here?" she asked.

Mario froze in the doorway with the plated sandwich and shot his eyes over to her. "A year?"

Sierra's breath hitched, and she felt her eyes grow wide for a second before she regained her composure. Nobody knew her parents' instructions. Nobody knew that the sisters would be selling the Sweetwater Café in a year.

"I can't stay here forever, Mario," she said, her voice soft but dismissive. She turned and headed toward the office as a cover to avoid any more questions. She heard Mario go through the door to deliver the sandwich order.

Sierra closed the office door behind her and ripped off the black apron. She threw it unsatisfyingly across the room, since it just lightly flopped to the floor. "Well, shit," she said to herself. "What am I supposed to do here for a year? Run the place and yet not do anything. Don't do anything here, but you can't go back to New York fucking City either. Argh, dammit." She plopped down into her father's desk chair, an old, uncomfortable wooden one from the eighties on black metal wheels.

This will not do, she told herself, plotting. She had already reorganized. Did she need to keep doing the inventory? Order supplies?

"That's gotta be what you spent your days doing, right, Dad?" she asked, clicking the screen on his computer and then looking through digital files. She heard the beat drop on Kesha's *Blow* through the wall and smiled to herself. *Take that, old ladies*, she told herself. Sierra hated slow music, country music, and jazz. Give her upbeat music day and night.

The door opened behind her, and Savannah came into the small office.

"The jukebox is broken," she said. Sierra smiled wider. "I pre-loaded like twenty songs to wake everybody up. I couldn't focus with those slow songs playing."

"It's 9 a.m., Sierra," Savannah said. "You don't think that's a bit much?"

"People are here to wake up, and that music was putting me to sleep," Sierra said, defending her playlist. "Besides, aren't you the music lover one?"

"Yeah, but like, music should fit the existing mood or help drive people to get into a particular mood. You've got it blasting like a nightclub at 3 a.m."

Sierra closed her eyes as if she were in a blissful memory. "Like an NYC nightclub. Exactly."

"It doesn't really fit the vibe of this café, sis."

Sierra popped her eyes open and turned toward her sister. "Yeah. I know. I don't like the vibe of this place. I don't like the vibe of Lincoln fucking Nebraska. I want to leave, but I'm stuck here in a windowless office trying to figure out what I'm supposed to do here for an entire year!"

Savannah crossed her arms but said nothing. She just glared down at Sierra and then turned and left the office, closing the door like closing the lid of a coffin. Sierra was a mix of anger, fear, sadness, and boredom.

"Fuck! The funeral!" she yelled, realizing she'd meant to call the funeral home and hadn't done it. They had been so distracted from working at the café that Sierra hadn't called to make arrangements or schedule any details. She might not relish the idea of planning her parents' funeral, but at least it was something to do other than sitting around on her hands at this damned café. She did a quick search on her phone for the contact details the firefighter had shared with her and called the funeral home. After making arrangements to pick up her parents' ashes, she decided that they'd have a wake at the café and then proceeded to schedule it for the following Sunday afternoon.

She just wanted to get it over with and assumed her sister would feel the same way. They could send out some messages and ask the employees to get the word out, also. Sierra was pretty sure that Millie would know all her parents' friends. Zadie would know all the regulars and previous employees.

Another thought interrupted her. Employees. Payroll. Was that automatic? Did she have to enter something to make sure the employees would get paid? She jumped up to go find Mario, hoping he knew, but couldn't find him anywhere in the kitchen. Zadie was with customers, so she waited patiently for her to finish ringing up the young couple.

"Hey, Zadie," Sierra said, coming up behind her.

"Yes, Sierra?" Zadie was always so cheerful and positive.

"Did my dad have to process your payroll, or is it automatic?"

"Oh yeah, we enter it into an app, and he just double-checks it, I think. On his computer. Not sure if he had to approve it or not, but our money is automatically deposited."

"That's a relief. I'll look to see what I need to approve. Thanks." She saw that Savannah was making a latte for the customer who had just ordered. "We'll have the wake here for our parents this Sunday afternoon, if you want to get the word out."

Zadie's smile faded, and Savannah nearly spilled the drink as she passed it over the counter. Both girls now looked directly at Sierra.

"Were you going to tell me?" Savannah asked.

"I'm telling you now," Sierra said.

"Why didn't you talk to me about scheduling it?" Savannah crossed her arms.

"Because I handle things like this and you handle things like that," Sierra waved toward the drink station.

"What the hell does that mean?" Savannah asked, her voice rising.

"Um, girls," Zadie said, trying to interrupt them. "We have customers. Could you scoot into the kitchen?"

Savannah shrugged at Zadie and started walking toward the kitchen, but Sierra didn't move.

"Stop being so dramatic, Savannah. I'm just trying to take care of things like scheduling the funeral, checking inventory, learning how to reorder inventory, and approving payroll while you're out here mixing drinks. You should be thanking me for staying here because out of the two of us, you're going to need that inheritance more than I will."

"I don't want to work the same shift as you," Savannah said, interrupting Sierra's angry tangent.

"Fine," Sierra answered. "You come in after the lunch shift and close. I will open and play whatever music I want to every morning, take care of business, then leave you to manage the nightlife."

"Fine," Savannah agreed, storming off toward the bathroom.

"Fine," Sierra said, heading back into the kitchen. Yelling at her sister had worked up an appetite, so she fired the cooktop back up and decided to make herself a grilled ham and cheese. She grabbed slices of wheat bread, slathered them with butter, and then laid them down on the stove. "Shit," she mumbled to herself, remembering her apron. She didn't want grease to get onto her Leset shirt.

She went into her dad's office to find where she'd tossed it onto the floor. A message on the computer screen caught her eye. It was a calendar reminder from Outlook. She crept closer to the screen to see that it read, "Payroll Due."

"Well, look at that." Sierra slid into the chair and started to dig for an app that hinted at payroll services. When she found it on his desktop, along with about a hundred other apps, she opened it and watched as lines populated in a neat little calendar.

All the employees had missed the days after her parents had died, of course, but every other day had entries. She scanned each name, date, and time and then looked for where she could approve them. One by one, she opened and selected an approve button. Sierra was starting to feel pretty proud of herself until the fire alarm blared at an ungodly volume. She covered her ears, crouching down as if she could escape the blast of noise. "My sandwich," she realized.

Sierra ran from the office and toward the stove. Luckily, the toast was just smoking; there was no fire. She grabbed at the bread with both hands and immediately burned the tips of her fingers, flinging the smoking toast across the room.

"Dammit, dammit, dammit," she mumbled. Zadie and Savannah ran into the kitchen with their hands covering their ears.

"What's on fire?" Zadie yelled over the alarms.

"How do we turn it off!?" Savannah screamed, her eyes searching the kitchen.

"Nothing is on fire! I don't know!" Sierra yelled in response.

Mario ran into the kitchen and over to a metal panel on the wall. He opened a metal door, pulled a lever, then pushed a button. The sirens immediately cut off. He turned and looked at the three girls, who were all still holding their hands over their ears, although the sound had stopped.

"What were you girls doing?" Mario asked, looking from one to the other until his eyes rested on the burnt toast lying on the kitchen floor.

Zadie and Savannah turned to Sierra as they all slowly lowered their hands.

"I was making a sandwich," Sierra said, shrugging and trying to mask her embarrassment. That's when she realized that her fingertips were burning. She tucked them behind her back so nobody would notice.

"Maybe you let me cook for you for a while, alright? I'll teach you first before you start on your own." Mario's tone was gentle, but she still felt reprimanded.

Savannah and Zadie went back out to the main floor, but Sierra walked straight to the office and closed the door, wanting to be alone. She held her hands up in front of her and blew on her fingertips, trying to cool them off. Sierra knew that she should go find a first aid kit or run cold water over her hands. Shit, even walking into the freezer could help, but she didn't want anyone to know that she had not only burned bread and set off the fire alarm on her second day but burned herself as well.

A few minutes later, someone knocked on the office door. Her hands hurt so badly by then that she wasn't sure if she could even turn the knob. She managed to grip the thing between both of her palms and turn it enough to pop it open. Looking up, she saw that it was the fireman, Caleb, decked out in full yellow fireproof gear.

"Hi, Sierra," he said, cautiously, as if approaching a tiger. "Fire alarm went off. Your, uh, sister said you burned toast, but I wanted to check on you. And the guys need to double-check the alarm panel."

He was in full uniform as if entering a burning building, but he held his helmet in his hands. Caleb's eyes were warm and kind, the hazel dark in the shadows of the kitchen, matching the color of his brown hair. He looked her over quickly, barely discernible with how fast his eyes moved down and then up again, but it was enough. He set his helmet down on the ground and then gently grabbed her wrists.

"Come here," he said in a tone so low it could have been a whisper. He guided her toward the walk-in freezer, pausing to grab a towel from a metal shelf. They walked into the giant metal enclosure, and he placed her palms face up. Her fingers were clearly burned, and she couldn't believe he'd noticed.

He laid the towel across her fingers, then grabbed a frozen bag of soup from the shelf and laid it on top of the towel. They locked eyes for a brief moment as the cool relief soaked into her fingertips.

"Now, I'm no doctor, but I think you burned your fingers." His words were so slowly spoken, and his lips curled up into a smile.

"Are you teasing me?" she asked, an uncontrollable smile threatening to curl up her own lips.

"I think you have a lot going on right now, Sierra."

The way her name sounded on his lips made her feel tingly all over. His soft-spoken tone, the tenderness in his eyes, lulled her into a trance. She felt like she was being pulled into his orbit and didn't want to fight it.

"And because you have a lot going on, I don't think you realize what you've done to your poor sweet little fingers." He still had his hands wrapped around her wrists, warmth from him contrasting with the coolness seeping through the towel on her fingers. His voice was quiet and intimately close.

"I don't want to parade you out through the café, but I think these need to be treated."

Sierra felt her head shaking, trying to pull herself back to reality and out of his dreamy eyes. She whispered the word, "No," and then, "I'm fine."

Caleb sighed a deep, heavy sound that sent another tingle through her body. His warm breath passed down across her face, and she had to stop herself from breathing it in like a maniac.

"I was afraid you'd say that, Sierra Sweetwater. Your parents were pretty stubborn, too."

"You knew them?" She suddenly perked up as if awoken from a dream.

"You think this is the first time that alarm's gone off since you moved away?" he asked, sounding ornery.

"Oh, that makes sense," she said.

"You are going to stay right here. I'm going to the truck to get something to put on your burns and to wrap up your fingers. Are you going to wait for me?"

Sierra just looked into his eyes, swimming there or drowning; she couldn't admit either feeling to herself. His voice was hypnotic, and she'd nearly forgotten that her fingers were burned.

"Sierra? Will you wait for me here?" he repeated.

Finally, she nodded.

Sierra watched Caleb leave in a daze, like she was in some drug-induced stupor. *Nope, nope, nope*, she told herself. *This is trauma. My parents died, and I burned my fingers. I'm trapped in Nebraska, running a café for a year. I'm experiencing trauma. This must be what they call a trauma bond. That's it.*

But she obediently sat down on a stool in the corner, her fingers extended with the towel covering them and the frozen soup on top, and waited.

13 SAVANNAH

The firetruck rolled away from Sweetwater Café and Bar, taking all its firemen with it—minus one. Savannah was curious, but not enough to go back into the kitchen to investigate why one man had stayed behind with her sister. Was her sister injured, or was she being lectured about the finer points of not burning toast?

Customers had resumed eating and ordering, and the front and back doors were wide open to let what little smoke was left out of the building. Savannah leaned against the counter and stared at the kitchen door, waiting.

Finally, the fireman came through the door, holding it open for Sierra, who followed closely behind with her hands bandaged up. The man's brown eyes lifted to meet Savannah's only after he ensured Sierra cleared the door. Savannah stood up straighter.

"Your sister asked me to drive her home in your dad's truck," the man explained. Savannah recognized the truck keys in one of his hands. "I'm Caleb, by the way. The fireman who called you about your parents."

Caleb walked up to her then, shifted her dad's truck keys to his left hand, and stuck out his meaty right one. Savannah took it and shook, still not taking her eyes off his. *Was her sister being rescued right now?* she wondered. "Hi," Savannah said, not knowing what else to say. She was honestly surprised for the second time today that her sister, the responsible one, the one who was supposed to be in charge of running this business while Savannah just 'made the drinks,' had not only set off the fire alarm but burned herself. What was happening?

"It's a good thing we switched shifts," Sierra said. "I'll be back to open in the morning." Then she turned and headed toward the back hallway. The fireman nodded at Savannah and then hurried to open the back door for Sierra.

"He's pretty good looking," Zadie said, suddenly so close to Savannah that she jumped, startled.

"I'm just glad she's leaving," Savannah said, feeling bitter, but a little guilty that she hadn't asked if Sierra was even OK. But then she remembered her sister's earlier tone and their fight. "With her gone, we'll have more room to relax and do our own thing for the rest of the evening."

"Party, party, party," Zadie said, playfully rocking her hips from side-to-side.

And in their own way, they did party. They pre-loaded the juke box with upbeat songs. They dimmed the lights, danced, and poured drinks for college kids who streamed in and out of the bar from after dinner until close. By the time they were locking the front door, Savannah was exhausted.

"How are you still so peppy?" she asked Zadie. The girl was still singing as she closed down the register and cleaned the bar, bouncing like she lived on caffeine.

"Just the way my mama made me," Zadie joked with a big smile on her face. "Your sister has the truck, right? I can drop you off on my way back."

Savannah realized that she didn't want to go back to her parents' house. She didn't want to deal with Sierra, especially after the fight they'd had. She was so tired; she didn't even want to get into a car. Then she remembered the upstairs apartment. Neither sister had ventured up there. They weren't ever interested in going up there when they were kids or teens, since the café was more fun with sodas, music, and school kids stopping by with their parents, so Savannah had nearly forgotten about it. She knew that her parents had slept there from time to time, especially when they'd worked full open-to-close shifts. At some point, their mom had switched to mornings and their dad to evenings, so it was just their dad who stayed in the apartment. Savannah was curious and decided to go see what condition it was in. If it was terrible, she could just get a ride-share car back to the house.

"No, I'm good, thanks," Savannah told Zadie. Savannah saw Zadie safely to her car from the back door, then closed it behind her, walking through the dark, quiet bar. She went through the kitchen and to a door that looked as if it were concealing a closet, but instead, it opened up to an old, narrow staircase.

"Shit, it's dark," she mumbled to herself. She went back to her father's office and dug out a flashlight from his desk drawer, made sure it worked, then headed back up, looking for light switches along the way.

There was one at the very top of the staircase, right outside of another door that she remembered would open straight into the apartment. She turned the ancient copper knob, noticing the lack of a lock, and pushed the old wooden door open. The only light in the room came from streetlights through the uncovered windows. She turned her flashlight to the wall, looking until she found a single switch, and flipped it on. Linear industrial lights flickered to life throughout the apartment, casting a harsh white light over the wooden floors and old, dusty furniture.

"Wow," she said, taking the space in. It wasn't like she remembered as a child. Overwhelming and scary as a child, now it seemed unique and cool. There was so much potential here. The living area was wide open, separated from the kitchen by a few vertical wood columns. Her dad had a television set up on a long worktable, where he'd clearly done all sorts of tinkering. He had boxes of nails next to empty coffee cans, a dead plant, light bulbs, and a broken apart radio laid open, waiting for a fix that will never come. There was one old red rug with undiscernible designs in the center of the room, and an old brown leather couch stained beyond saving, sitting on top of it, facing the television. A wood crate served as the ottoman and coffee table.

Savannah looked up to the ceiling, which was bare save for exposed wooden beams, electrical wires, and silver ductwork. Above the kitchen, a simple layout with appliances from the eighties, was a loft. She assumed that was the official bedroom, but figured her dad had just slept out on the couch, never making the trek up those stairs.

She carefully climbed the metal staircase, which looked like it had been added in the eighties when the kitchen was updated, but not when the building was actually built. At the top, there was a massive bed perfectly made with sheets and a maroon comforter covered in so much dust it looked grey, neatly tucked up under the mattress. There was a dresser, a vanity with a stool and mirror, a large wardrobe that must have been built where it stood, and a wingback chair so filthy, she couldn't make out its color.

"You didn't ever sleep in here, did you, Dad?"

She turned and looked at the entire space from the top of the loft.

"I. Love. This. Space."

And then, since nobody was in the building, she yelled it out into the hollow room. "I love this space!"

She turned back to look at the bed. "But God, are you dirty. That's all right. Let's see if there's dirt and dust under the covers."

Savannah took a deep breath and held it, then carefully drew back the heavy comforter, pulling it all the way to the foot of the bed and then onto the floor. The sheets underneath were pristine. However, many years ago, they were washed and then the bed made; nobody had touched them since. She could sleep here tonight, she knew. "I've slept in worse places."

She went back down to the kitchen to get her phone charger, a few towels, a spray bottle of surface cleaner to clear off a few spaces, and a glass of water. Then she made herself comfortable in her father's apartment above the café and slept better than she had in a long time.

Savannah woke up exactly eight hours later at 10:00 a.m., craving coffee. She knew her sister was downstairs, standing in her way of coffee. She wasn't ready to talk to her sister or even see her. And after spending the night in this apartment, she knew what she needed to do before her shift started.

She grabbed her wallet, headed down the stairs, and through the kitchen as quietly as possible. Sure enough, her sister was in their father's office, not standing in the way of a cup of coffee. Savannah said hi to Zadie, grabbed a to-go cup, served herself, grabbed the truck keys from a hook inside the kitchen, and then took her dad's old truck back home.

Back at her parents' house, she went to her room and packed up what little she'd brought, stopping only to brush her teeth and hair. Savannah loaded the truck up with clean sheets, a clean bedspread, and towels. She found an empty box in the garage and filled it up with some supplies she thought she'd need to both clean and live in the apartment. Digging through her dad's workbench, she found an unopened, lockable doorknob.

"You were going to get to it, right?" she asked, teasing his ghost. "I've got it, Dad." She threw the package and some tools into the box, then carried it to the truck. She spent the rest of the morning drinking coffee and cleaning up the loft apartment. She'd made a lot of progress and even started on changing the doorknob when it was nearly time to head down and take over for Sierra. Savannah sat against the doorframe and looked down the narrow staircase toward the kitchen. She didn't want to talk to her sister, but knew she needed to let her know that she'd be staying here now. She was certain that Sierra would be thrilled.

She went and cleaned herself up in the bathroom tucked away behind the loft kitchen, changed into some fresh clothes, then headed downstairs. Her sister came out of the office like a rocket, blocking Savannah's path to the front of the house. Sierra's arms were crossed.

"You didn't come home last night," Sierra said flatly.

"I stayed here." Savannah couldn't help but say it with a feeling of pride. She was an independent grown-up, and Sierra wasn't her mother.

"That's what Zadie said, but why?"

Savannah leaned back and crossed her own arms. "It was late, and I was tired. But I think it makes sense for me to just stay here. There's only one truck, and we are on opposite shifts."

"We can get another car," Sierra tried to say.

"For a year? No, that doesn't make sense. I can walk to everything I need from here. And besides, I love that apartment. It's perfect for me. The house fits your vibe." She wanted to add that they also wouldn't have to see or deal with each other, their differences, their annoyances, but she kept her mouth shut.

Sierra rolled her eyes. "Fine. Whatever. I don't care."

"Fine," Savannah agreed and headed to refill her coffee and start her evening shift. She served a customer and watched Sierra leave, swinging the truck keys in her hand on her way out.

"Howdy, miss."

Savannah's eyes snapped up to the tall cowboy standing in front of her. She cocked her head and smiled.

"Howdy?" she asked. "Is that really how you talk?"

He tipped his hat and winked. "She's curious about me." His voice was deep with a charming twang. He was tall, older than Savannah, but younger than thirty.

"Just curious about what you'd like to order, cowboy," Savannah said.

"Oh, well, you know my usual by now, right?" He put his hands on the counter, and she saw just how scarred and worn they were from actual hard labor. His fingernails were stained various shades of yellow, brown, and freshly purple from bruising. She wondered what work he did that would bruise his hands: roping, hauling hay, mending fences. What did cowboys do?

"Black coffee, whiskey neat, or a mix of both?" she asked, admittedly flirting a bit at this point.

"A woman after my own heart, knowing me so well already."

"Cowboy, I don't even know your name." Savannah stood up straight, realizing she'd been roped in like a calf at a rodeo.

"I thought you'd never ask," he said, his smile getting wider, showing off-white but clean-looking teeth, not perfectly straight but not terrible either. "Name's Waylon Hoffmann." He extended his right hand out to her.

Was he really trying to shake her hand? Did cowboys shake hands with women or just like, marry them and knock them up with babies? Savannah wasn't sure. She also didn't realize that 'cowboy' was still a legitimate career choice for people under thirty. Here was this handsome man living his life as a cowboy. It was mind-boggling.

She tentatively held her own hand out. His large hands swallowed her smaller ones, but his grip was gentle, his warmth permeating her skin in an intoxicating way.

"Savannah…" she paused, and her voice nearly cracked. "Sweetwater, obviously." She chuckled, feeling her cheeks flush with heat and embarrassment.

"It's nice to meet you, Savannah Sweetwater."

He kept shaking her hand gently, up and down, up and down, until Savannah started to feel dizzy. She actually giggled a little, and he finally let her go.

"So, what do you want?" she asked, then realizing what the question could insinuate, quickly clarified. "To order. To eat. Or drink. Um…"

What the hell was wrong with her? Sure, it had been a while since a man had hit on her, if that's what he was doing. She told herself that he was just being a polite cowboy, a southern gentleman. Weren't all cowboys this nice? Wasn't that their 'thing' to be charming with women or something?

"I'd love a whiskey with room for me to pour a drop of coffee into, if you still have any, and a turkey sandwich."

His eye-contact was unnatural, as if he was trying to see through her and to the wall of liquor beyond. Which would be a fun trick. *Stay cool*, she told herself. *Snap out of it.*

"Absolutely," she said, putting in the order, then turning around to pour his drink.

"I was sorry to hear about your parents, Savannah," he said, his tone changing from flirty to sorrowful. She pursed her lips, holding back her emotions. It still wasn't any easier to receive sympathy. Each word stung every time. "I haven't seen anything about a funeral."

"They've been cremated," Savannah said, handing him his whiskey. "We're having a wake here this coming Sunday."

"I'll be here," he confirmed as if that had been an invitation. She didn't mind terribly putting her eyes on his tanned face and green eyes.

Stop, she told herself, turning to the register. She told him the total and took his money.

"I'm glad to see that you and your sister came back to town to run this place, though," he said, taking his receipt.

"For a while," she said, more to herself than to him.

"You aren't here to stay?"

She looked up and met his eyes after sending the order through to Mario in the kitchen. "Well, I have a boyfriend out in Seattle and a couple of good jobs out there, an apartment, you know."

"A boyfriend, huh?" he asked. She wondered if she imagined the disappointment in his question. "How long have you two been together?"

"A couple of years now, I guess. I met him when I was working here in college. He was traveling through town with his band, and I went with them." Savannah cringed, knowing how that sounded.

"You have an artist's heart," he said, the mood lifting a little.

"Well, for someone without any artistic talent herself, I guess," she said. "I appreciate art." Savannah shrugged, feeling lame and wishing that handsome Waylon would go sit down somewhere. The café was currently empty, and Zadie was on her long break, off at a class or studying before her late-night shift.

Mario came out and delivered the sandwich to Waylon, who was still standing at the counter. The men were like old friends, the way they shook hands and talked. Savannah busied herself with pulling hot glasses from the dishwasher.

Mario went back to the kitchen, and Waylon just stood at the bar, chewing a bite of his sandwich. He didn't even move to a barstool, and she could feel him staring at her back.

"You and your boyfriend talk about marriage?" he asked. It felt like he'd been thinking about that question for some time.

She guffawed loudly, surprising herself. "Um, no."

"A woman like you, beautiful, kind, with an artistic heart, should be told how much she's loved every day. I hope he does that."

Jaxon did not do that.

Jaxon did not look at her the way Waylon was looking at her now.

Jaxon did not seem half as interested as the cowboy did while eating his turkey sandwich at the bar, as if he couldn't put even one more step of distance between them.

Savannah kept unloading the bar glasses, stacking them up neatly in preparation for the late rush. The best thing about being a business in a college town was that college students drank alcohol every single night.

Waylon finished his whiskey and sandwich, then pushed the plate across the bar.

"I need to get back to the ranch, Savannah," he said, sounding sad to leave.

"I hope you stay. There's a lot to love about Lincoln, and the city would be lucky to have you back for good."

Savannah looked up from straightening glasses and was nearly trapped in his piercing eyes. The look on his face was something she couldn't describe, even if she were an artist. The feeling it conveyed sent a warmth into the depths of her chest, and for some crazy reason, she felt like she could trust this complete and total stranger. And a cowboy at that. *Ridiculous*, she thought.

"Thank you," she said, not knowing how else to respond. He touched the edge of his hat and turned, heading out of the café toward the setting sun. He was a literal cowboy riding off into the sunset, and she was surprised to feel a little bit sad to see him go, but happier and more excited than she'd been in years.

14 SIERRA

The day of the wake came fast. Sierra had picked up her parents' urns from the crematorium. She'd rearranged the café furniture and set up a table at the back with pictures of her parents from throughout the years. She laid out a guest book and told the florist where to set up the flowers. She'd programmed a playlist of their favorite songs and written a eulogy.

Sierra did all this while her sister slept upstairs. Savannah was closing now, and Sierra had no idea how late her sister was staying up. For all she knew, she stayed up and kept drinking until dawn. Sierra rolled her eyes, feeling resentful about being in charge of every single thing. *Good thing I stayed here*, she thought to herself as she headed to the door to let in the caterer.

The kitchen was closed all day, but they would open the bar at 2 p.m. The wake was scheduled to start at noon, and the caterer had prepared finger foods like turkey pinwheels, veggie, fruit, meat, and cheese trays. Nothing too heavy or expensive, but Sierra hoped that meant the hungry people would go ahead and leave sooner than later.

She'd handled everything well so far. As long as she was busy, focused on what needed to get done, her checklist, she was good. As long as she didn't look too closely at the family photos, focusing instead on the size and positioning of the frames, she was fine. Strong. Resilient. Nothing would disrupt her calm focus.

"Good morning," Sierra said, greeting the caterer. The woman smiled demurely, clearly conscious that she was walking into a memorial.

"I've always liked this place," the woman said, glancing around. She set down a heavy tray covered in cellophane onto the bar. Then the woman put her hands on her hips and surveyed the space from the seating arrangement over to the table.

"Your parents were so kind," she said. The woman was middle-aged and about as heavy as you'd expect a full-time caterer to be, who properly tested her food. "I'm sorry for your loss. You have a sister too, right?"

Sierra smiled tightly and nodded, her eyes glancing toward the kitchen door. She supposed she needed to wake Savannah up and let her know that she'd brought designer dresses from New York City for her to wear. Lord knows what her bohemian sister would come out wearing if she didn't handle that, too.

When Sierra said nothing, the woman went back outside to resume bringing in food trays. Not wanting to make small talk, Sierra headed toward the door in the kitchen that led upstairs to her father's apartment. The stairs were narrow and dark, but she made her way up them and knocked on the locked door.

"Savannah," Sierra called after a few moments. Her sister unlocked and opened the door, letting it swing open as slowly as it was heavy.

"Hey," Savannah said, eyes squinting.

"Today is the wake," Sierra responded.

"I know," Savannah replied, rolling her eyes.

"I wanted to make sure you are up. And I brought you a few dresses to choose from. Black. Sleek. Designer." Sierra raised her eyebrows, expecting at least a little bit of gratitude, but received a shrug instead.

"I'm sure I have something," Savannah said.

"You haven't even thought about it or made sure?" Sierra scoffed. "I'll be right back. Stay there."

She marched down the stairs to the office, then returned with the dresses draped across her arm. "Here," Sierra said, thrusting them out to her sister. "The room is set up, the caterer is delivering the food now, and you have about an hour before people start showing up. Can you just… get your shit together and come downstairs." It was an order, not a question. Then she turned and went back to the kitchen.

People slowly began arriving a few minutes before noon. Sierra smoothed down the front of her black Theory shift dress. She smiled, stood near the café entrance, shook hands, accepted condolences one after another, then motioned for folks to enter and take seats.

Savannah came down five minutes *after* noon. She'd chosen the DVF wrap dress that hugged her thin frame. Sierra caught herself smiling when she really wanted to scowl at her tardy sister. But Savannah looked beautiful in the gown, even with her flat hair and makeup-free face. For a moment, Savannah was her little sister again, and not some flaky brat she was trapped running a bar with.

Sierra turned back to the door just as Caleb and his dog were walking up. Smokey was on a leash connected to a harness, and she hoped that in the week since the dog had knocked her over, it had received some behavioral lessons.

Caleb was dressed in a black, button-up dress shirt and dark blue jeans. Although more business-casual than funeral, he looked handsome. The clothes fit his muscled frame well, and his hair even looked to be trimmed up since the last time she'd seen him. She felt her cheeks redden as she looked him over. He leaned in close, catching her so off-guard that she froze like a possum playing dead. Caleb pressed his lips against her cheek, kissing her. His face was clean-shaven, and he smelled like cedar and soap.

He added no words to accompany his kiss, just walked past her, and headed toward a seat. She blinked herself back to life and smiled at the next person who entered. Sierra stood there receiving greetings and condolences, but her mind was on Caleb and that kiss. Sure, in New York, everybody kissed their cheeks in greeting. It was no big deal. But his scent, his touch, the outlines of his pecs in his shirt… what the hell was going on with her brain? This was her parents' memorial service. Their urns sat with their ashes next to all that was left of their lives; memories encapsulated in photographs.

"Sierra, darlin'," Millie threw her arms around Sierra's middle, about as far up as she could reach, and squeezed. As Sierra's eyes popped out of her head, she saw Zadie standing behind her mother. Both ladies were dressed in black dresses with pink, red, blue, and white flowers. They didn't match, but both dresses were similar in style and design. Millie leaned back and looked up at

Sierra. "How are you? How's your sister? I haven't seen you since…" she cut off before finishing.

"We are fine, Millie, thanks."

Zadie stepped up and hugged Sierra. Zadie was much closer to Savannah than Sierra, but she was a nice girl. There was usually a lot of energy and positivity with Zadie, but she seemed reserved today, as was to be expected.

More people filtered in, filling seats. Sierra recognized some, but there were many she hadn't ever seen before, including a tall, blonde man in a cowboy hat who seemed to head straight for her sister, she noticed.

She left the door propped open and headed toward the back table to begin the service. She had decided not to bring in any religious figure, since her parents had never gone to church, although she noticed a pastor in the crowd. Probably a regular. He was eyeing the psychic suspiciously. 'Tell me about it,' she almost wanted to say to him.

Savannah was talking with Zadie, but Sierra grabbed her by the wrist and pulled her toward the table, not sure if her sister had anything planned to say, but not wanting to kick everything off without her.

"Hello, friends, family, neighbors," Sierra started. The talking quieted down to nothing, and prickles climbed up her spine. "Thank you all for coming today to remember our parents." Sierra looked toward Savannah, nodding slightly. Savannah just blinked as if trying to hold back tears.

"Our parents, Dennis and Deborah, wanted to open this place not just to make money, but to foster a community," Sierra continued. "Each one of you is here today because, as much as you supported their business, they supported you as a community. They were here to serve you drinks and talk to you, get to know you, to become your friends, and to help you have a better day. They wanted that for you every day. I know this because that's what they wanted for us too."

Sierra turned to look at her parents' faces, smiling up at her from the photograph of some camping trip to some lake from a time she couldn't place. "They were good people who tried their best to be the best parents. Dad never raised his voice at us. Mom always knew how to put a positive spin on the most terrible of situations."

She laughed suddenly, catching herself off guard as she received a memory from childhood. Sierra looked up from the old photographs and into Savannah's eyes as if she could read the memory in Sierra's eyes, but knew she couldn't. Sierra wondered then if Savannah would say anything, but her sister was about to break down into hysterics. Sierra knew the signs. The shoulders hunched, the eyes red and swollen, the cheeks puffy, and her sister's chest beginning to heave in huge gulps of breath as if she hadn't been breathing this entire time. Zadie was there in a flash, wrapping her arms around Savannah and pulling her back toward the bathroom hallway.

Sierra looked back over the faces in front of her, on her own to handle yet another thing. She sighed. Resentment began to threaten to crack her controlled calm façade, but she knew she needed to bite it back and focus. Her eyes were drawn to Smokey, who started to scratch behind his gray ears as if nothing mattered. Then she looked up until she landed on Caleb's hazel eyes. His gaze was deeply inquisitive.

"I've always been the one to hold it together," Sierra said as if talking only to Caleb. "My parents didn't want me to leave, but they also didn't want to hold me back. I've always been ambitious, organized, and with a plan since I was a little girl. There's some quote about the best laid plans, right? I assumed that my parents would be running this café until they retired, still coming here in wheelchairs to sing along with the juke box and drink whiskey until nurses came to take them back to the home."

She cracked a smile, knowing she was being facetious and wondering what Caleb thought. "I hated this café at first," she admitted. "I might still hate it, actually. I lost my parents to this café and had to start making my own meals, getting my sister and myself ready for school, and sacrificing nights and weekends with friends to clean dishes. I see why you all love it; I do. But my life was never the same after they bought this place. And now that they are gone, I can't even be mad at them about it because a deer killed them coming back from a wedding. Not coming here. Not going home from here. Not a robbery or a burn or a fall down the stairs. No, this place didn't kill them. They truly *lived* here. They loved *being* here. They loved being with all of you."

Sierra took a deep breath. Had she said all she needed to say, she wondered. It's not like her parents were there listening, so it didn't really matter. What mattered was checking this off the list and moving on. This was a required part of the process of death. All she had to do now was say goodbye and move on.

"Thank you for coming to help us say goodbye to our parents," Sierra continued. "I would now like to invite each of you up here to share memories of our parents and to say your own goodbyes." Sierra left the back of the room and started to make her way to the bar. Behind her, she heard feet and people start to scoot chairs to get up and talk. She wasn't sure she wanted to hear it, but she wasn't going to duck out and cry like her sister had. Instead, she grabbed a glass and poured a whiskey. "To you," she said quietly before taking a sip. The heat felt good going down her throat.

"You OK?" Caleb asked from the other side of the counter. Smokey, however, did not stay on the other side of the counter. He squirmed his furry ass right up to her leg and put a paw on top of her Blahnik pump.

She tried to lightly shoo the pup away and said, "I will be."

"How are your fingers?" he asked, looking at the hand holding the whiskey glass. She followed his gaze. Her fingers had actually healed quickly thanks to his help.

"They are much better because of you," she said. Sierra's eyes lifted, and she allowed herself a moment to get lost in his. The sun seemed to be streaming in through the front windows, hitting his eyes in a way that sparked every hint of yellow to life. "Thank you."

A smile spread across his face, and she almost forgot she was at a funeral. "I'd love to hang out with you when you aren't in need of a rescue—although I'm happy to rescue you anytime."

Sierra felt stunned. Was he hitting on her now? Was he asking her out? What kind of a…

"What do you mean?" she asked, playing dumb. She heard a few people crying softly and sniffling in the background.

"If you don't need to be rescued, I'd like to take you out on a proper date," he said, standing up straight. His dog pawed at her bare ankle now. She blinked and looked down at the dog. Smokey looked up at her with amber eyes, seeking her attention. She set down the whiskey glass and, with both hands, grabbed Smokey's face. Her fingers got lost in the mass of fur, and she immediately relaxed. They hadn't grown up with animals because her parents were always too busy, but maybe she could deal with this mutt for a while longer. The idea of hanging out with a man and his dog sounded way better than listening to people mourning her parents. Besides, she'd checked the box. She'd paid for the cremation, picked up the ashes, scheduled, hosted, and spoken at the memorial. There was nothing that said she had to be here for the next few hours. She could always come back and help her sister close things up for the night.

And if Caleb was as capable and as gentle a lover as he was as a fireman, maybe she could use a little distraction and attention for her remaining time in Lincoln. She stood back up, finished the whiskey with one shot, and looked the handsome man up and down.

"Are you free now?" she asked.

15 SAVANNAH

Savannah walked with Zadie back into the dining area. Her sister was nowhere to be found, but people were taking turns getting up from their chairs and sharing memories.

"Are you ready to say something?" Zadie asked, her voice was gentle and quiet. For a second, Savannah thought she was, but then the voice of the speaker cracked. She didn't know the woman speaking, telling the room about the first time she'd met her mother, Deborah. Savannah shook her head no, feeling an empathetic reaction creeping up into her tear ducts.

Savannah wanted to be ready. She'd thought about different things to say over the last couple of nights lying in her bed, staring at the loft's beams. Of course, all those thoughts had muddied and blurred as she'd fallen asleep. But they had been her parents. They were her parents. She didn't need a rehearsed script to talk about them and their impact on her life, but she did need to refrain from crying for at least a few minutes. That was proving difficult.

And then Savannah saw Waylon standing near the door, the sun from the windows hitting his brown cowboy hat and casting a shadow across his eyes, but not his lips, which turned into a smile at seeing her. Something fluttered in her chest, replacing the sadness with another feeling… Excitement? Hope?

Waylon nodded at her, and she felt that nod push her toward the table where her parents' pictures were displayed. Savannah knew she could stay in control. She knew she had to talk—not because the people in the room expected it, but because it would be good for her. The woman who was speaking finished her story, wiped at tears, and sat back down. Savannah moved toward the table, drawn to a picture of her parents. Sierra was little and clinging to her mom's leg. Deborah was pregnant with Savannah in the picture, wearing a large floral dress that made her stomach look much bigger than it probably actually had been. Savannah smiled, trying to focus on the positives instead of the negatives. She started speaking as if to the picture, not looking at the crowd.

"They were really great people," Savannah said. "They loved us. They loved this town. They loved their house. They loved this café." Savannah set the picture frame down and turned, looking around at the old pictures on the walls, the historic pictures of downtown Lincoln. She looked over the wood floors and up to the wood beams on the ceiling.

"Sometimes I feel like this place became more of their home than their actual house, once they'd started spending so much time here," she continued. "Even though they were so busy running this place that I hardly saw them at the house, I never doubted how much they loved me. They dedicated so much time, effort, and money to this place because they loved it *for* us. They wanted to make a business, build a community, and make enough money to take care of us. I think my parents accomplished all of those things. I'm really proud of them and what they did. This café is a part of them. It's even named after them."

"It's named after you," an older woman's voice interjected.

Savannah looked up and around, trying to see who the voice came from. She spotted Laurel in the crowd and smiled at her. "Yes," Savannah said, agreeing with Laurel. "This is our Sweetwater family café and bar. We made a lot of memories here."

Her smile dimmed, realizing that those memories would fade over time, especially once Savannah and Sierra sold the business and moved back to their opposite ends of America. But she didn't want to think about that right now. Right now, she wanted to thank her parents, to remember them, and to love them.

Drawn in like a lasso had wrapped around her, she looked up and locked eyes with the cowboy at the back of the crowd. He nodded again, like a silent confirmation that he was with her. Butterflies flooded her belly, but she took a deep breath and settled herself.

"Thank you for coming, for loving my parents, and for loving this café as your own home away from home. Please keep sharing your stories. We'll open the bar up in a bit, and we can just keep sharing together."

Then she stepped into Zadie's open arms. The unconditional acceptance from this friend, whom she'd lost touch with, made her feel ashamed. Zadie was such a wonderful person, and Savannah had just gone off and left her. She'd also abandoned her parents, chasing a guitar player all the way to Seattle. Tears stung her eyes, and emotion burned her throat as she tried not to let the emotions wash her away again.

She released Zadie as her phone vibrated, where she'd left it lying on the bar. The tight black dress her sister loaned her had not come with pockets. Savannah picked up the phone, hesitating for a moment before saying hello.

"Savvy, baby, how are things?" Jaxon asked.

Savannah looked around the room but didn't see the cowboy. She wasn't sure why she'd done that, but she whispered her response to Jaxon. "I'm at my parents' memorial service. I can't really talk."

"Oh shit, that was today? I completely lost track of the days. I'm sorry I couldn't come. We had a gig last night, and there's no way I could have made it in time." Jaxon sounded sincere, but Savannah couldn't help but wonder how a man with a show schedule could forget what day it was. And obviously, he'd be playing on Saturday nights. She never would have expected him to fly down and show up for her on a Sunday morning.

Waylon walked into her line of sight, and her breath hitched in her throat. For a split second, she felt weak at the knees, and the only thing she wanted in the entire world was to fall into his arms. She shook the thought away, unable to believe that in this moment, on the phone with her boyfriend at her parents' memorial, she was allowing herself to be distracted by the idea of collapsing into a cowboy.

Jaxon was still talking, going on and on about this or that band member, his show, she wasn't really sure.

"Hey, Jax, I gotta go. Funeral," she whispered, since other people were talking and still sharing memories.

"Right, right, but babe, when are you coming back?"

A year? How would she tell Jaxon that it would be an entire year before she moved back? She definitely couldn't tell him with all these people standing around. They didn't know this situation was temporary. "Soon," she lied, disconnecting the call right as Waylon walked up to her.

"That was my boyfriend in Seattle," Savannah blurted out. Maybe if she kept Waylon at a distance, that would be good for both of them. No need to get attached to someone since she was just going back to Seattle in less than a year now.

"He couldn't come be with you today?" Waylon asked, his tone gentle but his words cutting her.

"He's in a band," she said, trying to sound cool and important. "He can't just leave without risking the band's reputation. He's the main guitarist and singer, so, you know."

"He sounds like a pretty big deal." Waylon's country accent curled words around her ears like fingers caressing. She pictured his big, meaty hands on her, teasing her, wrapping around her.

"He's working on it," Savannah said. "Their band is really good."

"What kind of music is it?" Waylon asked. They were keeping their voices low so as not disturb the mourners in the dining area. Leaning in close over the bar, whispering to each other felt way more intimate than it should have.

"A mix of rock, punk, and a little bit of country," Savannah answered.

"I like mostly mainstream country," Waylon said, "but from all decades since country began. I'll listen to it all."

"I never would have guessed," Savannah said, teasingly sarcastic.

Waylon leaned in dangerously close. "Are you teasing me, Savannah?" he asked, a devilish smile on his lips. She saw his eyes move to her lips and linger there for a moment before coming back up. Tingles. Butterflies.

What is wrong with me? she asked herself. *Boyfriend. Funeral. Not the place. Not the time. What the absolute hell is happening?* She slinked away from him and around to the back of the bar. She needed a drink. She pulled down two glasses, dropped ice into them both, then poured two generous amounts of Jack. She slid his glass to him wordlessly. Waylon kept his piercing green eyes locked on hers as he took a sip, his thick lips touching the glass in a way that seemed too sensual for a man. Savannah caught herself staring at his lips as he licked the whiskey off, and she quickly took her own drink. His eyes watched her lips, and she tried not to look sexy as she sipped.

She ran through a list of reasons in her mind for why being attracted to Waylon was a terrible idea. First, this man was a literal cowboy, working on a farm or ranch or something, with his dirty paws on God-knows-what animals or corn. She didn't know and didn't care. This was *not* her type. And even if cowboys were her type, she was only here for one year.

Oh God, she realized the final reason… she had a damn boyfriend.

"And you say you've been together what, two, three years?" Waylon asked, already knowing the answer, then took another sip.

"Since I left Lincoln a couple of years ago, yeah," she answered, feeling like he was fishing for as many details as he could.

"And he hasn't tried to tie you down?"

"We're young." And poor, and without direction, and maybe not as into each other as she'd once hoped they were…

"I know you got a lot going on with the loss of your parents, coming back home, and running this bar," Waylon said, his facial expression turning from flirty to sincere. "But we don't have to have it all figured out in our twenties."

"You don't have it all figured out, Waylon?" Savannah asked, being ornery.

"Nah, not by a long shot," he answered, leaning his towering six feet down across the bar to get closer to her. She kept her position, leaning a little forward herself, letting him get within inches of her face, their whiskey glasses nearly touching. "But I do know what I want."

For some reason him saying the word "want" sent excited shivers down to her thighs. She couldn't get the words out to ask him what exactly it was that he wanted. So, she raised her eyebrows in question instead.

"I want a strong partner, a best friend, a woman I can love every single day in unpredictable but reliable ways. Love is real, and I want a woman I can prove that to. I want to buy a house and have a family. I want to continue working, doing what I love, taking care of the world and the community just as God intended. Maybe I'm young yet, but I've got a plan."

All of a sudden, the juke box started to play "Don't Stop Believing," and the mourners shifted straight into karaoke mode. Zadie popped up beside Savannah, gave her a squeeze, and said it was time to pour the drinks. Both Waylon and Savannah slowly backed away from each other as they stood up on their opposite sides of the bar.

Savannah felt an odd mix of relief and sadness at pulling out of her transfixed moment with Waylon. But with Zadie singing next to her, her spirit lifted, and she moved into bartender mode, taking orders and pouring drinks for the people who had loved her parents. Savannah made sure to refill Waylon's glass, catching his glance like they had a secret between them.

Zadie hip-checked her as she filled a glass with soda. "What's happening with you and the cowboy?" Zadie asked.

Savannah felt her cheeks get red. "Nothing," she said. "I'm with Jaxon."

"But are you?" Zadie asked, squinting her face into a doubtful expression.

"What's that supposed to mean?" Savannah's voice pitched up, like a mouse caught in a trap.

"Do you still love Jaxon? He didn't show up for you today. Does he love you? Is he worth it?" Zadie peppered her with questions, and she found that she didn't have a good answer.

Did she love him? What was love? Did she love him the way her mom had loved her dad? Would she follow him across the country, to gigs, to record labels, to crazy life choices, on tours, into drug addiction and depression? Would it be unconditional both ways? What if she wanted to eventually settle down? Did Jaxon have a 'settle down' bone in his body? Would he ever truly commit to her or love her how she needed to be loved?

Would he love her the way Waylon had just described loving his future wife?

Savannah shrugged, trying to keep her eyes from searching for Waylon in the crowd.

16 SIERRA

Sierra pulled Caleb in through the front door of the house she'd grown up in. She'd parked her father's truck in the garage, and Caleb had parked in the driveway, following her home from the café. His truck was in the shade of their many trees, so Caleb left Smokey sleeping on the front seat with the windows all open.

She didn't care about being cordial or ladylike. She didn't say hello, welcome him inside, point out the living room where she'd learned to walk, or even share the memories behind the photographs lining the staircase walls. No pleasantries, just her arms around his shoulders and his mouth pressed to hers. They made out all the way up the stairs, and she was tugging apart his belt as she pulled him into her bedroom.

They were alone, so there was no need to close the door. They kept kissing as they tore each other's clothing off, letting it all fall to the floor. Caleb was trying to be gentle, she could tell, but she didn't want gentle. She didn't want polite. She didn't want questions about whether or not they should or if he was hurting her. So, she kept her mouth on his, moving her hands in a way that left no doubt or hesitation in his mind about what she wanted.

Forty or so minutes later, Caleb was snoring quietly in her childhood bed. She was wide awake, having received all his energy. She crept out of bed and put on a clean shirt and a pair of shorts. Sierra grabbed her designer dress and hung it up, leaving everything else scattered on the carpet. She'd deal with that later. For now, she wanted to leave the sweaty smell of the bedroom and go pour a drink.

In the kitchen, she grabbed a glass, two ice cubes to cool the whiskey, and opened the patio door, stepping into the sunshine. She felt good, satisfied. It was a nice distraction from the fact that her parents were dead and screwing her, imprisoning her, and essentially controlling her life from the grave. She took a sip and froze. Smokey was in her yard, looking at her quizzically.

"Smokey," she said flatly, surprised to see him. He waved his tail behind him in recognition and greeting. He started to move toward her, but she put her hand up. "I'm good." Sierra could have sworn the gray mutt rolled his eyes before turning sharply to go investigate the row of planters on the edge of the patio. Her tense shoulders relaxed again, knowing the dog would leave her alone, but she sighed seeing the yard and planters. "Shit," she said out loud, Smokey ignoring her curse word. "I have to take care of all of this."

Smokey turned his eyes toward her and shook his head. A thought came to her.

"You're right. Clever dog. If I can get your human to come over more often, maybe he'll do the yard. He is a hero, after all. I like how you think." In response, Smokey curled up into an awkward position to sniff and then lick his own butt. Sierra turned up her nose and looked away. "Dogs are gross."

She was on her second whiskey by the time Caleb joined her outside about half an hour later.

"Hey, there you are," he said, his tone relaxed and confident. She could feel her body respond as if ready for a second round. *Easy, tiger*, she told herself. *Don't appear too eager.* He'd pulled his jeans back on but had unhelpfully left his shirt inside.

"Hey," Sierra said. "Pour yourself a drink and join us." Sierra nodded toward Smokey, now lazily lounging in a sunny patch on the patio. She was sitting at an old metal bistro table, glad not to be in a dress since the rust was probably going to leave stains.

Birds were chirping, Smokey was snoring, and Sierra didn't have a care in the entire world when Caleb sat beside her with an iced whiskey in his hands. He leaned over and kissed her long on the lips. *Yep*, she thought, *there will be seconds. Maybe even thirds.*

He leaned back into the bistro chair and sighed before taking a sip of his drink. His eyes never left hers, as if he were transfixed. She felt her cheeks start to redden and looked away.

"Your parents have a nice place here," Caleb said.

A simple statement, and yet it sent a mix of emotions throughout Sierra. Her parents did have a nice place, she thought, looking around at the quaint yard with all her mother's touches everywhere. Gnomes, bird fountains, cobblestone walkways between scattered beds and planters, pinwheels spinning slowly in the breeze, and bird and squirrel houses either nailed to trees or dangling from branches. Every inch seemed to have been meticulously adorned without any concern for her daughters being left to caretake it all now. Would she be able to dismantle the junky decor, or would she sell it as-is, Sierra wondered. Part of her wanted to sit there, sip whiskey, and stare out at the yard every single day until she died, pretending that her parents would join her at the little table with their own cold drinks at any moment. The other part knew that she couldn't ignore the laundry list of work that lay before her.

Sierra smiled slightly and turned to Caleb, nodding. "When my mother wasn't working at the café, she was out here."

Caleb looked around, smiling wider at seeing how comfortable his dog was. Smokey had definitely made himself at home. "She must have really loved this yard," Caleb said, making small talk.

Maybe more than she loved her own daughters, Sierra thought bitterly, jealous of each hand-painted house built for useless birds. The café was her father's true love, but the backyard had been her mother's. Tending, tilling, and trimming until Deborah was too tired to sit and talk with Sierra or Savannah.

Granted, she knew now that her mother needed to decompress just like any other adult who worked, but the memories of not being chosen, not being sought-after, stung her now that she really looked at the love and care that her mother had placed here, in the yard.

Sierra felt her mood sinking, so she shot the rest of her glass and jumped up to get a refill. Caleb's eyebrows were furrowed in concern, clearly picking up on the shift. She smiled and placed a hand gently on his bare shoulder.

"Let's go refill and then..." Sierra winked, letting her fingers and eyes roam the tufts of blond hair on his chest. He smiled mischievously and then followed her into the house.

***

Sierra's life found a new pattern. Although technically on leave from her job in New York, she was able to do freelance assignments for the company, mainly in the area of online research and article editing. She woke up early, opened the café, supported the staff there with whatever they needed, then did both café and Fytté work. She managed Sweetwater's payroll, she wrote fashion blog articles, she did food and supplies inventory, she researched designer marketing trends, back and forth, while her sister slept upstairs in the loft apartment.

Savannah would make her appearance just as Sierra was heading out the door, into her dad's old truck, and back to their family home. Caleb would join her there after his firehouse shifts. They spent all their free time together. Somedays, he'd stop by the café for an early lunch or come in for a cup of coffee with the rest of his team if they were returning from a call that had turned out not to be an emergency.

Sierra couldn't help but smile every time he came into the café or when he showed up at the house to take her out. Smokey was always with Caleb, and Sierra found herself getting used to the shaggy mutt. Smokey usually stayed in the truck while they were out on a date or hung out in the backyard when she and Caleb enjoyed each other in her bedroom.

When Caleb wasn't available, Sierra found herself walking around the house, studying and thinking about what needed to be packed, sold, stored, or donated. She wondered if she could list the house with all the furniture in it as part of the deal. She could always rent it out as an Airbnb, but no, she told herself. She'd do all the work but still have to split the profits with Savannah. She rolled her eyes, thinking about her irresponsible sister. It just made more sense to sell the house and café, split the money, then go back to their opposite ends of the states. Sure, they might lose touch over the years, but Sierra was confident that the sisters would still visit each other at least once a year and text every once in a while. It would be fine.

17 SAVANNAH

Savannah felt giddy waking up in her loft apartment a few weeks after the funeral. She lay on her bed, wiggled her legs back and forth, and admired the wooden beams that held up the roof above her head. Happiness surged underneath her skin in a way that felt nostalgic because it seemed like years since she'd felt it.

A weight was starting to lift from her shoulders as she fell into a new routine, a new life. The best and most terrible part of her day was waking up and knowing that she would see Waylon at the beginning of her afternoon shift. She had a job she loved, an apartment all to herself that she was obsessed with, and didn't have to deal with her sister. Savannah still got teary-eyed thinking of her parents and even cried when she was alone in the shower, but she was starting to be OK. She was starting to move on from everything—except Jaxon.

He had been growing more and more impatient now that the funeral had passed. She had been putting him off with text messages promising that she'd be back soon after taking care of a few things, but she wasn't sure how much more time that would buy her.

Savannah knew she needed to be honest with him and suffer the uncomfortable feeling of conflict. She felt responsible for him, in a way. They were both living in the Seattle apartment. They had started building a little life there. Although they had drifted apart recently, it could have had more to do with her working schedule. She'd picked up multiple jobs that conflicted with his shows, and she knew that upset him. If things were different… if his band were more successful, if they got a record deal, then she could pull back on her bar job and attend more of his shows. Jaxon's steel blue eyes would find her front and center in the audience, and he'd look at her the way he used to, all dreamy intensity with their whole lives of possibilities ahead of them. The memories made her shiver even as warmth spread throughout her body, remembering those first nights with Jaxon.

His lean body had been slicked with sweat, and he'd smelled like whiskey. Jaxon had taken his time worshiping every inch of her in a way that still made her blush. Sex had become less intense, more one-sided, and more infrequent the longer they'd been together, however.

Her cell phone vibrated from the table beside her bed. She reached over with one hand and answered it without looking, thinking it was just her sister calling to tell her about some order or inventory or something.

"Savvy?" Jaxon asked in lieu of a greeting.

"Oh, hey, babe. How are you?" Savannah asked, jolting upright as if feeling caught in a wet dream. Anxiety replaced her euphoria.

"How am I?" Jaxon asked, sounding annoyed. "I have been trying to figure out exactly when you are getting back home, and it kinda feels like you've been ignoring me. All that clicks for me is that you're cheating on me."

Savannah blinked rapidly and squared her shoulders, guilt rushing in a hot wave through her body. "I'm not cheating on you!"

"Well, everybody thinks that you are, and I am starting to agree with them."

"Everybody?" Savannah tried to search her brain for who the hell everybody even was. His bandmates? They're various girlfriends or fuck buddies?

"Yeah, Savvy, everybody," Jaxon doubled down. "You left me here with an apartment to take care of, and you haven't sent me any money to pay the rent, even though your parents died and you should have an inheritance and be on your way back, and you're ignoring me. You never came to my shows. You just don't seem to care about me at all."

Her mind was a whirlwind of activity, not knowing which accusation to respond to first. She felt dizzy with a multitude of responses, but all she could come up with was, "I do care. I'm working. My parents fucking died, Jaxon."

"And I get that, Savannah, but they are gone, and I'm here, waiting on you to come home. When are you coming home? When can you send me some rent money?"

She shook her head. Was this really happening? Was he demanding rent money from her?

"Jaxon, I don't have rent money," she said, trying to slow down her words and her heart rate. "I'm working here for basically free, and we don't get the inheritance unless we…" she paused. Was she really telling him?

"Unless what? What are you talking about, working for free?" he asked, sounding angry and agitated.

Savannah took a deep breath before answering. "In my parents Will, they said we can't sell the properties and get the inheritance unless we run the café and bar for a full year."

"A full year?" Jaxon screamed into the phone, and she had to hold it away from her ear. She switched it onto speaker and held the thing in her lap. "What the hell am I supposed to do for a full year, Savannah? You got me into this mess, so you need to fix it. You need to figure out how to send me some money for rent, or I'm going to lose the apartment."

Savannah started biting her nails as she thought through ways to help. She liked their apartment and didn't want to lose it. And what about all their belongings? Could she afford to have it all moved into storage? Could she even pay for storage?

As she fretted, her eyes drifted aimlessly around her father's loft bedroom and out into the wide-open space above the living area. It was a whole world her father had left behind in an instant. The café, the house she'd grown up in, and every single memento, from framed pictures, televisions, chairs, to coffee cups collected like treasures over the years.

Savannah had followed Jaxon to Seattle with a couple of bags. She had returned home with even less and yet, looking around, she felt that she had all she really needed right there in her father's apartment above the café. It dawned on her that after years of obtaining material possessions, none if mattered once her parents died. The Seattle apartment didn't really matter; they could get another one. The furniture they'd collected from thrift stores and street corners could be easily replaced.

The legacy her parents built for Savannah and her sister couldn't be replaced. Her parents had worked hard for their business and house, and to walk away would be downright stupid. She shrugged before realizing Jaxon couldn't see her. "Then lose the apartment, Jaxon. I don't care. There's nothing I can do about it right now."

"This is bullshit," he said. "If you're telling me you can't send me money, and you can't come back for a year, then this is over. You go ahead and be with whoever you're cheating on me with, and let's just move on."

Savannah's breath caught in her throat, and her heart started beating even harder in her chest. Breakup? Was that what she wanted? It didn't really seem like he was giving her an option. If he couldn't wait for her, then were the two years for nothing? What about her sacrifice of moving with him to Seattle in the first place? Not to mention all the many months of full rent she covered for them because he just didn't make enough money pursuing his dream. Was that worth nothing to him? She started to feel betrayed. Maybe he felt like she was betraying him by refusing to come back to Seattle, but his unwillingness to wait, his inability to empathize with the complex situation she was in, was too much. She had fallen for a musician, hoping to be the girl he sang songs about, hoping to follow him across the globe on his path to stardom, but instead, she sat in her father's loft, lifted her chin, and accepted the dream coming to an end.

"Fine," she said. One word. Simple and done.

Jaxon groaned on the other end.

"Don't do that to me, Savannah. Savvy baby girl," Jaxon said. "You know I don't want to lose you."

Did she know that? she wondered.

"I'm just upset that you aren't coming home." Jaxon's voice had switched, swinging like a pendulum back from angry to charmingly calm. "Tell me more about what's happening there. I just feel like we haven't talked and you're keeping me in the dark."

Savannah signed and massaged her temples, staying quiet.

"Savannah? Are you still there?

"I'm here," she answered. "I'm sorry about keeping you in the dark, but I'm not cheating on you. I just didn't know how to tell you that in order to get my inheritance, I have to stay here until next June. We can't sell the properties until then."

"Properties?" he asked, suddenly curious. "The café and what, your parents' house or something?"

"Yes," she answered.

"You should have just told me that," Jaxon said. "I wouldn't have been so mad if you'd just been honest with me. You gotta tell me things. You know you aren't very good at communicating, right?" he asked with a chuckle.

Savannah nodded again, feeling dumb because he couldn't see her. "Yeah, I know," she said, shrinking into herself.

"I'll figure out the rent money," Jaxon said. "We got a while to go until next June, but we can do it, babe. We have a great thing here. We can make the long-distance thing work for a while, right, babe?"

Savannah took another deep breath and nodded, but still felt like she was standing in the eye of a hurricane that could kick up again at any moment.

"Right," she said, agreeing. They said their goodbyes and ended the call.

The giddy mood she'd woken up with was replaced with a somber one. Savannah moved slowly as she dressed, then headed downstairs to start work for the day. *Why do I feel so sad?* she wondered. *We aren't breaking up. I finally told Jaxon, and he understands. We'll be OK.*

Since she'd taken more time than usual getting ready, she'd already missed her sister, who'd left as soon as her shift had ended. It was fine. Savannah had already dealt with one downer already and wasn't interested in seeing another.

She'd actually been seeing less and less of her sister since Sierra had started spending more time with the fireman, Caleb. Part of her was happy that her sister found something else to put her attention into aside from driving Savannah crazy. But another part of her was almost a little jealous of them. They were happily spending time together, and Savannah felt lonelier than ever.

Zadie was already buzzing behind the bar, cleaning up after the lunch rush. It would be a slow trickle of customers until the dinner rush picked up. Savannah fell in beside Zadie, cleaning so the young woman could take a break if she needed it. They shared the work of order taking, pouring drinks, and serving until it slowed down enough for Zadie to run off to a class. Savannah waved her goodbye and then began tapping a pen against the bar.

This time of day, when the café emptied out, the juke box sat like a quiet sentinel, and the sun started to transition the sky to a bright orange through the front panel windows, tendrils of excitement curled beneath her skin. Savannah tried to ignore the feeling. She tried to lie to herself, wanting to believe it was just the eeriness of the calm. But she knew what it really was. Waylon was coming. Dependable as the hands on an ancient grandfather clock.

A shadow darkened the front of the café, then the door chimed as it opened, a shy tinkling that could only be heard when the room was empty. A tall silhouette entered with broad shoulders and a cowboy hat. Savannah hoped that one day the scene would grow old. She hoped to one day not feel that spark of desire that hid behind a veil of nerves. She wanted Waylon to strike her as "old hat" instead of "shiny new boots".

"Miss," Waylon said in his deep tone, nodding while touching the rim of his hat with one finger. He was dressed nicer than she was used to seeing him in a cream pearl snap button-up shirt with long sleeves, a collar, and brown vine-patterned stitching.

"You look sharp today," Savannah teased. "You want your usual?"

He smiled, nodded to confirm his order of whiskey in coffee, then pulled his arms up to admire his own shirt. "Well, yes," he said in a slow drawl. "Things got a little messy today on the ranch." He looked up and met her eyes as she returned with a hot mug of coffee. "One of our mares had a little foal today, so I opted to shower and change after helping her through it."

Savannah returned to the bar top with a bottle of whiskey in hand, freezing before adding it to the coffee. "A baby horse?" she asked. He chuckled.

"Yes, a big baby horse," Waylon confirmed. "A healthy colt."

"And you helped…deliver it? Like, catch it or something?" Savannah smiled, teasingly again, but was interested in hearing the story. She returned to pouring the whiskey into the coffee cup, measuring by heart. She didn't know much about horses or how they gave birth, other than maybe what she'd seen on television as a child. She didn't know if it happened standing up, lying down, or how exactly a man would help out.

"In a way," Waylon explained. "Once the mare lies down, I get on the ground beside her to keep her calm until the foal's feet appear. I watch to make sure the foal is coming out alright and, if need be, reach in and adjust the foal's position. That's what I needed to do today, hence getting a little more dirty than usual."

Savannah nodded in astonishment as she slid the mug across the bar top to the real cowboy. Curiosity came over her. "What else do you do on this ranch? And is it your ranch or your parents', or do you just work there? Do you deliver a lot of baby horses? What about cows? Goats?"

His earth-green eyes were wide with amusement as he smiled at her. She felt flushed with embarrassment for her questioning and closed her mouth. Waylon looked around the empty café.

"Why don't you grab a drink and come sit with me, and I'll tell you all about it," he said, as if asking a girl out on a date instead of talking to the server.

Savannah felt a shift in the air as if her acceptance of this request would mean something. Pouring herself a whiskey was nothing; the bottle was already there. She grabbed a glass, poured, and then took a step toward the end of the bar, feeling as if crossing the threshold would signal a distinct change from Waylon being just a customer. She shook away the silly thoughts and walked to join him at the table.

He stood back up and removed his hat, waiting until she sat before he placed it gently on the table. His shaggy blond hair was pressed down into an upside-down bowl shape. He tossed it loose with his fingers after he noticed her looking.

She felt underdressed next to him in his cowboy finery. Savannah had on a black Def Leppard tee-shirt, a black sweater cardigan rolled up to the elbows, and a pair of jeans. She slunk into the seat across from him and sipped her whiskey quickly.

"So," he started, leaning back into the chair as if readying himself for a long story. "Hoffmann Ranch has been in my family for three generations. My grandparents are still there in the main house, but retired now. We don't let them get out and work the farm, much to their dismay. Now, Memaw will go collect eggs from the hens, and Papa will stand about smoking his pipe as he oversees our work, but for the most part, they get to relax nowadays."

Waylon lifted the mug of coffee and whiskey to his lips and sipped, closing his eyes. Savannah caught herself watching his lips on the edge of the hot liquid and quickly turned away. "Main house?" she asked, trying to distract herself from how adorable he looked when talking about his grandparents.

"Yes," he said, leaning back again. "My parents have their own house on the acreage where my sisters and I grew up. Their house is actually larger than the main house since Dad built it, knowing they wanted to have three children. Of course, Dad was hoping for lots of boys to help him on the farm, but he only got me and two of the most prissy-princess girls a mother could dream of." Waylon chuckled and took another sip of coffee, looking proud despite how disappointed his father must have been.

"So, I'm guessing they don't help out on the farm?" Savannah asked.

"Oh, they can tend a garden and make tea so sweet it'll make your nose hairs curl, but as far as getting dirty goes, no. Papa, Dad, and I have been the primary caretakers of the animals and lands, but we hire out help."

Savannah nodded, trying to picture the ranch and his family and his life growing up there. It sounded like a little boy's dream.

"Do you live on the ranch too?" Savannah asked.

Waylon sat up slowly but straight, looking at her with a serious expression. "I do," he said, nodding slightly. "I built myself a cozy house with a fireplace for cold nights. It has an open living area from the kitchen to the dining to the living. Simple but comfortable."

Curiosity tingled the back of Savannah's neck, and although she wanted to keep it to herself, she just couldn't. "And did you just build it for yourself or for…" She stopped speaking and lifted her glass of whiskey instead. Savannah noticed how his green eyes dropped to watch her lips.

"For the family I might someday have," Waylon finished. "For now, I rent out the rooms to a couple of ranch hands when needed."

Savannah set her glass down and shook her head. She just couldn't imagine, at this age, under thirty, not only having plans but laying the groundwork for those plans. Something else struck Savannah about Waylon's life, and she had to ask another question.

"Have you ever wanted to leave?"

Waylon's eyes drifted from the table and out beyond the glass windows to the downtown area. He looked to be lost in thoughts—memories, maybe—or dreams of other places. It was a few moments before he returned his eyes to hers and answered.

"Running a ranch isn't easy," he started. "But I assume there's not much in this life that is. My dad taught me that if you want to get good at something, you have to keep working at it. No matter what it is. There's no such thing as an easy life or career. Going to school, I knew about all the interesting opportunities out there, and I knew what kind of work it would take to accomplish success in those various careers. But nothing made me happier than coming home to the ranch at the end of the day. Nothing. And…" Waylon paused and looked off again, taking a moment to sip his coffee before continuing. "And I love my family," he said, his tone softer. "I want to help them. I want to spend time with them. I want to enjoy holiday dinners with them and then walk back to my house and fall asleep knowing I've done my best for the day."

Savannah's stomach dropped as a feeling of despair sank in. She wouldn't get to spend holidays with her parents ever again. Her sister wanted to get as far away from her as possible, so once the café was sold, there'd literally be no family left, nothing left for Savannah to return home to.

"I'm sorry," Waylon said. "I didn't mean to upset you." His hand reached across the table and gripped hers tightly, protectively. The tingles of excitement were a blur of confusion as they blended with her abject depression. She shook her head and pulled her hands down to her lap, where he couldn't reach them.

"It's not your fault," she said, as a tear silently slid down her cheek. "What you describe is beautiful. When I moved to Seattle, I thought I would always still come back home, back here, for family and holidays. I didn't think… I couldn't have imagined…" She felt her nose running now as the tears were truly good and falling. "Excuse me," Savannah said, jumping up and darting for the bathroom. Waylon stood but didn't follow her.

In the bathroom, she let out a heavy sob over the sink, buckling at the waist as the moment gripped her. Savannah had taken the opportunity to leave the home, the business, the life she had known, and the guilt for that decision came in rogue waves, knocking her off balance. She let the emotions rock her for a moment before taking deep breaths to calm herself down. She was the only one working the café, so she had to get it together and go back to the dining room.

Savannah blew her nose and splashed water on her face, then took account of her reflection in the mirror. The black was fading out of her blond hair. Her brown eyes were red and puffy. Her nose was pink. But she was OK. She was breathing. She was alive. She tried to shift her mind from her parents and back to her conversation with Waylon.

Waylon's life, his choices, and his family did sound lovely. But what surprised her the most was how easy a decision that had seemed for him. He felt no shame living on the same land as his parents and grandparents. He felt no shame in doing the same work they did. He felt only joy in seeing them every day. If she had stayed, she wondered, would she feel the same way? If she had just decided to stay and work the family business with her parents, would that have been enough for her?

Now calm, she left the bathroom and returned to the dining room. Waylon was still standing beside the table, looking worried.

"Oh my gosh," she said, chuckling. "Sit, please."

"After you," he said, pulling the chair back slightly for her. She stepped up to the chair, mere inches from him, and turned to face the table. Feeling awkward, she began to sit as he slid the chair fluidly to follow her, bending down close to her ear. "Are you alright?" he asked. His breath on her sent shivers down her neck.

"Yes," she whispered. She'd never experienced a man push her chair in for her. It was exhilarating, and she felt her nostrils flare involuntarily as she tried to suck in as much air as possible to keep herself composed.

Waylon returned to his side of the round table and sat. They both sipped their drinks, eyes fixed on each other.

"I've been meaning to ask you," Waylon said with a twinkle in his eye. "Are you still talking to that guy in Seattle who doesn't know how good he has it?"

Savannah's heart did another flip. She hadn't been expecting that question, especially after the conversation they'd been having. She and Jaxon had just broken up, right? Or was that a misunderstanding, and they were actually still together? Jaxon was being a dick, but Savannah loved him. He embodied a rock star dream that excited Savannah. One day, she would be known as Jaxon Steele's girlfriend in all the magazines that covered his band's global success. They would eat expensive food and drink champagne from their hotel bed while he was on a European tour. Jaxon was going to be somebody someday, and Savannah was going to be right there beside him. That was the dream, right?

"Yes," Savannah said. "We are still together."

"That's too bad," Waylon said, just as the door to the café opened and signaled the arrival of another customer.

"Oops," Savannah said, shooting the last of her whiskey. "Customer. Gotta cut our date short." She jumped up to head behind the bar before realizing what she'd said. Savannah had used the word 'date.' Embarrassed, she gave the new customer her full attention and didn't look back at Waylon once.

18 SIERRA

Sierra had never believed that sex addiction was a real thing. But even after weeks of regular hookups with Caleb, she couldn't seem to get enough. Being with him had become an insatiable desire, and the only thing that kept Sierra from going stir crazy while trapped in the small town she had grown up in. Since she worked mornings and the lunch shift, she had evenings and nights blissfully free.

The nights when Caleb had to work were the opposite of blissful. It wasn't that Sierra couldn't handle being alone. She had moved across the country alone. She had walked back to her apartment in New York City alone. She had eaten tons of meals alone. Sierra was the queen of autonomy.

But something about sitting in her childhood home, listening to it creak unexpectedly, and seeing shadows out of the corner of her eye, made shivers crawl up her spine. Although the weeks since the funeral had flown by, the rest of the year stretched out ahead of her like a glacier.

To thwart the uncomfortable nights, she would call her New York friends, listen to music, do a little freelance work, read a book, and always pour a whiskey. But when those things didn't work, she almost wished for Smokey. Even a smelly dog shedding fur all over the furniture would be better than the eerie loneliness of a house full of memories she was trying to ignore.

The summer nights were hot, and the air conditioner could not keep her bedroom upstairs cool. Even at 24, she wasn't too old to admit to herself that she was too scared to sleep on the couch downstairs. Sierra needed to be able to close and lock her bedroom door, as if that could keep the ghosts out. The heat, the fear, and the whiskey made her toss and turn all night long. The early morning came too soon and yet, even with the terrible sleep, she felt wired.

Sierra washed her face, brushed her teeth, dressed quickly in a simple summer outfit of linen pants and a loose-fitting tee shirt, then grabbed her dad's truck keys and headed to the café. Once there, the morning passed as easily as the others. The regularity of it all, the tediousness, the lack of opportunity for challenges or creativity, frustrated Sierra to no end. She'd agreed with her sister to stay for the inheritance, but if she wasn't able to work on side projects for New York, she would go insane. Sure, there was comfort and nostalgia in the house and café. She knew the two places so intimately she could walk them with her eyes closed. But for every memory that made her smile, another reminded her of why she had left. Sierra had always wanted to leave. She loved her parents. She loved the house she'd grown up in, the café her parents had run, the friends she'd discovered life with, but she had loved the idea of moving on even more. As the regulars came in for their coffees and sandwiches, each hello and please come again made her feel like she was living in a Groundhog Day movie hell.

And then the door opened, and in walked Caleb to rescue her from her monotony. Out of uniform, in a pair of jeans and a blue shirt, he smiled a greeting so bright it could have rivaled the sun shining through the open front windows of the café. He was silhouetted at first, but she recognized his body immediately, and hers buzzed to life in response to his presence.

Sierra came out from behind the bar, and he scooped her up into a hug and a quick kiss.

"Hey," he said, hungrily looking her over. Sierra wasn't the only one craving sex 24/7. The electricity between their bodies could have lit up the café in a power outage.

"Hey, yourself," Sierra said.

"Just got off my nightshift and wanted to stop by for coffee before heading home."

Sierra felt the urge to both groan and growl. If Savannah wasn't asleep upstairs, Sierra would have pulled Caleb up there to her father's couch in a heartbeat. As it was, however, she would have to wait until the afternoon and pray he'd have enough energy for her. The night shift tended to inconveniently change his sleeping schedule. However, she also knew he wouldn't tell her no, even if he was dead tired. Sierra bit her lip while she poured him a coffee to go. Handing it to him, she nearly begged, "You'll be awake when I get off work, right?"

"Yeah, of course," he answered, taking the coffee. "I just need a quick nap. Call me and wake me up before you leave here, and I'll meet you at your place."

Not my place; my parents' place, she said to herself. To him, she smiled, hopefully.

"And hey, I'm off tomorrow night, and I want to take you out on a proper date. Like *really* out. Like, get dressed up in a skirt so short I won't be able to keep my hands off you all night *out*." His eyes roamed her body in anticipation of the sight.

Sierra smiled wider, her cheeks getting hot. Zadie laughed at something a customer told her, and Sierra snapped out of her sexual trance. "Sure," she said, nodding. "Let's go out." Sierra, although, could not imagine going out on a date in Lincoln, Nebraska, compared at all to going out on a date in New York City. She couldn't imagine a place where wearing a short skirt here wouldn't get her dirty looks from the locals.

"I'd better go help Zadie," Sierra said, shrugging toward the line of morning customers.

"OK, I'll see you later." Caleb kissed her on the cheek, but she could feel how much he wanted to do more. Or at least, that's what her body told her as it shivered underneath the touch of his hands on her bare arms. She headed back behind the counter to help with orders, watching him leave like a love-sick puppy.

No, she corrected herself. Just horny. Horny-sick? Horny-obsessed? Sierra shook her head and tried to focus on her work.

The following evening, Sierra found a shimmery sheer silver dress that was barely long enough to sit down in without revealing her goods to the world. Although she didn't need any help getting Caleb into bed, it was still nice to look in the mirror and feel sexy. Beautiful. For the briefest of moments, she saw her mother looking back at her in the reflection. There was something in the shape of her lips, the color and depth in her dark brown eyes, that reminded her of looking at her mother when Sierra was just a child. She pushed the thought away and replaced it with one of concern, hoping she wasn't overdressed for a night in Lincoln.

Caleb knocked lightly on the door at 7 p.m. Oddly nervous, Sierra shot the rest of her whiskey and went to greet him. Opening the door of her childhood home to a boy on the steps made her feel like she was back in high school, being picked up for prom. Caleb was dressed for a summer night with a pale blue cotton button-down shirt, sleeves rolled up just below the elbows, and collar buttons open. He had dark charcoal grey slacks on that complemented her silver dress perfectly. She hoped he had a blazer in his truck that she could wrap around her shoulders later if needed. She never could understand how in fashion, men, who were usually too hot, had to dress from head to toe, while women, usually freezing, wore the skimpy outfits. It made no sense, but she still appreciated the look Caleb gave her. Maybe that's why the women dress like this, she told herself, smiling.

He looked dumbfounded and seemed to be speechless. Sierra laughed, and he was jolted loose from his fixation. "What?" he asked, a silly smile on his lips. "Can't a man be stunned by beauty?"

Before she could tease him, he stepped across the threshold and wrapped his hands around her waist, pulling her into a kiss so passionate, she was glad she had gone with a clear lip gloss instead of lipstick.

"So, what's the plan?" Sierra asked when he finally stepped back to admire her attire some more.

"I am taking you to a place called Alchemy Aqua Vitae for drinks first," Caleb answered. "Are you ready?"

Sierra grabbed a small white clutch and followed Caleb to his truck. It was a precarious climb up into her seat with her short dress, but Caleb stood to block the view while enjoying it himself. He drove them to the Haymarket district, found street parking, then helped her out of the truck. Walking with her on his arm, she had never seen a man look so proud. As a firefighter, she assumed he knew a lot of locals. Sierra had lost touch with most people and wasn't sure she would recognize anyone who hadn't frequented their café. For a moment, she thought of her sister working nights at the bar. At least the Seattle boyfriend wasn't around to compete with date nights, Sierra thought gratefully. Sierra really did have a pretty good setup for being able to work mornings and then have her nights free, even if the ones without Caleb were lonely. She smiled and squeezed his bicep where she was holding onto him.

Alchemy Aqua Vitae was located in a beautifully restored 19th-century building with exposed brick and cedar beams. Walking in on Caleb's arm, she felt like she'd gone back in time or into a fantasy novel. Lanterns illuminated red brick walls and mahogany wood pillars. The hostess, a pretty girl with short black hair and a black dress, walked them past an area of black leather tufted chairs and stained-glass windows, depositing them at a small bistro-style wooden table with a view of an expansive bar.

"This place is beautiful," Sierra said, admiring everything from the table to the chandeliers. When she'd lived in Nebraska, she'd never imagined going to a nice bar. She had been a kid and then in college. It wasn't until she got a job in New York that she started to appreciate the finer things in life. This place was definitely in the finer things category. A nice surprise of a gem in her hometown.

They ordered smoky old fashions with an Elijah Craig small batch, clinked their glasses together, and sipped, enjoying the mix of smoke and vanilla.

"I always judge a place by how good their old fashions are," Sierra admitted, making small talk.

"I bet they have a lot of places in New York City with perfect old fashions," Caleb said.

Sierra shrugged. "Yes and no. It's like anywhere, I guess. The drinks at the expensive nightclubs can be absolute trash, while the ones at the hole-in-the-wall, so-dirty-you-squat-to-pee places, taste like they should be in gold-rimmed glasses. Of course, they all still cost $30 each." Sierra laughed at the ridiculousness of it, but sadness hit her unexpectedly. She missed the big city. She missed her friends. Her mood sank, and she inspected the contents of her drink with a dazed intensity.

"You OK?" Caleb asked.

"What? Oh, yeah, of course. This is really nice. This is a great place."

"But it isn't New York City?" Caleb asked, guessing, reading her so well already. She smiled in lieu of an answer.

"Have you ever wanted to leave Lincoln?" she asked him.

Caleb took a sip, set down his drink, then leaned back and let his eyes drift around the room. "I love Lincoln," he answered. "I have nothing against Nebraska. My family always teased that if any of us were to leave the state, it would be me. I guess I got caught up in my degree and in training for international disaster response, that I didn't make time to actually travel internationally or otherwise. My parents, my brothers, my friends are all still here. I don't necessarily crave travel. I don't feel the need to escape. But yeah, as a single man, I don't have anything tying me down, and I think it would be interesting to experience new places."

Sierra studied him as she finished her drink. He was a small-town boy, and she was now a city girl. Even if he claimed to be interested in leaving Lincoln, she knew that he would always need to return here to his family and friends. It was obvious that this was his home, but it was the home that Sierra wanted to escape… again.

They walked to dinner at a nearby Italian restaurant filled with that similar old-town charm and cozy atmosphere. After dinner, Caleb took her to another bar that was more focused on dancing than lounging. Sierra kept drinking, dancing, laughing, and snuggling into him, unable to keep her hands off. All she wanted by the end of the night was to get him back into her bed.

Hours later, Sierra was naked and breathless, sweating beneath the ceiling fan of her childhood bedroom. Caleb was beside her, still wide awake and looking at her as if she were some sort of goddess.

"What?" she asked, a sweet, teasing smile on her face as if expecting him to ask for another round.

"You're gorgeous," he said in a whisper.

She huffed slightly, but the compliment felt good to hear.

"I want to know more about you," he said. "Why did you leave Lincoln? Looking around, it looks like you had a great life, good parents, and the family business. Why choose New York over all of this?"

Something stirred in her belly. The drinks? The garlic from dinner? The dancing? She didn't want to answer his question. She didn't want to talk about her parents or her childhood or that damn café. Instead, she snuggled into him and enticed him into another round.

19 SAVANNAH

Fall in Lincoln

The summer months passed by in a blur. Although every day was the same, Savannah felt comfortable with her new normal. She knew her sister hated working at the café, but Savannah never hated it. Each day, waking up in the loft apartment felt like waking up in her daddy's arms. His smell, his belongings, his energy were all around her. She could almost hear him say, *"Good morning, sunshine. Time to wake that sleepy butt up."*

Savannah stretched her arms out wide above her and then quickly tucked herself back in. It was freezing. She'd gone to bed with the windows open and woken up to a fall chill. She wrapped a blanket around her to pad down to the bathroom and started getting ready for the day.

Down in the café, standing behind the bar to take orders, every time the door opened, it carried in the cool air and with it, the smell of wet, wilting tree leaves. The smell mixed with the burnt dust smell of the café's heater when it kicked on. The few trees she could see through the front windows were changing colors, but it wasn't enough. Savannah wanted to drive around town, through old neighborhoods, walk in all the parks, just to ogle each flamboyant display of transformation. Some might find it strange, but to Savannah, it was spiritual. She could stare at a bright red maple leaf for an uncomfortable amount of time, pondering how just a month ago that leaf had been green.

"What if we could do that?" Savannah asked out loud.

Zadie thanked a customer and then turned to Savannah with her dark eyebrows furrowed. "Do what?"

Savannah snapped out of her fixated gaze straight through the front windows and blinked at her friend.

"Go through a physical transformation," Savannah tried to clarify. "Have a sort of annual rebirth."

"Pretty sure born-again Christians do that all the time," Zadie said with a wink. "Oh, and people in Weight Watchers."

Savannah laughed. "No, I mean like the leaves. Or like snakes shedding their skin before they grow larger."

Zadie laughed with her now, rolling her eyes. "Isn't that what we do when we change our clothes? Or our hair? People are changing all the time."

Savannah considered Zadie's words as they worked on customer drink orders, maneuvering around each other in a well-rehearsed dance. People are changing all the time, but Savannah felt comfort in the routine of making drinks, handing them out, seeing Mario come out of the kitchen to deliver food, then heading back with a new order to make, while Zadie smiled and greeted one customer after another. There was poetry in their routine.

As another customer brought in a chilly breeze, a realization came to Savannah. She hadn't thought to bring any warm clothing. When she'd left Seattle, it was summer. Of course, summer in Seattle isn't nearly as hot as Lincoln, so she'd been able to make her small wardrobe stretch. But there was no way her light layers would keep her warm through the fall and into winter.

"I'm heading out for my split," Zadie said, giving a slight wave.

Savannah took up the primary position behind the register and leaned over her phone, changing her alarm to wake up early enough the next morning to walk to a local thrift store.

Suddenly, goosebumps skittered across her arms, and she looked up in time to see Waylon's silhouette approach the café door. Savannah set her phone down and stood up straighter, absent-mindedly pushing her hair behind her ears. The black dye was fading out, and it had grown since she'd arrived in Lincoln.

She couldn't help but smile as he sauntered over. He smiled back and tipped his hat toward her.

"The usual?" she asked.

"Yes, ma'am," he confirmed. There was something different in his energy, Savannah noticed. A hesitation, maybe. She turned to grab the whiskey bottle. He was unusually quiet. No questions about her day. No flirting. She poured the black coffee on top of the whiskey in the coffee mug, growing uncomfortable with his demeanor. The thought that Waylon wasn't interested in flirting with her anymore crossed her mind. What if he had started dating someone else? She was surprised to realize how that thought rattled her.

Savannah handed him the mug, and he took it, lifting his eyes to hers.

"I have a question," Waylon started to say as she rang him up. She looked back at him, and he seemed to shift from one foot to another. "A request for your… help."

Savannah's eyebrows rose, curious.

Waylon sipped his whiskey and coffee. "You see, fall is here, and we are prepping to host some harvest events at the ranch. Now, my sisters usually help, but they've got themselves tied up with college activities this year. I do all the heavy lifting, like dropping hay, moving benches, driving through the corn, but I'd like a woman's touch when it comes to decorating the main area for the kids who come through. I know you're busy here most days, but maybe on a slow day, a Sunday or Monday, you could come with me to the ranch to give me some ideas?"

Savannah was literally giddy at his request, her smile growing so wide her feelings were a dead giveaway. "That sounds—" her voice cracked with excited nerves, so she cleared it and tried to sound cool. "I mean, I'd be happy to help. I just need to make sure I'm covered here, sure. Monday. Probably. Yeah, Monday. Earlier, my sister could stay longer for me."

It was like she'd totally forgotten how English works as she stumbled over her response. *Is this a date?* she wondered. *Should I say no?* But looking at the relief in his eyes and how his shoulders relaxed, she knew she couldn't change her mind.

"What type of decorations? Do you have pictures?" Savannah asked.

His smile grew wider, and he pulled out his phone. They both leaned closer together over the counter, so he could scroll through an album. Kids were posing with scarecrows, a horse-drawn wagon filled with families, and pumpkins stacked up at booths showcasing various games like ring toss. It was so charming, and seeing how joyful Waylon seemed stirred something primal inside Savannah. It took everything for her not to deeply inhale him in and pull him to her by the collar of his pearl snap shirt.

Nearly overcome, she pulled herself back to standing upright on her side of the counter. *Counter, good. Being too close to Waylon, bad. But it isn't a date. I am just helping the community.*

Waylon took his coffee to his usual table, and she tried everything she could to keep from watching him, praying for customers to come in and distract her.

Monday morning came, and Savannah donned a burnt orange sweater that she'd found at the local thrift store, over a black band tee shirt, jeans, and black combat boots. She waved at Zadie and her sister as she headed outside to wait for Waylon. They both watched her with teasingly suspicious looks, although she had assured them both that this was *not* a date.

Stepping outside, she breathed in the cool air deeply. Chimney smoke, baking bread, and wet leaves stirred together in her senses. It smelled like winter was coming, and the realization that her parents wouldn't be here for the holidays jolted her unexpectedly. The joy she felt about the changing season contrasted painfully with the emptiness of going into the holidays without her parents. Since she rarely saw her sister, and with her boyfriend in Seattle, Savannah felt the weight of loneliness pressing down on her with every leaf that fell. She wondered if going to the ranch with Waylon was just a distraction from processing all the emotions of grief.

Before she could get lost in those thoughts, Waylon pulled up in a massive Ford F-250 Super Duty complete with a silver toolbox in the bed. She stepped up to the gray door, but before she could reach for the handle, Waylon was beside her, opening the door for her. He put his large hand on her back and helped guide her up into the seat. The touch and the gesture made her so foggy-brained she couldn't think of anything to say except to croak out a small thank you.

They made small talk along the half-hour drive, most of which consisted of dirt roads through farmlands. Savannah caught herself staring out across the fields, still wet from dew and glistening in the morning sunlight. The sky was clear, and her mind felt calm, despite knowing how close she was sitting to a masculine man who did things like open truck doors. She tried to stop herself from thinking about him like that.

As they pulled into a parking lot, which was half dirt and half loose gravel, he cleared his throat. "This is where the families will park when they come to visit."

Waylon pulled right up to a white sign that said welcome and entrance in big black letters. He parked and then jumped out. She watched him walk around the front of the truck, stilling her hand on the handle as she realized he was coming to open her door. Sure enough, he swung the heavy thing open and extended his hand. Looking down at him, knowing she could fling herself into him, picturing him catching her, made stars cross her vision. She thought she was going to swoon and faint for a moment before telling herself this was how he probably treated all women. Women are small, weak, and need to be tended to carefully. That's what all these southern cowboys thought. She was *not* supposed to fall for that nonsense. Savannah was supposed to be a strong, independent woman. She couldn't be feeling weak at the knees over simple gestures like ensuring she didn't fall and break an ankle while exiting an oversized truck.

Her hand was so small in his, and she felt as delicate as a flower stepping onto the dirt ground. He took his time letting her hand go, as if making sure she wouldn't fly away first. Her cheeks reddened, hoping he couldn't tell how much his proximity affected her.

"Let me give you a tour," he started, taking the lead toward a row of wooden stands. "We set up piles of pumpkins all around, but vendors like to bring in homemade breads and cookies. We leave the stands where they are, but just clean 'em out of dust and critters before harvest nights."

"Harvest nights?" Savannah asked, looking around. Strings of lights dangled between dozens of poles and booths, looking like a carnival.

"That's what we call it," Waylon said. "Hoffmann Harvest Nights at the Ranch. Starting up in the evening, before the sun sets early, the families come and pick out pumpkins, walk through the corn maze, take pictures in the fields, and eat corn and treats."

"I remember doing something like that as a kid, before our parents bought the café." Not wanting to get sucked into the memory, she looked out across the space. "How can I help?"

"I got a barn full of decorations," Waylon said. "There are harvest and Halloween decorations, posters, arches, and I just need a good eye on where to set everything up around here while I drive in and set down hay bales for seating. There are woven blankets in the barn, too, that can be draped over the hay bales."

As he talked, she could already see the area come to life around her. She could smell the corn, see the moms sitting on woven blankets, and hear the children laughing as they ran around piles of orange pumpkins. Savannah smiled. "Where's the barn?"

"Well, the shortcut is through the corn maze," he said.

"What?" She laughed, a childlike excitement filling her chest. Straight ahead was a framed entrance to a cornfield. She headed there immediately, with Waylon following her. Walking inside, the dry stalks towered over her.

There was a mixed smell of dust and mustiness of water that had sat gathered on the foliage. The world disappeared from view as she zig-zagged through the cut pathways. She came to her first fork and turned to the right. She assumed Waylon knew the quickest way through, but following him wouldn't be half as fun as trying to figure it out herself.

She heard his boots crunching on the flattened down stalks somewhere behind her and giggled as she picked up speed. "Shit," she said when she hit a dead end, smiling ear-to-ear. She turned around and lightly jogged backtracking to the last fork that had led her astray. Once she reached it, she took the corner quickly and crashed right into Waylon's chest.

His arms reached out around her, making sure she didn't bounce back and fall to the ground. She'd knocked the wind out of herself and looked up at him, unable to breathe. He laughed deeply, and she felt the rumble through their connected bodies.

"I got you," he said, as if he would never let anything hurt her. "You alright?"

She inhaled, and the scent of him nearly sent her spiraling. "Uh-huh," she said. Savannah was vaguely aware of his hands moving from stablizing her sides to up her arms, pulling the sleeves of her orange sweater up. His hands reached her shoulders when she realized they were staring into each other's eyes, their breathing heavier than it had been moments before.

She let out a very loud, unladylike laugh and took a huge step backward. "Woo, thanks," she said, looking past him for an escape from the maze. "I was having too much fun in here."

Something shifted, and Waylon's smile went from expectant to disappointed. "Tell me something," he said, respecting the distance she'd put between them. "Are you still waiting for that guitar player boyfriend of yours to write you a love song?"

Savannah furrowed her brow, not because he'd asked the question, but because she realized in that moment that no, Jaxon had never written her a love song. Not even when they were first dating. Not even when she followed him to Seattle.

She rolled her eyes and pointed down the flattened path behind him. "We've got work to do. Take me to the barn, cowboy."

20 SIERRA

Fall in Lincoln

Summer turned to fall, and even though Sierra and Caleb had spent all their free time together, Sierra still hadn't told him that she would only be in Lincoln until next summer. When the conversation started to turn more serious or long-term, Sierra steered them out of it and off into a more casual topic. She knew that most couples after a few months of dating would talk about where they were in the relationship, or at least, where they were going. But she also knew that people like Jaxon kept people like her sister in relationship limbo for years. It *was* possible to avoid the 'what are we' discussion, the words "I love you," and other such nonsense. She was having fun, and if they even made it to next summer, she'd thank Caleb for all the fun times, and she'd move back to New York City. There was no need for her to even refer to them as a couple.

Christmas was only a few months away, and Sierra knew she needed to start organizing the big annual Christmas party at the café for the regulars. It would be the last one, and a kind of homage to her parents, so she wanted to make sure it was absolutely perfect. There were boxes of decorations to put up, fresh trees to bring into the café, which would be donated to be planted, as her parents had always done.

Sierra sat in her father's office, typing a checklist of plans for the Christmas party. It was a slow Tuesday morning, and she took a moment for herself in between the breakfast and lunch rushes. Noticing her mug was low on coffee, she got up and headed into the café through the kitchen door. Sierra nearly ran straight into Savannah.

"Oh, hey, you're up early," Sierra said, hearing her own judgment in her tone.

"Yeah," Savannah said, holding a coffee mug with two hands. "The loft was cold, and I need to head back to the thrift store to find a winter coat before my shift starts."

Sierra maneuvered around her sister and poured herself coffee. "How are things?" she asked, realizing the two of them hadn't really talked since their paths rarely crossed nowadays.

Savannah shrugged. "Fine, I guess."

"What's going on with you and the cowboy?" Sierra asked. "You went to his ranch or something yesterday, right?" Although Zadie was with a customer, she could see the young woman glance in their direction. "Let's go sit," Sierra recommended, directing her sister out into the restaurant tables and out of earshot. She couldn't help but notice a mix of emotions that crossed her sister's face as they sat down at a small back table.

"Nothing is going on," Savannah said defensively. "We are friends, and he wanted my input."

"How are your friends?" Sierra asked. "Isn't he a customer?"

"Yeah, I mean, of course he comes in as a customer, but we talk and stuff, you know?" Savannah stumbled over her words. "His sisters weren't available to help set up decorations, and he thought I'd be good at it. It was fun. The ranch is lovely. It reminded me of when we were young, and we'd go with mom and dad to pick out pumpkins before…"

"Before they bought the café," Sierra finished, feeling their shared resentment resonating between them. They both took a moment to sip their coffee and look around the business that kept them trapped in more ways than one to their past.

"I think you're more than friends," Sierra said. "I've seen the way you look at each other. And you seem… happier today than normal. You're up early."

Savannah smiled slightly but then shook her head. "It was fun, but I am with Jaxon. I'm going back to Seattle. Waylon is just a nice man who hangs out here. He's a regular."

"A handsome regular," Sierra added.

"He's not my type!"

"Ha," Sierra scoffed, setting her mug down and looking at her sister's brown eyes. "What's your type then? Wannabe rockstars in black leather pants who can't survive without you paying their rent?"

"Jaxon is not a wannabe," Savannah said, defending her Seattle boyfriend. "He is insanely talented, and someday soon he's going to be picked up by a record label. I won't have to pay for anything after that."

"Listen, sis," Sierra said, putting her hand up in defense. "I'm all for feminism. But it's supposed to be equal, not one-sided. If you are taking care of everything for him, working so he can play music with his friends, that's not feminism. That's being taken advantage of."

"He's not…" Savannah started off, but then her voice dropped to a whisper, as if doubting the words as they came out, "taking advantage of me. He loves me."

Sierra scoffed again, and Savannah's eyes shot up at her like daggers.

"What about you and that fireman?" Savannah asked. "You're taking advantage of him."

"I am not! We're just dating," Sierra said defensively.

"Does he know that you're leaving?" Savannah pressed.

Sierra leaned forward toward her sister. "Shh," she warned. "Keep your voice down."

Savannah sat back and crossed her arms. "I'll take that as a no, then. You haven't told him. You are stringing him along, and you are going to break his heart. You are in no place to judge me and my relationship, sis."

Both sisters narrowed their mirror-brown eyes into glares at each other from across the tiny bistro table.

Savannah pushed back from the table, stood up, and grabbed her coffee mug. "Winter is coming, and I need to go buy a coat." Then she stormed off through the swinging door into the kitchen. Sierra could feel Zadie's curious eyes on her, but she refused to meet them. She sat at the table and quietly finished her coffee.

*** Winter in Lincoln ***

A few weeks before the Christmas party, Sierra held the door to the café open for Caleb, who carried in two trees from a local farm. He had picked them out to meet her specifications, put them into his truck, driven them across town, and hand-delivered them like some Hallmark Movie Hero. He wore a long-sleeved shirt to protect his arms from the prickly branches. His brown hair was messy, and the workman's gloves he wore made him look like such a prepared man. He had a truck, gloves, and the strength to carry out her every desire. Even Christmas trees.

Sierra would keep the trees in pots so they could be donated to a local school and planted after the party. It was a tradition her mother started, and to honor her, Sierra would do it one more time before selling the place. She knew she didn't have to host the Christmas party. But despite the resentment for being stuck in Lincoln, she did love the holidays. She had good memories of running around during these parties as kids, being showered with gifts and candies from the regulars, until finally falling asleep on a chair while the adults kept singing and dancing into the night.

Once she moved to New York, she still came back to visit for a couple of days around the holidays. It wasn't always on Christmas, and it wasn't usually during one of their parties, but she'd come back to see her parents and sister.

She closed the door against the cold and smiled at Caleb, who was positioning one of the trees in a planter they would fill with dirt and water to keep the evergreen alive until spring.

Is this really the last Christmas party? she wondered to herself, looking around at the pictures on the walls. College game days. Family pictures. Famous locals. Once it was all sold and she moved back to New York, Sierra would never return. She'd be done with this place. She could keep a few pictures as mementos.

"How's this?" Caleb asked her from the other side of the café.

"It's perfect," Sierra said, responding to how he'd placed the tree on either side of a make-shift stage where a local band would play Christmas music during the party.

Caleb helped her string strands of garland and twinkling warm lights throughout the café inside and out. The café was open, and Savannah was working behind the counter, barely making eye contact with her. They hadn't talked since they'd argued about the men they were or were not dating. Sierra told herself that it didn't matter. She was sure that they would reconcile around Christmas time, like everybody else. They'd finish out their half of the year, sell the properties, and go their separate ways.

Sierra was a little jealous as she strung the lights throughout the café, knowing that her sister would have more opportunities to enjoy the romantic twinkling, the magic of Christmas lights in the evenings, while Sierra would be back at her parents' house after her regular shifts.

Sierra designed a poster to hang on the front windows and in the bathrooms, advertising the party. The local band would play classic Christmas songs, sing-alongs, and she had created a special food and drink menu for the party. Sierra had worked with Mario to plan everything, then ordered the inventory. There would be spiced rum and cider, a white Christmas martini with vanilla vodka and white chocolate liqueur, Santa's old-fashioned, and bourbon hot chocolate. They would set out a grazing table with maple-glazed bacon sliders, brie crostini with cranberry sauce, and assortments of meats and cheeses all adorned with adorable little sprigs of mistletoe. Of course, Sierra wouldn't be allowed anywhere near the stove, but she could lay things out for people to grab and snack on throughout the evening.

Planning the event was actually fun, which she found surprising. Sierra could see why this was such an important event to her parents, and in some ways, recreating it felt like they were there with her. She hoped they'd be hanging out, listening to the music, and watching their daughters in the café they'd loved one more time.

In a way, it would be an extension of her parents' wake, giving them one more final goodbye, and allowing the community another chance to say goodbye through one last Sweetwater Café and Bar Christmas party. Of course, nobody would know that it would be the last party. But she could look back at this in six months and feel good about throwing one last event for the community, for the regulars, and in some ways, for her parents.

She sighed as she hung lights over a framed picture of her family from some camping trip pre-café. Sierra wasn't someone who thought about the past. She was always focused on planning for the future, setting and accomplishing goals. She knew the goal was to sell the business and house, split the proceeds, and continue pursuing goals in New York City. The lights, the trees, the decorations, and the memories surrounded her, pressing their nostalgia into her periphery in ways she couldn't completely ignore.

Will I regret letting all of this go? she wondered. Maybe not in the next few years, but eventually?

She shook her head at her thoughts, telling herself she was being silly. The next best step for her and her sister was to sell their past and return to the futures they were building.

21 SAVANNAH

Winter in Lincoln

Savannah found out about the Christmas party and special drink and appetizer menu from a flier beside the espresso machine. The party would be two days before Christmas on a Saturday night. She assumed her role was to dress nicely, show up, and serve these new special drinks all night.

She felt a little annoyed that her sister didn't talk to her about the idea before plastering announcements around the café. Was a Christmas party a good idea? *Sure.* Did a few new drinks and treats for the night fit right in with the theme of the party? *Yeah. Whatever.* But to not even talk to her about it?

Granted, the sisters had not talked much since their argument about men a couple of months prior. They'd stayed in their separate routines. Savannah woke up around noon, showered, texted Jaxon for a couple of minutes, then went downstairs to start her late lunch shift. Her routine had not included any nights off, unfortunately. Not that she had anyone to go out on the town with, anyway. Sierra had taken date nights with Caleb, but hadn't really missed any actual workdays. Living and working every day at the bar just made the months seem to fly by. She couldn't believe they would only have half a year left.

Melancholy mixed with the holiday decorations all around the café. That was another thing her sister had done without talking to her. Sierra had just started unpacking and hanging things while her boyfriend, or friend with benefits, whatever he was to her sister, carried in potted pines.

As the days had gotten shorter and nights lasted longer, college kids letting off steam between study sessions, or already on their holiday breaks, maybe even visiting from out of state, would fill the place. The bar was so busy that Mario and his wife, Edith, would help mix drinks. For anyone who wanted a time-consuming concoction, Savannah would steer them toward a pre-mixed trashcan punch she prepped before things got too crazy. Most of the kids just wanted something bitter, spicy, or sweet. If someone didn't know what he or she wanted, Savannah would ask them that question and then give them something easy that fits into the requested category. It was a trick she'd seen her dad use on busy nights.

They always reserved televisions for football, which was drowned out by the jukebox as the night went on. As the hordes became even happier, they would gather and impromptu karaoke together, hugging and swaying to songs by The Band or The Eagles. Laurel would show up on the weekends, decked out in her best flowery gown to read fortunes for the kids who had their whole lives ahead of them. Although Savannah was working while all the joy was happening around her, she had to remind herself that she, too, had her whole life ahead of her. She was only twenty-two, after all.

Zadie and Savannah would dance together behind the bar, refilling glasses with what felt like an ungodly amount of whiskey. She would take sips during her shifts, careful to keep her wits about her, kick everyone out at 1 a.m., lock up, clean away any evidence of fun, say goodnight to Zadie, and then head back upstairs to her bohemian loft apartment.

Savannah was happy with her routine. She enjoyed seeing the regulars and meeting new people. She liked sitting with Laurel when it was slow or listening to Zadie talk about her post-college dreams. She found herself watching the clock on slow afternoons, feeling both anxious and excited about Waylon coming in for a whiskey, coffee, or both mixed together. Savannah didn't want to admit this to herself, but there was a little twist in her stomach if he came in later than she expected, and a little excitement when he came in earlier.

Their afternoon talks had gotten longer and longer. She told him about growing up in Lincoln and about her time in Seattle, leaving Jaxon out of the stories. He told her about growing up on the ranch, childhood stories about falling off bulls and trying to herd sheep with the dogs. And always when it was time for him to leave, which was right about when a dinner crowd started to come in, he asked if she was still with her boyfriend. Her answer was always the same. When he left the café, she reminded herself that all of this would come to an end. Her sister would sell everything, and Savannah would go back to Seattle.

Savannah couldn't explain the tether Waylon seemed to have to her, but when he walked away, it was almost like something connected to her chest tugged a bit, wanting to follow him. She smiled to herself and checked the phone she'd left on the counter by the register. A text from Jaxon was waiting.

"What R U up 2?" he asked.

"Looking at a Christmas party flyer for the bar," she answered, since she was staring at the flyer they'd propped up to entice customers.

"I want to see," he texted. So, she took a picture of the flyer and sent it to him. "Those drinks sound fire," he responded, but with a fire emoji.

She nodded in agreement, then, feeling dumb, reacted to his text with a heart icon. Savannah set her phone down and turned to greet a guest coming in, switching herself into server mode, since Zadie hadn't arrived yet to start the last half of her split shift.

She took orders, passed food requests to Mario in the kitchen, and took care of the drinks herself, but every time she saw that flyer about the Christmas party, she rolled her eyes. She was excited about the party, but still just couldn't believe her sister hadn't included her in any of the planning. She'd woken up to trees being carried in, menus and advertisements printed and posted. She'd started her shift watching Christmas lights and garland being strung both in and out of the café. She'd started her shift to a menu, flyers, and everybody else was informed and excited about the plan. Everyone except her. It made her feel completely left out and useless. Sierra should have asked her for help. They should have decorated for the last Christmas party at Sweetwater Café and Bar together.

Zadie arrived for her shift cheerier than usual. "Oh my God, finals are done!" she squealed, coming around the counter and hugging Savannah.

"That's great," Savannah said. "How did you do?"

"I'll know for sure in a few days, but I feel really good. I knew everything. I wasn't stressed at all. Of course, Laurel told me I was going to do well, so that helped me be less stressed, I think."

"Oh, of course," Savannah agreed, looking over at Laurel, who was setting up her table for the evening rush. Laurel looked up and winked at her.

The girls worked through some more orders, but during a lull in activity, Savannah decided to go sit with the psychic. Something had been bothering her so much, but she was almost afraid to ask Laurel.

"Good afternoon, Savannah," Laurel said, her floral dress draped with a sweater to ward off the chill that came inside every time the door opened.

"Hi, Laurel," Savannah greeted, sitting down. "I've been wondering about something."

Laurel shuffled her Tarot cards. "About your boyfriend?"

Waylon's face, his hat, his smile suddenly popped into Savannah's head. Then she forced the image to switch to Jaxon: lean, long hair pulled into a high bun, earrings, tight pants. *That* boyfriend. Savannah nodded.

"I can pull cards, but no matter what I tell you, you have the free will to make decisions that make you happy. We all choose how we want to be treated. We choose what our relationships look like. We choose what happiness means to us. So, have you made any of these choices, or do you just go along with the flow?"

Savannah didn't know how to answer the question, feeling overwhelmed by everything Laurel had just said. Instead, she stared at the woman who shuffled her cards. Savannah did feel like most of her life had just been going with the flow from high school boyfriends, parties with friends, going to the school her parents loved, helping at the café, and then Jaxon in a hotel room, begging her to come with him to Seattle. Had she ever made a decision for herself, she wondered?

Laurel laid down one card: the fool. He was standing poised on the edge of a cliff, a little dog at his feet. Savannah's eyes shot up to Laurel's, feeling somewhat insulted, even though she knew the woman didn't pick this card on purpose. She swallowed back her pride. "What does this mean?" Savannah asked.

"You are a drifter, Savannah, dear," Laurel said, her tone gentle and quiet. "But you don't have to be a drifter. Upside down like he is, means you have perhaps let life happen to you. Did you choose to move to Seattle, or were you convinced to move to Seattle? Are you going with the flow when it comes to letting your sister run this place, while you just work here? Is that your choice or hers?"

Savannah pushed her chair back from the table and stood, feeling irritated. She didn't want to hear this. She tossed her hair back from her shoulders. Over the months, her short hair had grown, the dark dye fading out to reveal her lighter shade beneath. She sent selfies to Jaxon, and he hearted them, but sometimes she worried that he'd prefer her with the short black hair again. He had been understanding when she explained that she wouldn't be back in Seattle for a year, but he hadn't said anything about her hair growing out and going back to its natural dirty blond.

Choice. Had she made the choice to grow her hair back out? If she cut it again, would that choice be hers or Jaxon's? Her mind was going in a million different directions after listening to Laurel. She walked away from the little table, heading to the back of the bar to mix herself a drink. She needed to practice making the Christmas options for the party, so she figured she'd start on that.

Choice. Would she want to throw a Christmas party if her sister hadn't done all the planning? Would Savannah have chosen the same date, the menu items, the decorations? She looked at everything again: the lights, the menu, the trees. She shrugged, pouring vanilla vodka over ice. Savannah probably would have done most of the same things, but would she have been as organized and methodical as Sierra? She was so used to taking orders, not making decisions. She had managers at cafés, restaurants, bars, and clubs, all telling her where to be and what to do for years.

Before them, it was her parents. She cleaned the tables, served the food, and selected the music. She picked songs she knew her father loved, songs her mother liked to sing along to. Savannah thought she was making a brave decision moving to Seattle, but what if that never really was her choice? What if she just went with Jaxon because he seemed cool and exciting at the time? He'd picked out the apartment, the furniture, and connected her with people he knew to get her jobs.

Savannah finished mixing the white Christmas martini and sat down on a barstool, taking a sip. It was sweet and delicious. *Perfect*, she thought. Another great choice her infallible sister had made, she thought bitterly.

The picture of the fool came to her mind, and she saw him dancing, juggling, winking at her from within the card. Was that really who she was, she wondered. Here she was, sitting in her parents' café, working the bar, making drinks, her sister running the place, and Savannah just going with the flow of her sister's choices. Stuck for a year here because of her parents' choices.

"Hey, Savannah," Zadie said, popping out from the kitchen. "You good? Whatcha got there?"

Savannah looked down at her glass as if surprised to see it in her hand, but more surprised by how quickly she'd drunk it down. "A white Christmas martini," she said. Zadie rolled her eyes.

"That's racist," Zadie said. Then both girls barked out laughs. When they stopped laughing, Zadie asked about the ingredients, and the two of them discussed the upcoming Christmas party menu. Zadie always had a way of making Savannah feel better. She was more excited now about the party, picturing what she could wear, imagining Waylon complimenting her, and wanting to dance with her.

Waylon. She knew she couldn't choose Waylon. Sierra was going to list the café and the house for sale the first week of June. In six more months, both girls would be on their way back to Seattle and New York City. She knew that Sierra was hanging out with the fireman, Caleb, and didn't know how that was going, but she knew her sister. There was no way Sierra was giving up her career and her future in New York.

Savannah looked around Sweetwater Café and Bar, and for the first time, wondered if she had a choice.

22 SAVANNAH

Winter in Lincoln

Savannah woke up early the day of the Christmas party. Snow was lightly falling outside, flakes sparkling in the sunlight outside the large loft windows. According to the forecast, it would clear up by the afternoon. Although she'd stayed up and closed the bar the night before, she wanted to help her sister get ready for the party.

Sierra had planned everything, but she was also going to be working a full-day shift, opening the café for breakfast like usual, but staying up with Savannah to work the party. If Sierra was making the sacrifice by working all day, then Savannah would too.

She'd found time to dig out an old emerald, green gown from her closet. She'd worn it to a Christmas dance in high school and felt good about giving it a second chance at dancing. It had hung in a bag in her childhood closet for years, so aside from spraying it with some light fabric freshener, it was in great condition. Savannah placed the dress on her bed and pictured Waylon's admiring expression. Like a princess in a movie, she saw herself walking into the bar and his eyes brightening at seeing her. It was silly and romantic, she knew, and she was still with Jaxon and would never cheat on him, but it felt good to fantasize about a stolen romantic moment.

Savannah got dressed in jeans and a sweater, then headed downstairs to help open and prepare. Sierra was in the office. "I'm here to help with anything you need today," Savannah said through the open door.

"OK, thanks," Sierra said, dryly. "Can you get me more coffee?" Sierra held out an empty cup without looking up from the computer.

"Sure," Savannah said, taking the cup and walking to the machine in the dining area. She carried the hot cup back to her sister and set it down on the edge of the desk. Savannah didn't even thank her as she headed back to the bar to help take orders. Zadie was there already, smiling and chatting away.

"How are you always so well-rested and happy?" Savannah asked her. "You closed with me last night. You're up at the crack of dawn here. You're still in school. You have so much energy. How?"

Zadie laughed. "I nap during my split-shift break. I don't really need that much sleep, and I don't need to study much, either. When I'm in class, I'm able to remember most of what the professors tell us. It just sticks."

"That's lucky," Savannah said. Her brain had never worked that way. Although she hadn't struggled in school by any means, she had always needed to study, re-read passages, and write things down in order to pass tests. She'd decided to leave school around the time she'd met Jaxon, believing that school was more Sierra's thing and not something she wanted to compete with her sister on. Her parents were so focused on running their business, they hardly paid attention to grades anyway. Savannah had barely passed most of her college classes. When Jaxon and his band had come through town, that was it for her. Running away to a new city sounded way more exciting than finishing school and getting a degree.

Later that afternoon, Savannah and Sierra worked side-by-side in the kitchen, unwrapping meats, cheeses, and fruits. Sierra had ordered a bunch of mistletoe sprigs, and the sisters spent time setting up multiple charcuterie boards that they could carry out and lay across the bar. Both women were quiet and focused on their work, choosing tasks where they didn't have to stand together or interact.

As frustrated as Savannah was with Sierra most of the time, she missed how they used to be as children. They would work on tasks at the café for their father. Sierra would always lead the way, showing Savannah how to pour salt carefully from the metal nozzle into a shaker, then let her screw the metal top back on. Sierra had been a kind and protective sister. Sure, she'd had her moments when she'd push Savannah away. Sierra would get annoyed about something Savannah did, like leaving a mess in the small bathroom they shared, or get angry about something Savannah took, like borrowing a new pair of shoes without asking. Sister shit.

"I think we should pre-make all the various drinks," Sierra said, interrupting Savannah's memories. "That way, you and Zadie won't be stuck behind the bar all night." The words were considerate, but the tone was matter-of-fact.

Savannah smiled at her sister, anyway, giving her the benefit of the doubt that maybe the holidays were softening her up. "I like that idea," she said, and Sierra gave her a rare, albeit small, smile in response. Savannah took the opportunity to stir up a conversation. "How are you? How are you and Caleb?"

Sierra shrugged, unwrapping a round package of brie cheese. "We're good. Just having fun. Dating. Nothing serious."

"I see," Savannah said, turning to layer more meat down onto the board she was working on. "So, you won't be staying here to be with him or anything crazy like that?" Savannah was being facetious, but she was curious about whether or not her sister was still desperate to leave Lincoln. The two sisters had hardly spoken to each other in months.

"Absolutely not," Sierra said, definitively. She could tell that the question had shifted her sister's mood back to a negative, standoffish queen, which seemed to be Sierra's MO since returning to Lincoln. Although the sisters hadn't talked much when they'd been on opposite ends of the country, at least they'd been cordial, and Savannah hadn't had to deal with the boss bitch attitude.

"You should get started on the drinks," Sierra commanded. "I'll finish up these boards."

"Sure," Savannah said, wiping her hands on a towel. She left the kitchen and went to the bar, feeling relieved to escape and yet sad that even at Christmas, they couldn't get along. It was the first Christmas after their parents' passing. It would be the last Christmas at the café. It might potentially be their last Christmas together, once they've moved back to their new homes.

Savannah sighed as she gathered pitchers to start pre-mixing special drink batches. Having them ready in the fridge so she could just quickly pour them over ice would make things a lot easier, as long as people stuck to the holiday-themed drinks. She started mixing the holiday cocktail batches, watching the clock to make sure she left herself enough time to get ready. Zadie had gone home to change, and Mario left to pick up his wife, Edith. They locked the door and hung up another sign showing that although they were closed during dinner, they'd open up for the party at 7 pm.

Savannah finished her chore and headed upstairs, passing her sister. "I'm going to get changed," she said in passing. Sierra was still wearing jeans and a shirt with her sleeves rolled up.

"I'm finishing up now, so I'll run to the house and get changed. Caleb is going to pick me up from there."

"It feels like prom," Savannah said, heading up the stairs to her dad's apartment. Sierra didn't answer.

Savannah showered, brushed out her hair, curled her eyelashes, then put on the green dress that had been waiting for her where she'd left it on the bed.

It was a mermaid cut, low-back, with a slit opening on one side. She pictured Waylon's hand finding its way to her thigh through that slit and smiled. Forbidden tingles climbed up her neck at the thought of him following her back to her bedroom and helping her remove the dress at the end of the night.

Bad, bad, bad, she thought to herself, still smiling. "I am going back to Jaxon in Seattle in six months. Only six more months and everything will go back to normal." She spoke to her reflection in a full-length mirror on the wall. Savannah looked and felt good, and so she would enjoy the evening. She would drink and dance, maybe even dance with Waylon, but she would be good. She would *not* bring him upstairs to her apartment.

Savannah walked carefully down the stairs, now that she was in shoes with a slight heel and a tight dress, then headed to the bar to set out glasses. Mario and Edith showed up and helped carry out all the charcuterie boards to the bar.

"You look like you could get into trouble tonight," Edith told Savannah, winking. Her cheeks burned, but she smiled.

"I'm going to try my best not to," Savannah admitted.

"Well, that's no fun," Edith said, heading back toward the kitchen to bring in another board. Savannah watched Edith sashay her way like a queen in the deeply red dress she wore, feeling envious of the woman's wide hips and curves. Savannah began lining up glasses on the bar in preparation.

Caleb and her sister walked in together, hand-in-hand, from the back door. Savannah looked up, and for a moment, Sierra looked happy. She was beautiful in a golden gown, and she sparkled like a Christmas ornament in the warm glow of the lights strung throughout the café. Her blond hair was long and slightly wavy like a goddess. Caleb was in a dark navy suit that she guessed he'd already owned. It looked classic but polished. He stared at Sierra like the whole world revolved around her. They both stopped at the end of the hallway, and Sierra raised her eyebrows. Caleb turned his eyes up to the mistletoe hanging above their heads.

He smiled and then leaned down to kiss her in a way that was so passionate, intensity emanating from both of them, that Savannah had to look away. That kiss did *not* look like a temporary fling to her, but she'd never tell her sister that. Once the two separated, Sierra switched from a delicate princess who had just been kissed to an A-type show runner, clapping her hands together. She yelled out to ask if everybody was ready, but moved to the front door without waiting for a response.

"The band will be here to set up any minute," Sierra said. "They should start playing their set right when we reopen at seven. Boards look good. Savannah, are the drinks ready?"

"I'm ready to start pouring at seven, and then I'll mix up a few more batches to store in the fridge for the second round before I'm empty," Savannah confirmed.

"Perfect," Sierra said. "Tonight will be perfect."

Everything went according to her sister's plan. The band set up and started to play classic Christmas music. It was only three men: a crooner guitar player, a percussionist with a small drum set, and a man with a keyboard. For such a simple setup, she was surprised by how full of sound they made in the café's dining space. They would only play for a few hours before leaving. At that point, Savannah had been instructed to take over the jukebox duties. They would switch from the Christmas lounge to the party bar. She had no idea if she'd still be sober enough to even keep pouring drinks at that point, but she didn't care. It would all work out, she told herself.

Regular patrons, old and young, came pouring into the bar in their best attire. Laurel even came in, wearing a fur coat over a simple black dress. Savannah had an old-fashioned in her hand as she walked around the room, talking with people, singing along to Christmas songs, but keeping one eye on the door.

Waylon walked in wearing a pair of black cowboy boots she'd never seen before. They were clean, as if they'd never seen a speck of dust. He wore a charcoal suit, a white pearl snap shirt, a black leather belt with a tasteful silver buckle, and at his throat, a black bolo tie that came together around an emerald-colored pendant. It matched her dress in color, and she nearly choked on her sip of whiskey.

A wide smile spread across his face, and he walked straight to her, not even looking around the room to see who else was there.

"Merry Christmas, Savannah," Waylon said, looking down a little less since she was taller tonight in her heels.

"Merry Christmas," Savannah said in a whisper. His smile grew even wider, and his green eyes bore into hers. She looked up at his shaggy blond hair. "No hat tonight, cowboy?" she asked him.

"I didn't want anything to block my view or shield you from the light when I move in closer to dance with you."

"You dance?" she asked, surprise hitching up her voice.

"All good cowboys do," he answered. Then, without another word, he took her whiskey glass, finished it off in one shot, set the glass on the bar, and then pulled her into a space in front of the band that had been carved out for dancing.

He held her hand in his gently, then put his other hand on her lower back, directly onto her exposed skin, sending prickles of forbidden excitement throughout her body. Waylon pulled her body so close to his that she felt every groove of his belt buckle through the front of her dress. The band played the classic "I'll Be Home for Christmas."

Waylon's head was higher than hers, but he leaned his lips down to her ear. "I've been wanting to get you this close to me for months," he whispered.

Those illicit butterflies stirred in her stomach, some flying north to her heart, and others flying dangerously south.

"I think about you all the time," Waylon continued. "The best part of my day is coming here and seeing you. The worst part of my day is leaving. I know you have a boyfriend, and I've tried to keep my distance, but holding you like this…" his words trailed off, and she desperately wanted him to finish what he was saying.

Their bodies broke apart, and Savannah was suddenly cold. "Here," he said, pulling her from the dance floor and toward the hallway. She was confused and a little dizzy until she saw the mistletoe hanging above them. He looked down at her, his eyes pleading, asking her permission without saying a word. Savannah wanted to give in. She wanted to nod and let this man wrap his arms around her. She wanted this man to take her upstairs to her apartment bedroom.

"Savannah? Hey, have you seen Savannah?"

She heard her name on the lips of a man she hadn't seen in six months. She pushed away from Waylon and turned, searching for the man who was calling out for her in the crowded bar.

"Jaxon?" she asked, not truly believing what she was hearing.

"Savvy, baby!"

Jaxon was in black leather pants and a motorcycle jacket. He crossed the crowded dining room in seconds, pulled her into a tight hug, lifted her off the ground, and spun her around. "God, you look great," he said. "Did you miss me? Are you surprised?"

"Um, hi, yeah," was all she could utter. She was more than surprised. She felt like she'd just been pulled from a hot tub and dropped into an ice bath.

"Oh, great, perfect, come here," he seemed scattered and excited, full of that familiar energy. He pulled her toward the band before she could look back to see if Waylon was still standing under the mistletoe.

Jaxon interrupted the singer and took the microphone from the man's hands. A strange quiet, more eerie than romantic, fell over the room at the unnatural disturbance.

"Sorry, my guy," Jaxon said. "Hey, Lincoln, Nebraskans, hi." Jaxon held the mic in one hand and waved at the confused patrons with his other hand. "I'm sure you know who I am, but just in case, I'm Jaxon Steele, lead singer of Dusty Outlaws, and that woman's boyfriend. Savvy, baby, come here."

Savannah's cheeks flushed with heat. *What was he doing?* she wondered. She took one tentative step toward him and crossed her arms over her chest. She felt so uncomfortable with whatever was happening. This was a man she'd been planning to get back to, and yet, now that he was here, he felt like a complete stranger.

"As you know, when the Sweetwaters died, Savannah had to come run this place for a while," Jaxon continued into the microphone. "And baby, I've really missed you. I realize that I gotta shit or get off the pot, man, you know? We got a good thing, and I don't want to lose it. And since it's Christmas, the most romantic holiday aside from Valentine's or something, I wanted to ask you here, in front of everyone, if you'll marry me." Jaxon dug something out of his pocket and held it out toward her.

Realizing that he was holding a ring and this was some sort of half-baked proposal, Savannah's eyes went wide with shock. This man rarely used the word love, hadn't called her, had only texted, and although they'd been together for years, she still wasn't sure what they were. But here he was telling her exactly what they could be.

Engaged. Married. Forever.

"Savvy?" Jaxon asked, extending his hand out to her with the ring. She saw it was a vintage gold piece, big and bulky with what could be a few tiny diamonds or similar looking stone, in a circle in the middle.

She was very aware of the crowd murmuring, whispering, lingering, and lurking behind her. This was what she wanted, right? She wanted Jaxon to finally, truly commit to her? She wanted a life with him? There was a heavy presence of guilt with the people watching, and with Jaxon looking at her with excitement in his eyes. Those eyes were familiar. Even through different schedules, even with her abandoning him in Seattle, he was here smiling at her with those familiar steel blue eyes.

"Yes," she answered, not feeling confident in her own response.

Jaxon whooped and then lifted and spun her around again. With her eyes wide open, spinning, she caught a glimpse of Waylon walking out through the front doors into the night.

23 SIERRA

Caleb placed his hand tentatively onto Sierra's shoulder as if she might bite. They were standing at the bar, and Sierra's eyes were shooting laser beams across the dining and dancing areas at Jaxon, who had his arms around Savannah.

"You might consider wiping the expression of disgust off your face before going over there to congratulate them," Caleb said in a whisper, close to her ear. His being that close to her, whispering into her ear, would have normally sent excited shivers throughout her body, but at this moment, she was too… well, disgusted, to feel anything other than disappointment.

"I am not going to congratulate them," Sierra said firmly.

"They just got engaged. On Christmas. It's romantic." She heard the gentle reassurance in his tone, as if quelling a boiling volcano.

"My sister getting engaged to an idiot, a loser, a mooch, is *not* romantic," Sierra said, defending her stance on the matter.

"She must love him if she said yes. How long have they been together?"

Sierra's eyes jerked to the ceiling, calculating. "Two to three years? But love? They are basically roommates on opposite schedules. Savannah works hard so he can play music with his friends in a band that's never going to be successful. He's probably only here to desperately convince her to go back to Seattle." Which would be fine, Sierra thought. If both girls could just go back to their own states, back to the way things were before their parents' Will was read, everything would be fine.

"Dance with me?" Caleb asked, a big smile on his face as he so obviously tried to change her mood. He was flirty and attentive and always had a way of making her feel happier when she was stressed or irritated. It was nice, but she wasn't sure she was ready to move past the fact that her little sister was about to throw her life away—again.

She didn't answer, but he took her hands and pulled her to the dance floor anyway, spinning her around once and then pulling her body tight against his. They swayed side-to-side, his touch and the alcohol working their magic on her anger.

"You look gorgeous," Caleb said, his warm hazel eyes boring into hers with a hunger.

"You've already told me that at least ten times tonight," she said, finally starting to smile again since witnessing the worst proposal she'd ever seen. Sierra did feel caught up in the romance of the place. The grazing boards looked and tasted fantastic, the drinks were a big hit, but it was the twinkling lights, the classic Christmas songs, and the decorated trees that really touched her where nostalgia met dreamy in her heart.

Her parents loved Christmas. They loved throwing this party. They had danced with each other, with friends, and with their children. Sierra and Savannah had spun around in green and gold dresses, laughing, eating treats that people had brought for them as gifts. Many of those people were still here in this room with them tonight. In some way, her parents were still there, too. She could see them in her memory.

"Are you alright?" Caleb asked, sensing her.

"Remembering my parents," Sierra admitted, sharing a moment of vulnerability.

"They loved these parties?"

Sierra looked at him, then looked around the room at the lights and trees as they danced. "They loved this place, this café, the bar, the apartment upstairs, their neighbors, friends, Christmas, dancing, music, their house. They were really happy here."

"And you and your sister," Caleb said as if she was accidentally leaving them out. She felt a sting in the back of her nose as if sending a signal to flag her tear ducts. To stave off tears, she nodded and then lay her head against his shoulder, ending the conversation. He held her closer and swayed more gently. His arms around her, his hands sending warmth through the thin fabric of her gold dress, made her feel as if she'd never been this safe in her entire life. She closed her eyes for the remainder of the song. And then Jaxon yelled out, "Freebird!"

Her eyes went as wide as saucers, and she pushed off Caleb, looking up at him with her nostrils flared in renewed anger. "He said 'shit or get off the pot' in his proposal speech, Caleb."

Caleb's face scrunched up, showing all the sun-worn creases in his forehead. He shrugged, truly at a loss for how to defend his fellow man. His grip on her forearm told her wordlessly that he didn't support Sierra storming across the bar to confront her sister's new fiancé, but he let go as soon as she pulled away.

She knew Caleb was right behind her, and maybe embarrassed, but she didn't care. Sierra needed Savannah to know exactly what she thought about this engagement. Savannah was still her little sister, her family. It was bad enough that Savannah had followed this vagrant across the country, that it's taken him years to propose, and that he hadn't even come to their parents' memorial service, but to show up like this with a shitty proposal was preposterous.

Jaxon looked Sierra up and down with an approving expression, adding a creeped-out emotion on top of the disgust and agitation already propelling her forward. She narrowed her eyes as she approached.

"Wait, wait, wait?" Jaxon said, holding out his hands. "Is this your sister? What's it, um, Sandy?"

Savannah's cheeks flushed red. "Sierra," Savannah corrected, looking delicate in the green gown and much too beautiful to be standing next to a man in leather pants.

"Oh, Sierra and Savannah, I get it!" Jaxon laughed, clearly proud of himself for making the connection. "Your parents really liked the outdoors, huh?"

Caleb's hand tightened on her shoulder, either trying to calm her down or signaling in silent agreement with her that this man was truly stupid.

"Savannah?" Sierra asked, hoping her sister would know her thoughts without having to say the words out loud.

But instead, Savannah rolled her eyes. "I can't do anything right, can I?" Savannah asked. "I can't run this place, I can't work at bars in Seattle, I can't pick the right man, and I can't even get engaged in a way that you'd approve of. I'm so sick of all your judgments. You judged me for staying here for college after you left. You judged our parents for choosing to run this place. You judged me for moving to Seattle when I met Jaxon. And now this? What's wrong with this?" Savannah waved her hands, the gaudy engagement ring catching the light like a disco ball, around the space, indicating her fiancé and engagement happening here.

"Being proposed to here during the Christmas party made me feel like Mom and Dad were here; they were a part of it. They're with me and happy for me. Why can't you be!?" Even though Savannah yelled the words at her, Sierra heard something else in the tone, like Savannah was trying to convince herself as much as Sierra.

Sierra jolted back from her sister's yelling like she had been struck in the face. "I don't judge you, Savannah!" she yelled back. "I'm judging *him*." Sierra pointed to Jaxon, who had one arm dangling over Savannah's shoulders. "This guy is a loser. You deserve better than a wannabe rocker who mooches off his girlfriend. He's probably only here proposing because of the inheritance you'll get when we sell this place."

Sierra saw Savannah's eyes go wide, darting throughout the room. Everyone had grown quiet from the moment the girls had started yelling at each other, but it wasn't until that moment that Sierra realized just how quiet it was. Caleb's hand dropped from her shoulder, and he took the smallest of steps back.

"You're going to sell this place?" Caleb asked. It was so quiet now. The band was staring, and everyone had stopped dancing, drinking, breathing, waiting for Sierra to answer the question.

"It's why we're here," Sierra said, exasperated as if holding onto the secret for so long had been a heavy weight and she was finally setting it down.

"Sierra, no," Savannah said, trying to interrupt her. Her sister's eyes went to Zadie's, who was standing in the hallway beside them. Sierra saw Mario and Edith, Laurel, and others staring.

"Our parents won't let us get our inheritance until we run this place for an entire year together," Sierra said to Caleb, trying to lower her voice, but everybody heard.

All of a sudden, everyone spoke at once.

"You're only here for one year?" Zadie asked.

"You're gonna sell it?" Mario asked.

"It's only six more months, Savvy," Jaxon said as if trying to sound reassuring.

Murmurs in the crowd, questions, a few sobs, the sound of the band packing up.

Sierra's eyes were on Caleb's, waiting for his reaction. It was true that she'd been leading him on, but they were having fun, right? It's not like they were falling in love. This was always meant to be a one-year thing for her, but his eyes were somewhere between heartache and betrayal.

"Sierra," he said, his voice quiet. "What are you going to do after you sell this place? Are you selling the house too? Are you going back to New York?"

"Yeah, man," Jaxon answered for Sierra, sounding as if Caleb were the dumbest man on Earth. "The girls are selling all their parents' shit, and then Savvy is coming back to Seattle with me, and her sis is headed back to N.Y.C. Right, babe?" Jaxon pulled Savannah into him even closer, shaking her a little bit beneath his grip as if to shake out her confirmation.

Savannah smiled, but no joy met her eyes. She nodded at her fiancé and then looked at Sierra, shrugging.

Sierra turned back to Caleb, a spark of fear igniting deep within her chest, although she didn't understand what she was afraid of. And then it happened. He shook his head.

It was the most subtle of movements, but it was enough. He turned around, walked away from her, and left the bar. That spark grew inside Siera like flames, sending panic into her chest. She wanted to run after him, but she forced her feet to stay planted on the hardwoods. This was for the best, she told herself. She was always going to leave.

"Can we go?" Savannah asked Jaxon.

"No way, babe," Jaxon said. "We're going to get more drinks. The party is just getting started. We gotta celebrate!"

Sierra stayed in place as her sister got dragged back to the pitchers of drinks sitting on the bar between the picked-over charcuterie boards. All at once, she was surrounded.

Edith came up first with her arms crossed and a scowl on her face. Mario stood behind her with his eyebrows scrunched, and his mouth turned down into a frown.

"When exactly were you going to tell us about selling this place?" Edith demanded.

Sierra put her head into her hands and started rubbing at her temples. "Soon," she said through her fingers. "I would have told you all soon. I just wanted to get through the holidays."

Zadie also stepped up, and Sierra noticed her mother, Millie, had conveniently already gone home.

"How could you do this to me?" Zadie asked. "How could you do this to your parents?"

Sierra's head shot up, and she glared at Zadie. "Do this to my parents? My parents did this to me!" Sierra jabbed herself in the chest. "I never wanted to own this place or run this place. I left Lincoln, remember? I didn't want to be here. I didn't know that my parents would hamstring us in their Will. None of this is my fault, OK?" Sierra started to hyperventilate, and through her clouded vision, she saw people leaving the bar. The night had turned out to be a disaster.

"I didn't…" Sierra gasped, trying to regain control of her hysteria. "Know… they would die. This isn't… my fault."

Zadie's hands were on Sierra's shoulders, and the young woman was staring her in the face, all the anger gone. "Sierra, breathe." And then Zadie took exaggerated deep breaths in order for Sierra to attempt to follow her lead.

As Sierra tried to take deep breaths, she wondered if she was having a panic attack. The thought embarrassed her. She didn't want to believe that she could be weak or that there was something she couldn't handle. She fought harder to regain control of herself, looking into Zadie's dark eyes.

Sierra stood back up straight, and Zadie removed her hands from her shoulders. She looked around at the people left: Zadie, Edith, and Mario, who now looked more concerned than angry, and her sister standing with the idiot musician at the bar, worried more about drinking than Sierra.

She had to get out of there, but she realized in horror that Caleb had driven her. Her eyes lifted back to meet Zadie's, probably the best option out of all available present company. "Will you give me a ride home, please?" Sierra asked, trying to sound lost and pathetic to thwart any further attacks.

Zadie rolled her eyes and took a step back. "Sure, let's go," she said.

Sierra grabbed her coat from the back room and then followed Zadie to the front door. Edith and Mario didn't say another word as they left. Before Sierra walked outside, she cast one last glance back at her sister. Savannah looked not happy but content, taking shots with her fiancé on opposite sides of the bar. She looked up briefly and made eye contact. Sierra tapped the lock on the door as if she just wanted to make sure her sister was sober enough to lock up. Savannah nodded once, then returned her attention to Jaxon.

Sierra's heart ached as she left the bar entirely too sober.

24 SAVANNAH

The café was so quiet that Savannah could hear the sound her socked feet made with every step on the hardwood floors. Slightly hungover, she'd woken up early to help Zadie and her sister clean up before the café opened for breakfast. She poured herself a strong double shot of espresso, then mixed in some Bailey's for good measure. She'd only slept a couple of hours, so what did it matter, she thought.

She heard Zadie and Millie arguing before they'd even punched the code into the back door. Feeling embarrassed, she started to rearrange the furniture herself.

"I'm just saying, we tell each other everything. I trusted you," Zadie said, coming in before her mother.

"This is my job, Zadie," Millie explained. "I couldn't divulge the personal wishes of my clients, even if they are all my friends."

"What am I supposed to do, though?" Zadie continued. "This is my job."

"You are about to graduate from college, sweetie," Millie defended. "I knew you'd be finished with school and moving on from this place soon after. You wouldn't just keep on working here with a Business Administration degree, baby."

Both women froze when they saw Savannah cleaning up in the dining area.

"Oh," Millie said, startled. But her mood softened, and she smiled. "Good morning, dear," Zadie said, and went to put on the coffee. Savannah could almost hear her roll her eyes.

"How can we help?" Millie asked. Savannah asked her to grab the edge of a table, and the two women went about putting the entire café back into its original layout. No more stage area. No more dance floor.

They moved on to cleaning up any leftover napkins, plates, and glasses. They cleared away the remnants of the charcuterie boards and then began wiping down surfaces with sanitized rags.

Zadie did her usual opening activities, still pouting, and eventually unlocked the front door and turned the sign around to open. The Christmas lights were all still twinkling, and Savannah thought it best to leave them on to help with the mood of things. There was something about Christmas magic soothing hearts and minds.

"Alright, girls," Millie said, wiping off her hands onto a towel. "I'm going to head into my office. Have a good day." She blew a kiss toward Zadie, who ignored her, and left through the back door.

Savannah contemplated running back to her apartment upstairs before her sister showed up for her shift, but she hesitated. She hated seeing Zadie upset, and Savannah knew the girl probably felt betrayed. Savannah had already abandoned the girl once.

"Hey, I'm sorry I didn't tell you," Savannah said safely from the other side of the bar counter.

Zadie looked up, her face stern but giving way to emotion. Her brow furrowed, and her mouth turned down into a frown. "Why didn't you tell me?" she asked.

"Sierra and I didn't tell anyone," Savannah said. "We weren't sure how people would react. We still need people to work here. And I don't know, I guess we just figured we would tell you all later, when we were closer to listing it for sale."

"But it's not just about losing this place," Zadie said, sounding exasperated as she threw her hands up. "You're going to leave."

Savannah shrugged, not meaning to dismiss the emotions as she shoved them down. Of course, selling, leaving, and marrying Jaxon all made her feel a bit lost, overwhelmed, and confused, but she had to accept that it was her path.

"We've been gone for so long, and now we'll just be leaving again. I can't run this place."

Savannah knew she was sounding way too pragmatic and dismissive about the situation. She had to admit to herself that she sounded more like Sierra in that moment.

"But you are running this place," Zadie said. "You've been running it."

Savannah shook her head. "Sierra has been running it. I don't know how to do payroll or inventory. I don't deal with cash, receipts, or taxes. I need to go back to Seattle with Jaxon.

Zadie's lip started to quiver, and guilt washed over Savannah.

"I'm so sorry, Zadie," Savannah said, her own eyes starting to pinch with the threat of tears.

"I thought you were back, you know, for good," Zadie said, about to cry. Savannah rushed around the bar and hugged the girl.

"I didn't know my being here meant that much to you," Savannah said, honestly. She'd lost touch when she'd moved away. Aside from a few check-in texts, she hadn't realized how much the girl looked up to her.

"It's not just me," Zadie said. "With your parents gone, if you and your sister leave this place again, it will fall apart. Our town won't be the same. The people who come here now will have lost this place forever. We will have all lost your parents forever."

Savannah thought about this, and then her sister spoke up from behind her. Apparently, Sierra had come in during their conversation, and neither one of them had heard her.

"Somebody else will buy it," Sierra stated bluntly. "They might give it a new name, a new sign, but it'll be the same damn place drawing the same damn crowd of old locals in the morning and rowdy college kids in the evening. It'll be fine. You can keep working if you want, but you're getting a degree. I'd highly advise putting it to use so you don't waste your mother's money."

Then Sierra went through the kitchen door to the office. Zadie wiped away a few tears, staring at the kitchen door as it swung back and forth until it stopped.

"Your sister is kind of a bitch," Zadie said, finally. Savannah laughed, agreeing. "Are you really gonna marry that White boy?" Zadie said it as if she didn't expect her to marry *any* White boy, but Savannah knew that wasn't what she meant.

"We've been together a really long time," Savannah said, thinking out loud.

"Do you love him, though? I saw you with that cowboy."

"You saw me with Waylon?" Savannah asked, embarrassed.

"Everybody saw you dancing with him. He's a country snack. I half-expected him to carry you out of here and ride off on a horse with you."

Savannah blushed but considered the question. Yes, Waylon was handsome, but she didn't really know him. She'd known Jaxon for a long time. There was a time she was so obsessed with Jaxon that she'd told him just how much she loved him regularly. She yelled it from the crowd at his shows. She whispered it over his sleeping body when he was passed out drunk. She was pretty sure she'd said it during sex at least a dozen times. But that had been in the beginning. The first time she'd used the word love, Jaxon had responded by saying, "That's scary." So, Savannah had kept the word to herself after that. She'd just decided that he was a non-traditional sort. But last night at the party, he had somewhat traditionally proposed marriage to her in front of a crowd of people.

"Jaxon is great," Savannah said, without answering the question. "I've known him forever, and we've been working toward something. I hardly know Waylon." Something twisted in her stomach at hearing herself say his name. "He's just a cowboy, and he belongs here on the ranch he's working. I belong in Seattle or traveling the world with my boyfriend… my *fiancé* and his band."

Zadie did not look like she believed what Savannah was telling her. But she didn't think there was anything she could say that would convince her old friend that marrying Jaxon would be a reasonable choice. An idea popped into her head, and she spun toward the espresso machine. She made two Americanos, grabbed two pastries from the fridge, and headed upstairs to where her fiancé was sleeping.

Fiancé. The world felt strange in her mind. Weird? *Wrong*? *No*, she thought, *just surprising*. It wasn't that she hadn't thought about marrying Jaxon; she just hadn't thought about it in a long time. She walked up the stairs with her breakfast surprise in her hands, carefully opening the door and then kicking it closed behind her. She laid the goodies out on the kitchen countertop and then took the coffee upstairs.

Savannah watched him sleep while she drank her entire cup, not wanting to wake him up. She left his cup beside the bed and eventually went to take a shower, getting ready for her afternoon shift. When she got out of the shower, he was still asleep, so she ate both pastries. For a moment, she considered going upstairs to wake him up by sitting on top of him. But then, she considered how she'd have to shower again and talked herself out of it.

Savannah wiped off her hands, threw away the sugary evidence, and went downstairs to start her shift. Zadie had left for her split, and Sierra was at the counter. The café was empty.

"Slow day?" Savannah asked.

"All the regulars are hungover," Sierra deadpanned, staring into the vacant dining area.

"About last night—" They both started talking at once, paused, then smiled awkwardly.

"I shouldn't have told the entire bar that we were selling and leaving," Sierra admitted. "Mario hasn't spoken to me all morning, but his wife texted me that he's looking for another job now. I know Zadie is graduating, so she'll go off and start a career doing something, but she shouldn't have found out that way. The busboys will find out eventually, if not already. I'm pretty sure their parents were here last night. Hopefully, they'll stick it out through the transition to new owners, but you never know. I should have been smarter; more in control of my emotions."

Savannah nodded. "Yes, you are usually the one totally in control of your emotions." And everything else, she finished to herself. "Don't you feel bad about all of them having to look for new jobs?"

Sierra turned slowly toward her sister; her brow furrowed so aggressively she looked like she was solving a complex math problem.

"They are all capable of finding new jobs, Savannah," Sierra said, putting a lot of attitude into her name. "Besides, this is a hot spot for a restaurant, upscale bar, sports bar. Some investors will scoop this up and probably keep everyone who works here. If they quit, it'll be because they're pissed at me, and I can handle that. It'll just be more work for us for a while. I'm not worried about Zadie. With her degree, she will find a real job. The cook will go cook somewhere else if he's too angry at me to stay. The busboys are children. They'll be fine no matter what they do. I have my own career to worry about. I'm going to list both of these properties and never look back."

Savannah felt torn for the first time since hearing her parents' Will. Her sister sounded so confident, so sure of the decision and of the timeline, but Savannah was starting to feel something else. Attachment? Hesitation?

"What about Caleb? Don't you like him?" Savannah asked. The second the words came out of her mouth, she regretted them. Her sister's face morphed into a dozen different expressions like a psychopath in a movie: warm happiness, disappointment, panicked regret, shallow anger, irritation, and then finally, eyes glowering into Savannah's in an expression that could only be stubborn resolve.

"Of course, I like the man. He's handsome, good in bed, and not annoying or clingy," Sierra admitted. "But I'm going back to New York City. That's my dream. My career in fashion is there. There's nothing I can do in Lincoln, Nebraska. I'm not going to design skirts for milkmaids, Savannah. And I'd rather die than spend the rest of my life working here."

Her words cut deep and sharp because their parents had died working here. They lived here. Dreamed here. Loved here. And died just a few miles away from here. They hadn't even had the luxury of dying peacefully in their own beds, in the home they'd worked so hard for.

"Amen to that!" Jaxon burst through the swinging kitchen door, grabbing Savannah from behind and lifting her into the air. He kissed her neck, his stubble scratching her skin. "See, your sister and I agree on something already, like a real family."

Sierra's glare narrowed like a laser beam of destruction at his face.

"When are you going to sell this place and get out of here?" he asked Sierra, although he already knew the answer. Savannah had told him multiple times.

"Six more months," Sierra answered, dryly. She sounded as if they would be the most painful months of her life. "When are you leaving?"

"Ah, I gotta be back up to Seattle in a few days," Jaxon answered. "Figured I'd spend a couple of days with my girl here. My betrothed."

Savannah saw Sierra roll her eyes.

"And I'm out," Sierra said, skirting around them as if they had the plague.

"Later," Jaxon said, still gripping Savannah uncomfortably. She tried to gently tug herself free.

"I gotta work, Jaxon," she said.

"Cool, cool, cool, yeah," he replied. "You got some coffee down here? And maybe a sandwich or something? I'm starving."

Three young women walked into the café, chatting and laughing. Savannah recognized them as regulars who worked nearby. They always came in during their afternoon break together to get cappuccinos.

"Good afternoon," Savannah greeted, moving toward the register. "Ready for your pick-me-up?" The women still had a few more hours to go, but Savannah knew they mostly came in for a moment to gossip amongst themselves, outside of their office. She'd learned their names over the last six months. The shortest woman had long, wavy brown hair and translucent green eyes. The second-tallest woman had light brown skin and thick dark hair. The tallest woman looked like a supermodel with long legs and a thin, beautiful face. If Savannah had planned on staying in Lincoln, she would have tried to become friends with these three. They always seemed to be having a good laugh and interesting conversations.

Savannah rang them up and started to make their orders. While she stood behind the bar, Jaxon sauntered over to the women, who were talking together while waiting for their drinks.

For the first time in at least a year, Savannah felt a jealous claw climb up the back of her neck. Then, when she heard the girls giggling, her stomach twisted. Jaxon was definitely flirting. She finished the drinks and carried them to the end of the counter.

"We play all over the U.S., though," Jaxon was saying. "Maybe we'll do a European tour soon. You should come out to see us."

"But you don't play here?" the tallest woman asked.

Jaxon laughed. "I did. That's how I met my bride-to-be." He gestured toward Savannah, and she smiled, immediately feeling better. The young women congratulated her as they took their drinks.

"I'm sure we'll be back here to play at the college bars, like this one," Jaxon shouted after them as they headed back to their jobs.

"Would you really consider coming back here to play?" Savannah asked, her emotional rollercoaster giving way to nostalgia, tender longing. If he did come back six months from now, this place wouldn't be here. Or it would be owned by someone else. What if it were turned into a furniture store? Or a sushi restaurant?

"Babe, we aren't coming back here," Jaxon said. "This is small. We're getting big-time crowds in the northwest. When we get a recording contract, we'll go to really big cities like Chicago, Austin, and San Diego. Not here. I'm gonna hit the shower."

Savannah watched him grab a coffee and go into the kitchen, back to her apartment. The silence that loomed after he left felt heavier than normal. We aren't coming back here, he had said. Ever. Never. She looked around the empty dining area and could see ghosts of memories floating through the space. Her mom delivering sandwiches, customers laughing together, her dad slow dancing in front of the jukebox with a whiskey in his hand, little Sierra and Savannah chasing each other around tables at the end of the night. And there were new memories, now. Her parents' wake, Laurel flipping over her Tarot cards for stunned college kids, the Christmas party, and Waylon walking through the door.

Never?

Alone at the counter, she turned her head toward the front door. It was late afternoon, and the sun was dipping lower in the sky. Her body tensed in anticipation. This was when Waylon's silhouette would come into view, the edges of his cowboy hat unmistakable.

But he didn't come.

Days went by, and he didn't come.

Savannah thought that with each day, she would miss Waylon less. She would enjoy Jaxon more. She would get more excited about moving back to Seattle. She would be more comfortable with the idea of never coming back to Lincoln, Nebraska. She would accept selling and forever walking away from the Sweetwater Café and Bar. She would want to start planning her wedding.

But she was wrong.

25 SIERRA

Sierra's skin crawled when she saw Jaxon that morning at the café. There was something about that guy she hated—and yet, if he ended up being the catalyst that took Savannah back to Seattle, maybe that wouldn't be a bad thing.

Then she wondered if she could talk Savannah into moving to New York with her instead. At the end of the day, Savannah was her sister. Now that it was just the two of them, Sierra, as the eldest sister, had a responsibility to help save the flaky girl from herself. They could find space for her at the apartment. Hell, with all the inheritance, they could rent a bigger space for just the two of them. If Savannah wanted to spend her days waiting tables and serving drinks, there were plenty of those jobs in the city. As long as Savannah worked and stayed out of her way, and didn't bring home rocker losers, it could work out. Maybe there could be hope for Savannah to live a somewhat successful existence. Sierra made a mental note to talk to her sister about it at the end of the following day's shift, as long as Jaxon wasn't there, of course.

Back at her parents' house, she spent the rest of her afternoon working on a blog post, doing laundry, then grilled some chicken and mixed it with baby spinach, apples, raspberries, and vinaigrette. The house was quiet, and for some reason, she kept looking out the back door as if Smokey would appear there any minute, waiting to see her.

"Nope. Stop it," she told herself. "I don't even like dogs. They bring dirt inside. They slobber. They shed."

She took a bite of her chicken salad, trying to ignore what felt like a tear stinging her right eye. Sierra opened up her group chat with her NYC besties and tried to participate, but their updates about happy hour and their plans for later that night just made her feel even more depressed.

After she cleaned up, she made a hot toddy and curled up under a blanket on the couch. Tomorrow would be Christmas. The sisters hadn't been able to come home for Christmas Day since they'd moved away, and now Sierra really regretted it. Sure, they had tried to come back around the holidays, but never on Christmas Day. Tomorrow, Savannah would be with Jaxon. Sierra's friends in New York would have each other or go to friends' and family homes. Sierra would sit alone in her dead parents' house, drinking herself into a stupor.

Her phone buzzed, and for a moment she hoped that it was Caleb. Of course, it wasn't. It was just her friend's group chat going off about Christmas plans. What would she even say to Caleb if he texted? Was he still mad at her? Would he forgive her and keep her company for the next six months if she called and asked him nicely? Would he invite her over to his parents' house for Christmas dinner?

On Christmas Day, Sierra stayed in her brown silk Lunya pajamas all day. She ordered enough Chinese food in the early afternoon to cover her for both lunch and dinner. She watched Christmas movies, texted her friends and her sister simple, cheery messages about having a Merry Christmas, and ate entirely too much food. She ate so much that by the time she went to bed, she didn't feel drunk, although she'd had a ton of hot toddies.

The next day, the café would reopen, and the march through the final six months of Sierra's incarceration in Lincoln would begin. She showered off the remnants of her depressing holiday, dressed in a pair of vintage Levi's and an oversized black sweatshirt, then climbed into her father's truck. She was the first one to arrive at the café and began the process of opening everything up. Zadie was late, so when the first customer came in, Sierra moved behind the bar to take the order.

The woman who came in was tall, thin, brunette, and dressed in a tailored pencil skirt suit with classy winter boots. Sierra greeted her with a smile.

"Good morning," Sierra said.

"Sierra Sweetwater," the woman answered. Her voice and the shape of her cheeks struck Sierra with familiarity. "Do you not remember me?" And then it clicked.

"Regan?" Sierra asked. The woman squealed and leaned over the counter to hug Sierra.

"It is so good to see you," Regan mumbled into Sierra's hair. The woman released her and stood back up straight on her side of the counter. "You've been gone for too long. New York City, right? Ah, your parents told us all about it. They were so proud of you. I'm real sorry for your loss. So tragic. Just both gone in one night. You and your sister must be happy to be back, though. Back home. Back here."

Regan looked around the space, but her expression did not match her words. She looked like she knew they definitely were *not* happy about being back here.

"Can I get you something to drink?" Sierra asked, suddenly suspicious of this old high school 'friend' coming into the café for the first time in six months.

"Oh yes," Regan said, whipping back to look at Sierra. "A matcha latte, extra hot, no foam."

Sierra just stared at the woman and blinked. "We don't have anything matcha here, sorry. My parents were… old-fashioned?"

"Right, right, of course," Regan said. "How about a flat white with oat milk?"

"Is almond milk OK?"

"Sure, sure, sure," Regan said, waving nonchalantly as if she'd take a gas station brew if she could just get on with why she's here. "So, I'm not sure if you've heard…" Regan started to say to Sierra's back while Sierra started working on the espresso shots.

Here we go, Sierra thought to herself.

"I'm a commercial realtor in Lincoln. Just so happens, my best friend Emma—you remember her—was here for your Christmas party the other night. She told me that aside from your sister getting engaged, it also came out that you two plan on selling this place in June. Well, when I heard that, I just had to come over and see if you already have a realtor. I would love to work with my old bestie. I have so many investors and developers on speed dial, as they say. I can get so many rich men outbidding each other, it'll make your head spin."

Old bestie? At what point in high school had they been besties? she wondered. The woman had been snobby as a kid, ruling over a new group of snobs at every grade level. Sierra had spent time in one of her cliques at some point, but her hours at the café had interfered with enough party invitations that the invitations had just stopped coming.

Sierra sighed as she finished layering the steamed milk onto the espresso. She didn't know any other realtors, and this one, foaming at the mouth to get her commission, was probably a good thing. If Regan were as ruthless as she had been in high school, she'd be a formidable ally in selling both the café and the house. Sierra put a smile on her face and turned around, handing over the hot beverage.

"Tell me a bit about your local experience," Sierra started, not wanting to just hand the woman everything she demanded all at once. She took the woman's credit card and rang up the order as Regan talked about how many small shops she'd sold to investors in the college town who had come in and completely revitalized and gentrified the neighborhoods. They were all hot, in-demand businesses run by respectable people that Regan took full credit for making happen.

"This place," Regan said, turning around to seemingly admire the high ceilings, wood beams, and tall windows. "Well, it has the kind of charm that is hot right now. A brewery or distillery could come in here, make a few local concoctions on site. It's really big for customers to be able to see what's brewing. If we busted out the apartment upstairs, a brewery could have a pretty big space for tall fermentation tanks." Regan delicately sipped her coffee, and then, as if the caffeine had kicked her brain into gear, she spun again.

"Or sports!" Regan said with even more excitement. "I know there are a lot of sports bars already, but this one could be huge. Fill the space with even more screens, and they could have Friday, Saturday, Sunday, Monday, and Thursday night football. High school through the NFL. I'm sure a lot of national chains would love to get that local college and adult male crowd."

Sierra was grateful when another customer came into the café. She was already exhausted listening to Regan, but Sierra knew it was probably best to go ahead and join forces with the woman. Regan sat at a small table near the bar while Sierra took orders and made drinks. Zadie came in without any smile or apologies and took over at the register. When things died down, Sierra went and sat beside her high school 'bestie.'

"Can you sell residential too?" Sierra asked, not really knowing the rules.

"Absolutely," Regan said, sitting up with her back as straight as a rod, brown eyes big and hungry.

"Then let's do it," Sierra agreed. "Let's list them both early enough so that we can get deals and close the first week of June."

"I will start with getting the appraisals, and when I have those, I'll bring you the paperwork." Regan looked around again. "Should I find you here or at your parents' house?"

"I do morning and lunch shifts here, then I'm at my parents', but here's my number." Sierra opened her phone to share her contact information.

"Oh, a New York area code—how fancy."

Sierra couldn't tell if she was being serious or sarcastic.

She watched the woman leave and then turned to find Zadie glaring at her.

"What?" Sierra asked.

"You're just going to throw it all away?" Zadie asked.

"No," Sierra said firmly. She turned and headed toward the office in the kitchen. "I'm going to sell it."

26 SAVANNAH

Jaxon was cuddled into Savannah, pressing his body into hers, nuzzling his nose into her neck.

"You want breakfast?" he asked in a whisper. Jaxon had never made her breakfast, let alone asked if she wanted any. They rarely had time to drink coffee together before heading their separate ways in Seattle. This was a first.

"You're gonna make me breakfast?" Savannah asked. Maybe she was still in a dream.

"No," he said, still whispering even though they were both awake now and completely alone in her apartment above the café. "I'm going to get that fat Mexican downstairs to make it."

Her eyes shot open like she'd been punched. What had she just heard?

"You mean Mario?" she asked.

"Isn't that an Italian name? Like Mario and Luigi?" Jaxon asked, chuckling.

Savannah sat up and pulled the sheet across her chest. "His name is Mario, and he's American. And he's not fat, not that it would matter if he were."

Jaxon sat up, got out of bed, and laughed. "Don't be so sensitive," he said. "I didn't know the guy's name, but now I do, and I'm going to ask him to make us some breakfast sandwiches."

She watched him get dressed and wondered when he would be flying back to Seattle. They'd spent Christmas day sleeping, eating, and drinking directly from the empty café kitchen below them. They'd watched Christmas movies, and Savannah had cried like a baby throughout most of them. The first time she lost it, Jaxon hugged and kissed her, but by the third time, he was over it.

Every scene with a complete, full, happy family or a couple romantically overcoming all odds, sitting around a table, Christmas tree, or fireplace, devastated Savannah like bittersweet ray guns. Pure light pulses just kept beaming themselves into her heart over and over, reminding her of her childhood, her parents, every Christmas tree that ended up planted in the yard or illegally in the closest park. The mom on the screen would do or say something wholesome, as her own mother had. The movie's dad would make a joke that was so corny it reminded her of her own father. The romance was so honest and easy…

Savannah had looked at Jaxon from time to time to see if the movies affected him in any way. He was mostly on his phone texting, watching videos, or scrolling. She hadn't been sure of exactly what he was doing on his phone, since she stayed cuddled up under her blanket with a box of tissues at the other end of the sofa through most of the movies. After the first night of them getting engaged, and aside from sleeping side-by-side, Jaxon hadn't made many attempts to touch her.

She was supposed to feel blissful, swept off her feet, dreamy like the young women in the movies. They were all so sure of the relationship. From the moment they all locked their eyes, it was meant to be. In all honesty, looking at Jaxon, she wasn't sure if this was meant to be.

They had been together for a long time. And yes, Savannah had given up everything to follow the musician to Seattle. It had been sudden and romantic. And the night he proposed, that had also been a sudden, romantic gesture.

Savannah got out of bed and got dressed. She would have to head back to her regular bar days starting later that afternoon, and she was glad. Sitting with Jaxon on Christmas had felt, well, boring. She was bored and missed being in the café.

She finished getting ready for her workday and headed to the loft's kitchen as Jaxon was coming up from the café kitchen with two breakfast sandwiches.

"That guy's kind of a dick," Jaxon said, setting the sandwiches onto the kitchen counter. "You should fire him." He grabbed his sandwich from the serving basket and took a bite, chewing with his mouth partially open due to the heat of the eggs.

Savannah blinked slowly, and then, in a condescending tone she couldn't help, she said, "The café is going up for sale in six months. We aren't going to fire anybody, unless you want to stay and make all the food for us?"

He laughed, not catching her tone. "That's right, I forgot. It's going to be so awesome to have you back home and out of this shithole town. I mean, there's nothing to do and absolutely no good music. How much do you think you'll get from this place? Or like, overall, after you split with your sister?"

He took another bite, not making eye contact, and something about the question sent a shiver up her spine.

"I don't know," she said.

"But like, ballpark," he said. "Half a million? A million? We could get such a nice place for that. What do you think about Capitol Hill? Or maybe closer to downtown?"

"I don't know," Savannah repeated. He still hadn't looked at her as he dug into his sandwich, some kitchen 'dick' had made for him. For free. Asking her about money. "I gotta go to work." She started walking toward the staircase down.

"Right, only six more months to go! You got this. Hey, you gonna eat your sandwich?"

"No, go ahead," she said, barely audible as she headed down to the kitchen. All she needed was a strong cup of coffee to clear her head. Savannah had the sudden urge to talk to Laurel, but knew she had to first make sure everything was ready for her shift.

Savannah nearly ran into Sierra as they both tried to come through the swinging kitchen door at the same time.

"Oh, hey," Savannah said.

"Good, I need to let you know that I have a realtor," Sierra said. She looked like she had something else to say and didn't move to the side to let Savannah pass.

"OK," Savannah said, stringing out the word.

"Regan, from high school," Sierra said, after a pause. "She'll schedule it to try to get us closing in early June, meeting our one-year commitment."

"Fine," Savannah said, clearly not needed in any conversation when it came to this massive decision.

Again, Sierra just stood there, not saying anything else, but not moving aside either.

"Is there something else?" Savannah asked. Sierra shifted from one foot to the other, as if considering the question carefully.

"Your engagement," Sierra started, sounding more like she was at a business meeting than in a conversation with her sister. Again, she paused, and Savannah was getting impatient.

Savannah raised her eyebrows high, "Yes?"

Sierra cleared her throat and said, "Let me know if you need anything with that." Then Sierra finally moved to the side and walked by Savannah into the kitchen. Savannah didn't have time to feel confused as the entrance door opened with customers. She slipped into place by the register.

All afternoon and into the evening, she couldn't shake the strange feeling that had washed over her when Jaxon asked about the money. And Savannah knew there was something Sierra wasn't saying. She was holding something back.

Zadie, still upset at both sisters, returned to the café for her evening shift, and things started to get busy. Laurel arrived in a calm flurry of fur over a floral dress and laid her cards out onto a table. Savannah watched the older woman meet with one college girl after another, telling their fortunes, telling them things they wanted to hear, and maybe a few things they didn't. She took their money in cash or Venmo. Laurel put the 'hip' into hippie, staying ahead of the trends.

Finally, Savannah had a free moment when Laurel was between customers, and she slipped into the chair across from her.

"I figured I would be seeing you back here," Laurel said, like any good psychic.

"I have a strange feeling, like something is wrong or is going to be wrong," Savannah explained.

Laurel was wearing a long-sleeved, floral dress with her fur coat draped behind her on the chair. Her hair was wild as ever, a curly but controlled gray mess on her shoulders. The woman shuffled the cards, not looking at Savannah. Savannah was starting to feel insecure with all the lack of eye-contact today.

Savannah nervously wrung her hands under the table as Laurel wordlessly shuffled the deck. It felt like a few minutes had passed when Laurel lifted her eyes, finally looking at Savannah, who nearly jumped, startled by the sudden attention.

"The first card is what is bothering you the most," Laurel explained. She flipped over and laid down a picture of a man with horns. Savannah's heart sank, knowing this was not a good way to kick off the reading, and she squeezed her own hands tighter under the table.

Laurel took in a deep breath, let it out, then took in another. Savannah was going crazy waiting for the woman to tell her what the hell it meant. "Temptation. Manipulation. Greed." Laurel looked from the card to Savannah. "Someone close to you is not being honest about their motivation."

"Is it Jaxon?" Savannah whispered, leaning in. He wasn't in the dining area, still upstairs on his phone, or maybe napping, but she still kept her voice quiet.

"If that's what your intuition is telling you," Laurel answered.

Savannah was annoyed by that response. Couldn't the woman just say yes or no? Is he just waiting to get access to her inheritance? Jaxon wasn't really the lovey-dovey romantic type, and now, all of a sudden, he wants to get married?

The next card Laurel laid on the table was upside down. It was a card she recognized by the two people entwined on the cover.

"The Lovers, reversed," Laurel stated. "Disharmony. False love. But Savannah, this card isn't about love or your relationship." Laurel reached across the table, grabbing Savannah's arms with both of her thin, bony hands. "Regardless of the cards, you have the power to make choices in your life.

Some turn out good, some are good for a turn, some are mistakes. We live. We learn. But only you get to choose. Nobody else can choose for you. Do you understand?"

Savannah nodded. "I have the choice to marry Jaxon, yeah. But if I don't…" she leaned in even closer to Laurel, over the cards, and whispered. "If I don't marry Jaxon. If I don't stay in this relationship. Why would I go back to Seattle?"

Laurel released her arms and sat up straighter, almost looking proud.

"If I don't go back to Seattle, that means I stay here." The realization of the true choice crept in like a storm cloud. Sierra wanted to sell. Sierra already had a realtor. Sierra was going back to New York City with a windfall of cash to fund her future dreams.

Leaning in even more, whispering even more quietly, Savannah said, "Sierra would be mad if I didn't sell, and if I decided to stay."

Without a word, Laurel dropped down another card right underneath Savannah's nose. There was a tall tower in the middle of the card with fire coming from the windows and people flying through the air on a collision course with the ground. Savannah sat back up sharply.

"That's worse than the first card, right?" Savannah asked. This reading was unfortunately going exactly as she'd predicted, or at least, as much as her intuition had predicted.

"It is a warning, yes," Laurel said, again, not really answering the question directly. "Tarot is simply a conduit for the Universe, God, and Spirit to help you confirm what you already know. Savannah, you don't need me or these cards to tell you that your world was shaken and will continue to receive aftershocks until you make a choice. The choice has to be yours and yours alone. This is your life. You don't have to do what Jaxon wants. You don't have to do what Sierra wants. You don't have to do what your parents wanted."

Savannah sat and stared at the cards, taking them and Laurel's words into her memory like capturing a momentous occasion. When Jaxon had first come to Lincoln with his band, Savannah was unhappy and directionless, wandering between college classes that she hated. Working at the café and bar with her parents was comfortable, so she'd kept doing it. But Jaxon had begged her to come to his hotel. After a night together, he'd begged her to come back with him to Seattle. She'd felt swept off her feet. She saw their future traveling all over the world together. It would be full of adventure, new places, great music, and tons of sex.

But that dream had only been a fantasy. None of it had come true, minus a couple of shows from time to time. Late nights ended in whiskey dick more times than not, that magical feeling of love never manifested, and most mornings she woke up feeling like she was still chasing the man she'd chased to Seattle.

"Thank you, Laurel," Savannah said, pushing back from the table. The woman smiled in response, nodding with sympathy.

Savannah went to the bar and poured herself a whiskey before sending Laurel a Venmo with a sizable tip.

The message had been coming to Savannah through her own intuition, through her parents, or something. She'd never been religious, but tonight she planned on praying before going to bed. She needed guidance. She wanted to make the right choice, not for Sierra and not for Jaxon. Savannah was ready to make the right decision for herself.

27 SIERRA

A few weeks after the new year, Sierra stood in the living room of her childhood home surrounded by piles of flat boxes. She'd ordered them online and had them delivered. Regan had advised her to start packing up 'clutter' and 'mementos' as soon as possible to prepare for staging.

Regan was very optimistic about getting over $300,000 for the house and close to $500,000 for the café. She claimed to know interested investors and that the café would require no clean out or staging. The house, however, looked too old. It needed fresh paint and carpet, and a complete removal of every dated object. Regan would bring in rented furniture to stage it for photos. She would front Sierra for the paint and carpet, then take the payment out of the sale proceeds.

After packing just one box, Sierra collapsed onto the worn floral couch. She had once moved from her bedroom to a dorm, then to an apartment at fashion school, then to the one she shared with her current friends. Aside from a few trips in a small, rented truck, she'd never truly moved. Looking at the boxes and at all the things around her, she felt overwhelmed. She knew she needed help.

More than help, she knew that she needed Savannah to do this with her. Although her younger sister would be more sentimental and emotional, it would be good for her to be a part of the process to help her let go of the past before they both moved away again forever.

Sierra picked up a framed photograph of the sisters together at a lake. They are sitting in the sand, surrounded by plastic toys, looking up at the camera and smiling. They had been best friends once. They were the only friends they had. And years later, when their parents had started the café and bar, the sisters were still the only ones they had. All their school friends faded away, never able to come play because the girls were never home after school. There were no activities other than cleaning tables and doing homework at the bar.

She missed the ease of being a carefree child, looking out for her little sister, and running barefoot through the yard on a summer day. It was currently cold outside and snowing. She had a long way before summer, but still closed her eyes, looking forward to being back in New York City in June. She had no doubt that Regan would sell the properties, and Sierra could be on her way back out of Lincoln.

Soon, she told herself. Just gotta take care of this stuff first. Sierra texted Savannah.

"Hey, I'm packing up the house. Do you think you could come over while I'm on shift and help a bit with this, too? I'm not sure what you want to keep or donate, but I'll mark some boxes."

Her sister, who was currently working her late afternoon shift, replied with a simple thumbs-up icon. Good, Sierra thought, she'd leave the truck for her sister to bring back here, and maybe Savannah could make a dent. The two of them, trading shifts, should be able to get through a lot of the house. It would be better if she could get extra hands to help at the café while Savannah and Sierra packed up the house together. But Sierra didn't know how she could convince their skeleton crew, who were all looking for new jobs, to pick up extra shifts or to find random people to come in and work the place while she and Savannah took off.

Caleb popped into her mind, as he often did. She could see his handsome, stubble-covered face and brown hair, his smile spreading across his face. He would know where to donate the furniture, her parents' clothing, and the dishes, things that the sisters wouldn't need or want. Any of the firefighters off shift could maybe come pack up and carry out boxes of donations. It would just take one text asking him for help, and he'd show up. She sighed, knowing that he wouldn't let his anger stop him from helping her. Even though she'd let their relationship go on, fully knowing not just that it would end but the exact month it would end, and keeping it from him, he'd still probably show up like a hero with a band of strong men behind him. She knew that about him, and it cracked her heart just a little bit.

First things first. Sierra jumped up from the couch and went in search of a notepad. Whatever desperate funk she'd slumped into, she was actively pulling herself out of now. She set a pad of paper on the kitchen counter and started to make a list, organizing what was left to do in this house without complicating her tasks with insignificant details like emotions or nostalgia or boyfriends that could have been.

First, she needed to ensure that her room and her sister's room were untouched spaces where they could store things they wanted to take with them back to Seattle and New York City. Pictures, photo albums, records, a fuzzy blanket, a jewelry box, etc. It needed to be clear that this was where she and her sister would be storing these items to be shipped to their final destinations at a later date.

Second, items that could be sold for a profit needed to have a special place. She couldn't put them in the primary suite because, more than likely, her parents' furniture was too old to be sold and would need to be donated. The dining area of the home was mostly empty except for a table and a buffet. If she could move those things out, then that would be an easy space for 'sale' items to be stored.

Oh no, she thought… Should she have a garage sale first? Did she have time for a garage sale?

"Nope, no, no, no. None of this stuff is going to make enough money in a garage sale, and we just don't have the time with us already working at the café and me doing freelance work for Fytté. It has to be donated." Sierra nodded at her list as she wrote down on line number three: no garage sale. *If anything has real value, we will put it into the dining room area to sell online.*

Everything else was over twenty years old: the furniture, dishes, rugs, picture frames, blankets, throw pillows, everything. They would just rent a truck and have the firehouse men load it all up to be donated. Line four: donate everything that wasn't too old or damaged.

Five, trash everything else.

Sierra took a step back. Trash. Throwing away. Disposing. Out. Gone. Done.

A shiver ran down her spine that she couldn't explain, and she shook her head back and forth. *What was that?* she wondered. Had she just had a physical response to the word trash?

No, that would be silly, she told herself. Then, referring to her list, she decided that the first room she would clean out would be her own. She would go through the clothes she'd left behind, old pictures she'd taped to her walls, pictures that said things like "Girls Can Be Anything" in pink frames. She would reduce everything to just the items that were worthy of being shipped back to New York, but leave her bed to the end. She did have to sleep there for six more months, after all. Maybe she would get some nicer sheets and a comforter to help stage the room for prospective buyers.

Sierra poured herself a very large amount of whiskey before heading to her room to begin the purge. Two hours later, she was on her bed, staring at her historic text exchange with Caleb.

She started and deleted at least twenty drafts.

I want you.

I miss you.

I'm sorry, but…

I know I'm leaving in June, but…

Hi.

Hey.

So, the thing is…

People do casual all the time.

I'm not looking for anything serious, but…

I'm sure you're still mad at me.

I hope you're not still mad at me.

Are you mad at me?

Can we see each other casually for a few more months?

How do you feel about something casual?

I really enjoyed our time together.

Until finally, she found a message that stuck.

"I wanted to reach out and talk about what happened, what you heard at the Christmas party at the bar. I know I should have told you sooner. The truth is, I wasn't expecting to have so much fun with you for so long. My sister and I had to run the café for a year in order to be able to sell the properties and get our inheritance. I have always planned on going back to New York. I'm sorry I didn't tell you. I am now starting to pack up my parents' house and was hoping you'd have some ideas about where I could donate a majority of the items, especially furniture. It would be great if you and some guys could help my sister and me out, and it would be nice to see you again."

Sierra sent the message and turned her phone over, so she wouldn't be tempted to watch it for a response. She kept her phone on silent for the rest of the afternoon as she packed up items from her room and from the bathroom she had grown up sharing with her sister. She moved the boxes of items out into the living room, lining them up neatly against one wall. Her plan was to systematically stack and label them, so as to make it easier to move them all out.

It was a little before 9 p.m. when Sierra, feeling drunk by then, finally slowed down on packing and started to get ready for bed. She had to be up early enough to open the café, which always meant an early bedtime. After washing her face and brushing her teeth, she went back to her bedroom. It felt strange, walking into a blank canvas space where her own footsteps sounded different. There were no more pictures on the walls, no miscellaneous items, no knick-knacks or decorations. Aside from the bed and blankets she'd slept in most of her life, there was no more Sierra left at all. Moving toward her bed, she realized she hadn't looked at her phone in hours. She'd been so afraid of what Caleb's reply might be that she'd wanted to pretend like she'd never even messaged him.

She turned the phone over and unlocked the screen. A new message indicator showed on the screen, and she opened it.

"Hi Sierra," Caleb texted. *"I was upset learning that you were leaving at the party, yes. But I understand why you didn't tell me. I can still have some guys come and help you out with packing and donations. Let me know when you're available, and we can try to schedule something."*

She read the words over and over, her heart beating loudly in her chest. He *had* been upset. *Did that mean he wasn't upset any longer?* she wondered. He said he understood, or at least texted that he understood. He was going to help her out, help her pack, and help her donate her parents' household. Did that mean he forgave her, since he understood her reasons, and he was going to help her out?

Sierra couldn't understand why she was so obsessed with Caleb's reply. It wasn't just his response, even though that felt really good to receive, but it was his words. Or maybe it was the lack of words. He admitted to being upset, but he understood. What did that mean? Would he be interested in her still? Did he still like her?

She spun herself around, tossing her phone onto the bed.

"Am I being insecure right now?" she asked herself out loud, her voice sounding strange in the room, hollow without anything on the walls. It felt cavernous and lonely.

She really enjoyed the time she'd had with Caleb and would be with him again in a heartbeat. If they were both in New York, this would be a no-brainer. But he was here, in Lincoln, and Sierra would be leaving this place behind.

28 SAVANNAH

Savannah drove her dad's truck from the café, where Sierra was working her morning shift, to her parents' house a few neighborhoods away. Pulling up, she marveled again at the yard full of planted Christmas trees. They had been selected to live long lives instead of being doomed to decorate a room for a single holiday. Savannah smiled, remembering all her mother's sweetness. She didn't think that Deborah had ever made a single enemy in her life. Savannah's mother had been kind, generous, and positive, no matter the situation.

She parked the red and cream truck in the garage and went into the house. Maybe it was her parents' kindness, their naïve sense of positivity, that had frustrated Savannah and Sierra so much. The sisters couldn't complain to their hard-working parents about how much time the whole family sacrificed to the café. It would have been negative and selfish. Both sisters had become passive and decided to flee their small town instead of telling their parents how much they resented them for abandoning their kids, their house, all those trees…

The eeriness of the house remained as the old floors creaked beneath her every step into the living room and then the kitchen. Was it too early for whiskey? What about a drop into the cup of coffee she'd brought with her from the café? But she knew she needed to focus.

Sierra had given her instructions, of course. Whatever items Savannah wanted to keep, she needed to put them into her childhood room. She needed to sort everything else into donation, trash, or sale boxes, which Sierra had labeled and spread throughout the house. Sierra had also clearly instructed that the sale pile should only be items that are actually worth money, not just nostalgic mementos. They both doubted very much that their parents were hiding priceless relics.

She rolled her head around on her neck and pulled back her shoulders, as if stretching things out before a fight. Then she literally rolled up the sleeves of her long-sleeved shirt and got to work. She started in the kitchen, leaving just a couple of items she thought Sierra might need over the remaining months to cook herself an egg or something.

In the quiet, tediousness of the sorting, the three tarot cards from her reading kept floating into her mind. Jaxon had flown back to Seattle the day before, after showering her with compliments about how she was going to be a beautiful bride, how he couldn't wait to have her back home, and the like. Savannah had felt so out of sorts that she'd just smiled and let him kiss her. This was still her boyfriend, after all, and a man she'd known and loved for a long time. She told herself she was going to break things off, but every customer seemed to gush over her ring, her engagement, and she felt silly about wanting to end it. Wasn't this what she'd wanted when she'd followed her dream man to Seattle just a couple of years ago?

Savannah opened a kitchen drawer that mostly held miscellaneous items like chip bag clips, Post-it notes, and scissors. She started to box up the donations when a picture caught her eye. She picked it up and saw that it was one she'd mailed to her mother of herself and Jaxon standing on a pier at the Seattle Waterfront, Elliott Bay stretching out behind them. There was something in the water behind Jaxon's head. Savannah brought the picture closer to her eyes to see, and whatever it was, maybe a boat, was positioned in a way that made it look like Jaxon had devil horns.

"The Devil," Savannah whispered, tossing the picture back into the drawer and closing it. She felt momentarily off balance in the kitchen, as if the floor was moving below her feet. She leaned onto the countertop, steadying herself. Savanah knew she was just being paranoid. She'd always had an overactive imagination and was definitely emotional. She knew it.

"Maybe we take a break from the kitchen," Savannah said out loud. But then, feeling silly, she considered the possibility of talking directly to her parents. Or at least, to her mom. She left the kitchen, walked through the living room toward the foyer, then turned toward the staircase leading up to her and her sister's bedrooms.

"Mom?" Savannah called up the stairs. "I got engaged at the café on Christmas. And I should feel happy. But I feel… off. So, I asked Laurel to read my cards. I think the cards she read for me mean that I need to do something, but I don't know what to do. They are trying to tell me something, but I don't know what."

Something crashed to the floor at the top of the stairs, and Savannah, scared, ran to the front door. She grabbed the doorknob, ready to unlock it and run outside. But instead, she took a deep breath.

"I can't fear messages from my mom," she told herself. "I can't fear messages." Savannah turned back to face the staircase. She flipped on every single light switch on her way back from the foyer and up the stairs. At the very top, right around the corner, a picture had fallen off the wall. It was leaning against the floor trim, backward and upside down. She turned it around and gasped.

It was her parents' wedding picture, and the frame had landed upside down; The Lovers Reversed.

"Shiiiiiiiiiiiiiiiiiiiiiiiiiiiiiiiiiiiiiiiiiiiiiiiiiiiiiiiiiiiiiiiiiiiiiit," Savannah said, landing extra hard on the 't'. She stood back up and looked toward her room, at the bathroom behind her, flipping the light on, of course, then over to Sierra's room. *Please don't manifest, please don't manifest,* she thought to herself. Then, out loud, "Just, please don't manifest. I don't think I could handle that."

Savannah went to both bedrooms, turned on the lights, and peeked in. With a deep breath, she walked all the way to each bedroom closet, holding the frame up in case she needed to knock out a real-life burglar. Finding the closets empty, she went back to the hallway where the frame had fallen. The nail in the wall looked undamaged, as did the latch on the back of the frame. She shook her head, not wanting to believe that her mom's ghost had knocked the frame off the wall to send Savannah the message she'd asked for. But there was no other reason for that frame to have fallen. Her mom was there. Or maybe her dad—or both. It both comforted and frightened her. *Were her parents always listening and watching?* she wondered.

"OK, I have to focus," she said to them and to herself. "Sierra is going to be so angry if I don't make progress while I'm here." Savannah walked to her bedroom, thinking that maybe it would be easier to clean out that space first. She'd moved away so long ago that she thought for sure she'd already taken everything she'd wanted to keep.

She started by pulling posters off the walls. Then she took out an old jewelry box full of cheap rings, bracelets, and earrings she would never wear again. She pictured a kid discovering these treasures in a thrift store and smiled.

About an hour later, she'd done good work clearing out old clothing and shoes from the closet, knick-knacks like cat figurines and candle holders. Her old desk was still in pretty good shape, since she'd done most of her homework sitting on her bed. Sierra had told her about Caleb and friends agreeing to come carry some furniture out to be donated, but Savannah had to clear the clutter out first. It was a good size for a teenager, just a spot to write on top with three drawers going down the right side. She pulled open the bottom drawer and froze. Staring up at her was a research paper she'd presented in high school on the World Trade Center terrorist attack in 2001. Underneath the title of the paper was a picture of the North Tower still standing after the South Tower collapsed.

"The fucking Tower," Savannah said. She pulled the paper out of the drawer and tossed it into the trash pile, feeling stunned.

They hadn't grown up religious or spiritual. In fact, Savannah and Sierra had both been surprised to see that their mother had partnered with a psychic, with Laurel. But there was no denying that Savannah was getting signs. Even if Laurel had purposefully placed each of those cards in front of Savannah, there was no way she was here making these signs; these confirmations pop up in front of her.

Was she just seeing what she wanted to see?

No, she told herself. That picture frame could not have thrown itself to the floor. But beyond the card reading, aside from the strange signs, she felt her parents in the house. Talking to them as if they were there was as natural as breathing.

Savannah continued working in a daze, watching the clock, knowing she had to go switch shifts with Sierra soon. She had worked up a sweat and needed to make time for a shower now, too. She moved boxes from her room and into their respective piles. She took all the frames off all the common walls, then sat down on the couch to drink some water and take each picture carefully out of each frame. The frames would be donated, but the girls would divide the family photos.

As she sat there on the couch that had been in the house for her entire life, carefully pulling out the photographs and placing them gently on the wooden coffee table, tears started to fall. With every back she removed, with every picture she slid out and laid down, Savannah felt like she was dismantling her family. Instead of creating, putting pictures into frames and hanging them onto walls, she was tearing it all down, taking it all away from the home she'd loved. Her parents smiled up at her from the photos, and it made her feel worse. She was tearing down everything they had built for herself and for Sierra. What would happen to the pictures? Would they go into shoeboxes and be pushed to the backs of their closets?

Savannah had to rub her face, protecting the memories from the wetness of her tears as they dripped, fell, then poured. She hunched over and balled, feeling guilty for packing up the house, for donating things that were precious to her parents. She hated that she couldn't talk to them face-to-face about her hesitations in marrying Jaxon. She felt like she had abandoned her own parents, the last chances to see her parents alive, at the chance to be with a man that she now wasn't sure about staying with, let alone marry.

Her skin burned, and her heart raced as she cried deep sobs, soaking the knees of her pants and her sleeves. But then, as if a heavy blanket was being draped across her shoulders, a calm wave washed over her. The sound of the room changed, and she sniffled herself into silence. Savannah couldn't explain it; it was like when you ran cold water, trying to get it hot. The sound of the water changes once the water is hot. It was like that. The way the room sounded just *changed* from heaviness to lightness.

Savannah took a deep breath.

"I think you're here with me," she said to her parents. "I need to talk to you." She picked up a picture of just the three of them: her mom, her dad, and Savannah. Savannah was in a pink dress, holding an award she got in elementary school. Her parents were smiling proudly.

"I like Seattle," Savannah started, talking to the picture but feeling her parents in the room with her. "I like Jaxon. But I think I love being back here. I love how everything and everybody is just a little bit familiar. Dad, I love your loft apartment."

Savannah looked up and around the living room and into the kitchen. It was a classic craftsman that had never been upgraded, so it had all the quirky, broken, chipped charm. "But I love this house too," she said. "I could see myself having a family here someday. Or maybe even Sierra. I can at least see her coming back to visit my family here."

She looked down at the picture, worry creasing her brow. "But I can't keep the house and the café. Sierra deserves to get an inheritance. She's going to want half of the sale of the properties. If I give her the house to sell, and keep the café, that still isn't half. The café and bar are worth more than the house."

Savannah closed her eyes and shook her head, feeling crazy for talking to her dead parents, feeling crazy for even considering that she could run Sweetwater Café and Bar on her own—crazy for thinking she could tell any of this to her sister.

"I would be sadder to lose the café and to lose this house than I would be to lose Jaxon, and I don't think that's what love is supposed to feel like," she finally admitted out loud to herself (and her parents). "If I break things off with Jaxon and Sierra still forces me to sell, then I'll have nothing, not even Jaxon to go back to in Seattle. If I go back to Jaxon and let Sierra sell everything, I'll never forgive myself. But I'm scared. Why am I so scared?"

She set down her parents' picture and put her face into her hands, smelling a mix of dust and saline. She didn't expect an answer, but she was afraid. She was afraid of breaking things off with Jaxon. She was afraid of asking her sister for the café. She was afraid to suggest they also keep the house.

Sierra had always been a pragmatic planner. Savannah had always been the flighty one, and because of that, Sierra had always looked down on her decisions as silly, frivolous, emotional, and just not well thought-out. Well, Savannah *was* thinking now. And yes, she was emotional *too,* and a lot of her decision was based on attachment, but she wasn't ready to let her past go. She didn't have experience breaking up with men, but she was certain it could be a text. If letting Jaxon go meant she could keep the café, then it was worth it. It would be scary, especially if he called and begged her to stay, but she would stand her ground to keep the café. The idea of losing the café felt much more painful and scary than breaking things off with Jaxon did. She was trading one love for another. One dream for another. The more she looked at her parents together, happily smiling in pictures, the more she realized that she and Jaxon were not and would never be that kind of couple. He would never be the love of her life. He was just a love for a time. Her love for her parents and her love for their café was stronger.

Her heart perked up thinking about telling Zadie and Mario that they wouldn't have to look for new jobs. And then it sank right back down, picturing her sister's reaction.

"I have six more months to grow a pair," she told herself (not her parents). Then she washed her hands and gathered her things, heading back to the shower and starting her shift at the café.

Her café.

29 SIERRA

Two weeks later, Savannah and Sierra had enough items boxed up that it was time for a truck to haul them all away. Sierra coordinated a time with Caleb where he and two of his firehouse friends would be off their shifts for long enough to help her load up most of the donation boxes into trailers that the men would bring with them. Apparently, every man with a truck in Nebraska knew how to get a trailer at the drop of a hat.

Sierra paced back and forth in the foyer, wringing her hands like a boy was about to pick her up for prom. Her stomach was twisted into knots, and her mouth was dry. Although it was after her shift, she hadn't poured a drink to calm her nerves, scared the liquid courage would make her too calm, and she'd start admitting things to Caleb that she'd rather keep locked up tight.

The man was handsome, polite, respectful, great in bed, and had shown genuine interest and care in her. Sierra missed him in every way, but she was moving, and he was staying in Lincoln. There was no future for them. Honestly, to Sierra, that didn't really matter. She would have happily continued dating him and sleeping with him up until the hour before her flight back to New York, but she knew it wasn't fair to him. When Caleb looked at her, it was with depth and intensity that reminded her of how her parents used to look at each other. It wasn't that she didn't want what her parents had enjoyed since high school; it was that Sierra didn't want it yet, and definitely didn't want it in Lincoln, Nebraska.

When her parents first opened the café, she and her sister had been excited. It was new and something they'd all be a part of together. But as the years went by, Sierra had this strange feeling that the café had trapped them. They never went on family vacations, not even camping. They didn't have time for family dinners. Their parents couldn't make it to their school concerts, plays, or any other events. There was never anyone available to babysit the café and bar for them. On nights when Sierra would have been off with friends, going to parties, or even hosting a few of her own, she was stuck helping her parents work in the business.

The feeling of being trapped again, in a relationship, in this house, in this town, sent creepy crawlies up her spine and all down her arms. She shook them off with a shudder.

No, she told herself. No matter how great Caleb was, to Seirra, it wasn't worth giving up her sense of independence. Living as an adult in New York had given her the freedom to go and do whatever, whenever, wherever she wanted. Sierra was pursuing her dreams, making friends, and having fun.

She heard the rumble of a diesel engine and the rattling of metal, so she opened the door and walked out onto the front porch. Three trucks of different models and different colors rolled down her street, pulling trailers of varying sizes behind them. The first truck, Caleb's, pulled right up into her parents' driveway, making it all the way to the garage door with the trailer behind it barely hanging over the edge of the street. The other two pulled into neat lines along the curb. She couldn't help but think of a circus caravan pulling up.

Seeing Caleb jump down from his truck sent a shock wave of hormones and adrenaline through her body, as if it was trying to manipulate her into throwing herself into him. She almost told her subconscious to stop it as she resisted the pull. Sierra crossed her arms before walking toward him, not wanting to send mixed signals. But then Smokey barked and launched himself out of the truck, zigging around Caleb and zagging right into her feet, nearly knocking her down. Her arms unfolded in self-defense and in need of stabilization, but she found herself betrayed by her emotions as her hands reached down and grabbed both sides of Smokey's massive gray, furry head, rubbing him, petting him, and smiling with complete abandon.

Dammit, Smokey, she thought.

"Why are you so soft and cute?" she asked the pup, who lolled his tongue out at her. "Did you miss me?" She could not believe herself. Petting and asking the dog questions. Weak… so weak. Sierra tried to mute her smile and pull her arms back into a tight chest hug, standing fully upright like a nun.

"Hey," she said to Caleb, who was now standing beside Smokey and entirely too close to her.

Instead of responding, he smiled. His eyes were soft, gentle, not angry at all, as she'd hoped. Caleb looked at her crossed arms and smiled more widely. "You look good," he said.

She felt her cheeks start to redden.

"You brought friends!" she said, entirely too loudly for how close they were standing. And yeah, she obviously knew he was bringing friends, but she walked past him and toward them like they were water, and she was a thirsty man in the desert.

The first man climbed down from what looked like a newer model Ram. Of course, Sierra wouldn't know, not really caring about things like that. The truck was red, and so was the man's thick hair and beard. His skin was pasty white with red splotches. He was a big man, tall with broad shoulders, and definitely capable of pulling a full-grown man out of a burning house.

"Hi, I'm Sierra," she said, extending her hand to the man. "Thank you so much for—oomph," she spat out, unladylike as the man pulled her straight into some sort of bear hug. He smelled like both soap and sweat, as if no shower on earth could rid this man of what was inherently his natural musk. Smooshed into the man's chest, she couldn't say anything, couldn't push away or escape. If he didn't save lives for a living, she would have been more concerned. He finally released her but still held her out in front of him by the shoulders.

"Sierra, it's nice to meet you, and don't you thank us for doing what God put us here on this planet to do." His voice was just as loud as you'd expect from a man of this size.

"Sierra, this is Red," Caleb said, standing behind her. His voice was like a life raft back to reality.

"Ah, that's right, yes, hi. I'm Red," he said as if just learning manners for the first time.

"Is that your real name, or is it because of your hair and beard?" she asked, trying to soften the situation a bit, and out of genuine curiosity.

"Mainly the hair," Red answered.

Another man came up from the other truck, which was a much more reasonable shade of black.

"And this is Dante," Caleb introduced. Dante was the polar opposite of the tall, bearded man of Irish descent.

"Hi, Dante Ruiz. Good to meet you." Dante extended his hand, and Sierra took it and shook it lightly. He was her height of about 5'8" or maybe 5'9". He was Latino, lean, with tattoos on his arms from fist to as far up his arms as she could see before disappearing into his short-sleeved shirt. He had a friendly, very approachable expression and demeanor. She liked these friends that Caleb had brought over to help, even if she could do without Red's bear hugs.

"Thank you for coming to help me, guys," Sierra said, trying to look more at Dante and Red, although she knew Caleb was the reason they were here, and she was the reason Caleb was here. Smokey barked from the porch.

"Come on in, and I'll show you what needs to be taken out," Sierra said. They followed her to the front door and into the house. She pointed out the boxes, clearly labeled for what was going to the dump and what was going to the donation center. She had put blue painters' tape on all the furniture that would be donated. Even though she knew Regan would be having their house staged, she'd decided to leave her bed and just update the bedding. But everything else was going. Savannah's room would be staged; all the furniture would be replaced. Her sister had already taken the items she wanted to keep back to the apartment over the bar.

Sierra had watched her sister carry box after box of mementos up the stairs with a frown heavy on her face, shaking her head at how many things Savannah had clung onto. Didn't she know how expensive shipping things back to Seattle would be, she'd wondered.

Sierra started to help the men by carrying out lighter boxes, but the three of them stopped her.

"I can carry some stuff," she said, defending herself.

Red and Dante each had an end of the couch and were carrying it through the front door. Caleb walked up to her, placing his hand on her arm, gently.

"We know you can, Sierra," he said, his voice almost a whisper. He smelled like cedar, like the trees in the front yard, like a cool breeze on a spring day. "But we know how much you've been through and how hard you work. This is hard," he said, motioning around to her childhood reduced to boxes stacked around her. "And we want you to just take a deep breath and let these things go. Let us do this for you, OK?"

She nodded, knowing that she would agree to just about anything he said to her when using that tone. Why wasn't she with him again? His eyes reflected bits of yellow from the light coming in through the open door. His muscles bulged from beneath his tight T-shirt. She could remember the feel of his lips against hers.

Smokey was beside her, nudging her leg, asking for pets. Sierra was thankful for the distraction and reached down to pet the dog. When she looked up, Caleb had walked away carrying the box they'd made her set down.

With every item the men carried out, the more and more empty her parents' house felt. It sounded different. It felt different, like the floor had fallen out from below her feet. And with some sick twist, it felt like they were stealing from her.

She stopped petting the dog, stood up, and tried to fight off the feeling that what she was doing was wrong. Sierra ran up the stairs to her room, and Smokey followed her. She stood in her childhood bedroom, looking at the boxes that she needed to push out into the hallway. They were the last remaining anchors to her past. Remnants of a girl she used to be, with hopes, dreams, wishes, and fantasies. That little girl had never imagined that her parents would die while she was still in her twenties. That little girl had never imagined that there would be no father to walk her down the aisle. That there would be no mother to hold her first baby. Tears began to fall as she realized that her baby would never have a Grandma Deborah…

Sierra felt something touch her leg. Startled, she kicked out her foot and smacked Smokey in the face. He yelped.

"Oh, my God, Smokey," Sierra said, crumbling onto the floor beside the dog. "I'm so sorry, baby. I'm so sorry." She pulled the dog into her arms like a lifeline and sobbed into his fur. Arms came out of nowhere and folded around her and the dog, a cuddle puddle on the floor of her childhood bedroom.

Sierra sat up after only a minute of crying, sniffling it all back, tucking it away for another ten years. But the arms around her didn't pull away. She turned toward Caleb's face, so close she could smell his minty breath.

"You're right," she whispered, hoping her breath was just as fresh as his. "This is hard." The admission, the vulnerability in it, sent another round of needles behind her eyes, triggering a spring of tears and sobs she could not control. It was so unlike her, or at least unlike the person she tried so hard to be. Sierra had always been the responsible one, the strong one, the one who had her entire life planned out, structured, and organized. She was in control of her emotions, her desires. She could turn it off just as quickly as it came on. But not now.

With a fluffy grey dog beneath her and the strong arms of a handsome man wrapped around her, she melted. Sierra lost the woman she had spent years trying to perfect. The wall she'd spent years building crumbled like a sandcastle in a storm.

She wasn't sure how long she cried, sitting on the floor of her room, cradled like a baby in the arms of a beautiful man. Sierra finally wiped her face onto the sleeves of her faded blue vintage sweatshirt and looked up into Caleb's hazel eyes. Although she'd felt him with her the entire time, she was almost surprised to see him there, as if she were seeing him for the first time in days. And then she realized she hadn't seen him since the Christmas party at the café.

"I'm sorry," Sierra said, suddenly overwhelmed with guilt. Apparently, guilt followed grief. "I should have told you from the beginning that I was planning on going back to New York. My job is there. Our parents, in their

Will, said we can't get our inheritance unless we work at the café and bar together for a year after their deaths. That's why we came back and stayed."

Caleb nodded, blinking slowly, but said nothing.

"I think you're amazing," Sierra admitted, realizing that she could be drunk on grief and guilt and say too much without a drop of alcohol. She may as well have had a damn drink at this point. "And if I were staying, I'd want to be with you. I do want to be with you, but I love New York City. I love my job there. I want to have a career in fashion, and I don't think I can do that from here. At least, I can't start that career here. I'm so sorry that I met you and did this."

"I'm not." Caleb's voice was strong, not a whisper. He readjusted their positioning on the floor to lift her off Smokey a bit, poor dog, and pull her closer to his lap. "Being with you is one of the best things that's ever happened to me," he said.

"What?" Sierra asked, convinced she hadn't heard him right. He smiled slightly.

"I was upset that you planned on leaving without telling me," Caleb admitted. "But the past few weeks without you have been torture. I hate it. I can't focus. I want to text you, to call you, to see you. I understand why you didn't tell me, although I don't like it. But now I know. You're moving away. But before you do, I'd rather spend the next however many months with you, enjoying every piece of you, before you go. I miss you. We miss you." Caleb jerked his head toward Smokey, who was staring at her with a dopey expression on his fuzzy face, waiting for them to stop talking so he could get himself some more cuddles. Sierra reached out, put her arm around Smokey's neck, and pulled him in close to her.

"I miss you both, too," she admitted.

"Can we spend some more time together before you leave for good, then?" Caleb asked. Relief flooded her body like a warm spring. She felt suddenly light and happy.

January was wrapping up, the house would be on the market next month, but they couldn't close until early June. She would be in town for at least five more months. Most relationships didn't last that long anyway. She was sure it would come to a natural conclusion before she flew back to New York. The idea of getting Caleb into bed again was also another strong motivator for giving this a chance for a round two.

"I would love that," Sierra said.

30 SAVANNAH

Savannah pulled on a pair of black skinny jeans with holes in the knees and a band t-shirt from one of the many concerts that had rolled through the bar she used to work at. *Used to*, she thought to herself. Would she really never go back to Seattle to work? A smile curled up her mouth. Savannah felt good about that decision, finally. She'd made a choice; she just hadn't told anybody about it yet…

The engagement ring sat on the kitchen counter, where she'd left it for days now. She'd thought about mailing it back to the apartment with a note that simply said 'sorry,' or with no note at all. She'd started multiple texts to break things off with Jaxon, but she felt sick about ending a two-year relationship and an engagement over text. Of course, the thought of calling him made her feel even sicker, so that hadn't happened either.

Savannah went down the stairs from the loft bedroom, smiling even bigger. She'd brought home many framed pictures from her parents' house and hung them throughout the apartment. The mismatched sizes, styles, and colors, collected and hung over decades, fit the bohemian aesthetic feel of the apartment perfectly. Seeing her family smiling at her every morning sent warmth flooding through her body and made her feel sure that her parents were still with her. Of course, the signs and energy shifts she'd experienced back at the house had also convinced her that her parents had stuck around.

She talked to them more, too. Having their pictures, feeling them around, she felt more comfortable telling them about her day, patrons at the bar the night before, little worries like how she needed to learn to do inventory, to big worries like telling her sister about her decision to stay.

"Sierra is gonna kill me," she would say out loud, hoping her parents' ghosts could somehow alleviate her trepidation, or reassure her that her sister would not, in fact, kill her. Of course, there was no response, which meant the response was that Savannah was on her own. She'd made the choice, and now she needed to be brave enough to tell Sierra.

Savannah walked down the stairs to the kitchen, said hi to Mario, then went out to the café to start her slow afternoon shift. They'd taken down all the holiday decorations, so the place felt much less festive. Even with February around the corner, nobody mentioned putting up Valentine's Day décor. Moods had definitely tanked throughout the winter months.

Sierra was sitting at a table having coffee with the realtor, Regan. Savannah's smile vanished, and her mood soured. She didn't say hi to them, and instead, averted her eyes to look more interested in organizing glasses behind the counter.

"I'm going to put a sign outside anyway," Savannah heard Regan telling Sierra. "But honestly, the commercial listing already has so many hits that it might be a bidding war. I reached out to some friends of mine at Brothers & Barrels, and the owners are really interested in getting the chain into this market. Smoked meats are so hot right now, so Brothers & Barrels focuses on smoked meats, smoked whiskeys, and the high ceilings in here would be perfect for pulling that smoke up and out, you know? Anyway, we'll throw up a sign, but we may not even need it, is what I'm saying. Are you so excited? This is great news, right?"

Savannah couldn't hear Sierra's response, and she didn't want to look like she was eavesdropping. A customer came in, and Savannah greeted the man without her usual positive energy. By the time she finished his order, Regan and Sierra were gone. The next day, a commercial real estate for sale sign was taped to one of the front windows. She was certain there was a sign in her parents' front yard, also.

When Zadie came in for her shift, Savannah was biting her lip and the insides of her cheeks and fidgeting with her nail cuticles.

"What's wrong?" Zadie asked.

"Nothing," Savannah lied.

"You're sweating like a whore in Church," Zadie said, using a southern colloquialism. Savannah's eyes popped open in shock, but then both girls started to laugh, the mood lightening a little bit. "Seriously," Zadie continued. "I've never seen you like this. I know you, Savannah. What's up?"

Instead of answering, Savannah went back to worrying the inside of her mouth with her teeth, gently shaving off whatever that skin in there was called, one nibble at a time.

"Oh my God, stop, are you chewing your face from the inside-out? Stop it right now. You need a drink. Go sit down. You're useless to me." Zadie shoved Savannah out from behind the bar and forced her into a chair. Then she went to pour Savannah a whiskey and brought it back, setting it down in front of her like it was medicine. In this case, maybe it was.

Savannah took the cool glass in between her hands, lifted it to her mouth, and sipped. She felt tears coming into her eyes. She didn't want to admit to anyone or say out loud what she'd been thinking about for days. If she ignored Jaxon, maybe he'd just go away and forget that he wanted to get married. If she ignored Sierra, the sale of the properties, just shown up and signed everything away, maybe she'd still be OK. She'd take her parents' pictures with her somewhere else. Alaska? Tahiti? Is Calcutta a real place?

"Spill it," Zadie ordered. Savannah looked up at the beautiful Black girl who had turned into a strong woman seemingly overnight. She'd watched Zadie grow up in this café, making sure she didn't spill on herself or burn herself or slip on a wet spot on the floor, and now Zadie was looking over her and looking out for her like a friend. Zadie might just be her only friend, she realized. Savannah had spent so much time either working here or working in Seattle, trying to help Jaxon have a music career, that she'd never really focused on friendships.

"I don't want to leave," Savannah admitted in the mousiest whisper ever.

"What?" Zadie asked, trying to sound gentle through her frustrated impatience.

"I don't want to leave," Savannah repeated, her voice louder but laced with fear and insecurity.

Zadie cocked her head as if she had not heard that correctly, furrowed her brow, and asked, "What do you mean? Like, you don't want to leave this room? You don't want to leave Lincoln? What are you talking about?"

Savannah picked at the wood grain on the tabletop, not looking up. "I don't want to leave the café," she whispered, tears forming in her eyes. "I don't want to leave my dad's apartment." The tears started falling as she saw him dancing by the juke box. "I don't want to leave you, Mario, Laurel, Edith, this place." Her voice grew louder, more confident, and she looked up to meet Zadie's eyes. "I don't want to go back to Seattle. I want to stay here. I want to stay home."

Zadie dropped down into the chair beside her, shocked and looking like she was trying not to get her hopes up. She grabbed Savannah's hands and leaned forward conspiratorially, lowering her voice. "Have you told Sierra? Have you told Jaxon?" Zadie looked down and saw the ring was missing from Savannah's hand, and then back up at her. "Where's your ring? Did you break off the engagement?" Her question was laced with excitement.

Savannah shook her head back and forth, tears spilling from her eyes, streaming down her face. Why could she never control her emotions, she wondered, feeling embarrassed to be crying in the café. There were only a few customers eating and drinking, talking with each other, and not paying the young women any attention.

"Oh, sweetie, why not?" Zadie asked, her voice empathetic and gentle now. "You need to tell them."

"I can't." And Savannah truly felt like she physically could not tell them. She could not look her sister in the eye and ask to keep the café. Savannah could not ask the woman not to sell the house, not to take any inheritance. It wasn't fair to Sierra. She was also a little bit afraid of how Sierra would react.

And then there was Jaxon. Savannah had been obsessed with that man, but now she felt only indifference. She wasn't afraid of him getting angry; she was afraid that breaking things off with him would be a mistake. What if they were meant to be together? What if no man ever loved her again? Would she be giving up her dreams of being with a successful musician, traveling the world, and cheering him on from the crowd? She had fantasized about a life with Jaxon for so long that no longer wanting that life felt like giving up a piece of herself.

"OK, deep breath," Zadie coached, handing Savannah a pile of napkins. Savannah tried to follow her instructions while wiping her eyes and nose. "How about we just focus on one of these things. Jaxon. Do you love him?"

Savannah shook her head, not able to say the word no. But then, she reconsidered. "Well, I care about him. But I'm not *in* love with him."

"Not enough to marry him?" Zadie clarified.

"Right. I don't want to marry him. I don't want to be with him anymore, either. I think we've been over for a long time, and we've just been hanging out."

Zadie nodded in understanding. "Why haven't you called him and told him that?"

Savannah shrugged and took a large pull of whiskey. "I don't know," she said. Zadie narrowed her eyes, not believing her. Then she raised her eyebrows and blinked rapidly, prompting Savannah to speak.

"If this place sells, I don't have anywhere else to go but back to Jaxon in Seattle," Savannah admitted.

"No, girl," Zadie said, sitting back up straight and crossing her arms. "You can't do that. You can't keep that man around because it's comfortable or 'just in case' other things don't work out for you. If you're done with him, then you need to be done with him. No amount of hanging around is ever going to change that. Feelings don't just magically reappear because you don't have a place to live."

Savannah leaned forward and put her face into her hands, ashamed that her friend was right. Totally right. Whether or not Savannah stayed in Lincoln had nothing to do with Jaxon, and she knew it.

"So, what do I do?" she asked, taking another gulp from the whiskey glass.

"You go upstairs right now, and you call that man. You leave him a message if he doesn't answer. You tell him that you want to talk, then you tell him that you don't want to marry him. Everything else is logistics."

Savannah sat back up straight and looked at Zadie. "When did you grow up?"

"When you were in Seattle, I guess," Zadie answered with a smirk.

A group of college kids came in, and Zadie headed back to the register. Although Savannah knew that Zadie might need help, she ran upstairs anyway, not wanting to lose either the friendship courage or the liquid courage from the whiskey. Once in the apartment, she hit the button in her favorite contacts to call Jaxon, then she paced, looking up at the smiling pictures from her youth, the ones that had always been there through every struggle, every drama, every happy event, every holiday.

"Hey, Savvy," Jaxon answered, sounding surprised. "Everything OK?" What was unsaid was that they never actually called one another. They always texted. There were no late-night, good night calls where they could hear each other's voices or video calls to see each other's faces. There was no longing, no desire, no desperate need to be back in the same room together.

"Yes, I need to talk," Savannah said, trying to remember Zadie's advice.

"I'm all ears," he said. She hated that phrase. It always made her picture the person's face covered in ears. Then again, maybe picturing his handsome face infested with ear holes, ear wax, and ear lobes of varying sizes could help her in this conversation.

"Do you still have the apartment?" she asked, a thought popping into her mind.

"Um, yeah, yeah, why?" His tone changed to something akin to fear, nervousness?

"How?" she asked. Savannah had been the one who made enough money to keep the apartment.

"I-uh, got one of my friends to rent out the bedroom. I'm staying on the couch. Just subletting, you know. I didn't want you to worry. We'll be alright once the inheritance comes in."

The inheritance. She suddenly didn't feel sad about this any longer. He needed her more than she needed him. There was something empowering in that.

"I don't want to get married," she said bluntly. "I am going to stay here. I don't want to come back to Seattle. I'm sorry, you'll have to figure something out with the apartment."

He was quiet for a few moments before responding in a desperate squeal. "Savvy? What? Are you kidding me right now? No, Savvy, this isn't right, baby, babe. I want to marry you. You're coming back. We have this whole life here."

She closed her eyes tightly together, dumbfounded. "What life do we have, exactly, Jaxon? We don't go on dates. We don't have sex. We hardly talk. We don't miss each other. We are like an old couple, but we're in our twenties. We are on different shifts, and I'm the only one making a living, paying for you to have an apartment, a crash pad for you in between your gigs. I'm over this, Jaxon. I'm sorry."

And she was sorry. She was sorry that she'd kept dating him long after she'd stopped being in love with him just because it was the easy thing to do. She was sorry that she'd waited so long for him to be in love with her, and sorry she said yes to a proposal that was probably more about her inheritance than his love for her. Engagement was the next best step to keep her connected to him, and not a romantic gesture after all.

But she was glad to be breaking up with him over the phone, finally, sitting on her dad's couch in his loft apartment above the Sweetwater Café and Bar. She felt her parents there with her, supporting her, encouraging her, and loving her no matter what. She was allowed to make mistakes. Maybe it had been a mistake to leave Lincoln for Seattle. Maybe it had been a mistake to chase a wannabe rockstar over a thousand miles away. Maybe it had been a mistake not to be here when her parents passed away. Maybe it had been a mistake to accept Jaxon's proposal. But humans make mistakes, she told herself. What mattered was that she was now correcting a very big one.

Jaxon was begging her to change her mind, but she wasn't interested in that. She wasn't interested in him, and she had finally made a choice that was entirely hers. She owned it.

"No, Jaxon," Savannah said, confirming her decision a final time. "I'll mail the ring back to you. We are over."

"But Savvy—" he tried one last time.

"I hate being called Savvy!" she yelled. And then she hung up feeling stronger than she ever had. Not strong enough to tell Sierra that she didn't want to sell the properties, but hey, baby steps.

31 SAVANNAH

Spring in Lincoln

Two months went by, and Savannah still hadn't told Sierra her wishes. Being on different shifts, they hardly saw each other unless Sierra was staying late to take a meeting with her realtor. There was never a private opportunity for the sisters to talk. At least, that's what Savannah told herself.

April was alive with trees and flowers blossoming across Lincoln. Savannah slept with her windows open, the fragrant breezes blowing into the apartment all night. She was falling more and more in love with her current life, the spring feeling like a new chance for her to make her own choices. She woke up, got coffee, worked the late shift, got to know all the college night regulars, closed things down, went to bed, and did it all again the next day.

Zadie had given up on trying to convince Savannah to tell Sierra that she wanted to stay and not sell. Zadie was so frustrated that she wasn't talking much to Savannah anymore, giving her the cold shoulder.

Savannah knew that time was running out, but without offers on the properties, she felt like it was OK for now. She had two more months to find the courage to confront her sister.

And then one early spring day, while Savannah was starting her shift in the café, Sierra just happened to be standing behind the bar, finishing up a customer's order. Her sister looked down at Savannah's hands and squinted her eyes as if she couldn't find what she was looking for. Sierra's sharp eyes darted back up to meet hers.

"Where's your ring?" Sierra asked.

Savannah stupidly looked at her hand as if she herself was surprised. "Uh… well. I broke things off with Jaxon."

"Really?" Sierra at first looked relieved, happy almost, but then something in her expression changed. "But you're still going back to Seattle in June, right?"

Savannah looked away, glad that the time of day when they changed shifts was always slow. Sierra's last customer had taken his coffee order to go. It was after lunch but before happy hour, so it was just the sisters in their parents' café, the brick walls suddenly closing in on Savannah.

"Actually..." Savannah started. Nothing to do now but be honest, she realized. "I was hoping I could stay here." Her words were quiet, slow, with long gaps between each of them as if the words themselves were treading through mud.

"But like where?" Sierra asked, her tone suddenly aggressive and loud. "You can't stay in the apartment, Savannah. We are selling the café. That means we are selling the apartment that's attached to it. You do realize what we are doing, right?"

The condescension was everything Savannah had feared. That affirmation that she was indeed a complete idiot. She would never succeed at anything. She shouldn't make important decisions. She wasn't good enough or smart enough or capable enough to even survive this harsh world without someone else making decisions for her. Savannah closed her eyes as if she could disappear, and maybe her sister couldn't see her, and this conversation could end.

"Savannah?" Sierra asked, her voice firm and probing.

Savannah was crying. She hadn't meant to do it, but that was the story of her life. As relaxed and calm as she appeared, she could never control her emotions. She was like a broken sprinkler.

"Seriously, why are you crying?" Sierra pressed. "What is going on?"

"I didn't love Jaxon," Savannah finally said. "I didn't love Seattle. I missed being home. I love being here. I want to stay here. I've always worked here or at other bars and restaurants. I want to work at one I love in a place I love with friends I love."

Savannah was good and balling now, snot mixing with the salty tears, running down and dripping onto the countertop.

"I can't do this right now. Just go upstairs and calm down. Go get yourself together, Jesus," Sierra said, pushing Savannah toward the kitchen. With blurry vision, Savannah moved through the kitchen to her stairs and up to her apartment.

Oh, God, she thought. *This is my apartment, but what if Sierra sells it and it isn't mine anymore? I've wasted so much time hoping things would work out without facing that woman, and now, what if it's too late to change anything? Would telling her months ago even have made a difference?*

Tears.

Fears.

Savannah collapsed onto her father's couch, crying hysterically into the cushions. A stillness came over the room as the energy shifted. Something heavy but light. Something changed the silence of the room. Her parents were there.

The tears slowed down to a small trickle. She sniffed, found a tissue, blew her nose, and looked around at the memories surrounding her. A calm realization settled in her bones. She was her parents' legacy. This was her legacy. This was her apartment. This was her café. She could do this.

Savannah didn't think that these thoughts were her own, but that they were being influenced by her parents. Her parents wanted her to run the business as long as it would make her happy.

She knew she had to go back downstairs. She had to finish her conversation with her sister, and she had to take over the shift at the very least. Savannah took deep breaths, trying to calm herself down. She splashed water from the kitchen tap onto her face. She blew her nose, she slapped her cheeks, as if hyping herself up before a caged fight.

Then Savannah took the stairs back down, through the kitchen, and out to the café where Sierra was standing behind the register, texting on her phone. Sierra looked annoyed. She set her phone down and turned to face Savannah.

"All good now?" she asked.

"No!" Savannah nearly yelled. "I'm not all good. I have to tell you…" her words caught in her throat, her courage suddenly draining from her brain, face, and body, trickling down, running away. She thought of Zadie's words of encouragement, of Mario losing his job, of losing her dad's apartment forever, the house, and then, for no reason whatsoever, Waylon's smiling face popped into her mind. He was holding her, dancing her over to the mistletoe. He was leaning in for a kiss.

"I can run this place," Savannah blurted out. "I want to try to run this place."

Sierra blinked and then started laughing. Literally. Bending over, grabbing her belly with one hand and the counter with the other as if she might fall over laughing.

"You?" Sierra asked. "Running this place? A business? Savannah, sweetie, you don't know a single thing about being professional. You can barely run a hairdryer, let alone a business."

Savannah cocked her head to the side. The hairdryer comment was what really stuck. It was true. She never used a hairdryer, preferring that her hair just air-dry naturally. She could style out the haphazard waves into a form. She could control the untamed nature of her wild locks. But she didn't. It was just another part of her bohemian nature. She let her hair just be whatever it wanted to be. After months of no cuts and no color to fit in with the rocker girlfriends in Seattle, she was looking and feeling more like herself. The black was fading out back to her natural blond. The length was now over her shoulders, giving her loving touches when she looked from side to side. And the waves were more pronounced the older she got. Her hair was getting healthier, more natural, and it was feeling right.

Savannah didn't like hairdryers. But she liked this café and bar. She liked the apartment. She liked the life she was now living, and she would work to keep it. Her sister was wrong.

"I *can* do this," Savannah said, feeling brave. "You can teach me everything that you've been doing. I can learn. I want to keep this place—not just for our parents but because it's what I want to do. I think I could run this place for the rest of my life and truly be happy here. I think this is what I'm supposed to do; it's my purpose."

Sierra scoffed, clearly shocked by this new epiphany her sister was experiencing. Savannah took advantage of the silence.

"And I don't think we should sell the house either," Savannah added. "We should rent it out instead. Then just wait and see. Maybe one of us will want to raise a family there. Maybe we will want to host holidays there. I don't want to wipe away everything our parents spent years building with just one stroke of a pen. All this is ours, yes. But not to sell."

"Stop," Sierra said, holding out her hand. "I'm not going to listen to this. You were engaged and changed your mind. You followed some random stranger across the country one night after meeting him. You have only worked service jobs, not learning anything about how to run businesses or even how to run your own life. You are emotional. You've always been the emotional one, the unhinged one, and you make emotional decisions. You are still a child, Savannah. There is no way you could run a business like this. I am the one who has been keeping everything afloat for the last ten months, and now, all of a sudden, you think you can handle things? You're delusional."

Sierra turned toward the front of the café and started to walk there, casting herself into a silhouette.

"I love you; I do. You're my sister," Sierra continued. "But no, you can't decide that you want to make the type of decision that will negatively impact *our* lives. I could really use the money from the sale of these properties to set up my life and career in New York City. Maybe it's best if you just go back to Seattle and pick up where you left off with Jaxon before our parents died. I can't keep worrying about you or taking care of you. There's no way that I could trust you with this place. You'd end up losing it after a year, and then we'd both be screwed."

Sierra turned around and walked back toward Savannah. Savannah's chest was tight with stress and fear, and something that felt like the heaviest weight of the world crushing down on her chest, pushing her deep into the wood floor below her feet.

"Listen," Sierra said, softening her tone as if to sound more like a sister and less like a manager. "This has been hard for both of us. We haven't spent much time together. Maybe we should hang out on Monday at the house, take some time off. Regan has it all staged; it looks amazing. We'll have some lunch and talk. Let's talk about what you can start planning for your life.

Sierra reached out and put both her hands on Savannah's shoulders. Savannah felt trapped instead of comforted. "If you don't want to go back to Seattle, then come to New York with me. There are a ton of bars for you to work at up there. We can be roommates. You'll love my friends. We'll start over in the city. OK?" Sierra's tone was that of a mother cooing a child, soothing one after a temper-tantrum while trying to get it to calm down.

. Savannah felt helpless knowing she couldn't keep the conversation going. She'd been told no. She'd been laughed at, belittled, insulted. Running a business was beyond Savannah's capabilities. Sierra had better ideas. Sierra was in charge, and things were going to move forward with or without Savannah's emotional resistance.

Yeah, she got the message. Savannah shut down, pushing her fear and emotions, all her desires and wishes, deep down, back into the depths of her gut, and nodded.

Her sister walked away, and Savannah started her afternoon shift feeling like a complete failure.

32 SIERRA

Spring in Lincoln

The café was buzzing with activity, but Regan said that it would be a good thing for the owners of Brothers & Barrels to see. Sierra tried to keep her attention on taking orders and making drinks, but her eyes kept shooting toward the front windows for signs that business tycoons were about to enter.

These would be the richest men she'd ever met; even richer than the men in her Fytté office. Regan walked in wearing a red suit jacket and matching pants, a low-cut, lacey black top peeking out from beneath the jacket. She was sexy but reserved in an outfit carefully crafted to get attention from two wealthy men in the safest way possible. The outfit said, "I'm smart, not slutty, so if you find me sexy, that's just good luck."

Regan raised her eyebrows at her, asking a silent, "Are you ready?" Sierra nodded, handed off the drink to a customer, then turned the counter over to Zadie. Sierra made sure her hands were dry, smoothed down the nice but not *too* nice blue Reformation dress, and went to sit beside Regan at a table she'd reserved earlier with a simple piece of paper. She crumbled the paper up and tossed it before sitting down.

"If they like the place, we could have an offer on the table by end of day," Regan said, in lieu of a greeting.

"But we can't close until June," Sierra said. It was late in April, and she wasn't sure how long these things took. Regan brushed it off as if that timing was nothing.

"Closings can take 30 to 90 days at the most," Regan said. "They will have brokers, lawyers, all sorts of hot shots looking things over before they sit and sign anything. Trust me. There isn't a rush. The timing should be perfect."

Sierra looked toward the doors again, and Regan snapped her fingers at her.

"Don't look so nervous or eager," Regan instructed. "Pour a drink if you need to, but calm down, relax. Just tell yourself that you are a pro and sell properties all the time. This is nothing, just another day in the office. OK?"

Sierra nodded and tried to look calm. She was a professional woman, just like Regan. She had been working very successfully in New York City before getting sucked back to this town. She took a deep breath and considered pouring herself a drink when two men in their fifties walked into Sweetwater Café and Bar looking completely out of place.

They were dressed in black suits. One had a dark blue shirt and black tie, the other a white shirt and sky blue tie with light grey stripes. Both men were graying, with the one with the dark suit having slightly thicker hair. They were tall, broad-shouldered, and clearly related, having similar noses, eye shapes, and bushy eyebrows.

Sierra stood up; a professional smile plastered across her face. Regan turned and stood as well, cranking up the sales charm. The men who had been looking around the café zeroed in on the two well-dressed ladies standing in waiting and approached in long strides.

"Mr. Montgomery," Regan said, the tone in her voice much more formal than it had been a few minutes before. She shook the hand of one man and then the other. "I'm Regan Whitmore, Lincoln residential and commercial real estate agent. And this is my friend and café owner, Sierra Sweetwater."

Sierra stepped forward and extended her hand to shake theirs. She tried to make sure her handshake was firm and trustworthy, knowing that men like these would appreciate a strong handshake.

"Mr. Montgomery," Sierra said. "And Mr. Montgomery."

The two men smiled down at her. They were both at least six feet tall, she realized, now that she was looking up at them.

"I'm Barry, and this is Bill," said the man with the darker shirt. "No need to be formal, Regan and Sierra. We are looking forward to seeing this place."

And with that, Sierra started the tour with details about the age of the building, the history of the area, drawing attention to original wood floors below, wood beams above, and a bar once refinished and updated for a clean look. They admired the bar's whiskey collection, the espresso machine, and gave a nod toward the wall that held the menu. The more Sierra talked, the prouder she felt about the space her parents had founded, updated, and maintained. Showing it to these men was like seeing it through fresh eyes.

Sierra led them through the kitchen, the stocked pantry, fridge, freezer, appliances, and back office. "And those are the stairs to the apartment above."

"An apartment," Barry said. "Now that is a good little extra perk. With space above, we could have a quiet tasting room, a VIP room. Lots of options."

Something jolted Sierra—an uncomfortable violation at the thought of someone using her father's personal apartment, the apartment that had become her sister's temporary home as a 'tasting room.' She shook the odd feeling off and smiled.

The four of them returned to the café and sat down at the reserved table where Regan had left her briefcase. The place was still busy, so nobody paid much attention to them.

"Do you own this place outright, Sierra?" Bill, the one with the white shirt, asked.

"My parents own it, but they passed away in June," Sierra explained. "According to our records, it is paid off. Regan can provide you with the tax statement from last year and our insurance costs. My sister and I are set to officially inherit this place in June, which is when we can legally sell it."

"I see," Bill said, nodding.

"We have had our fair share of estate dealings over the years, so there shouldn't be any issues as long as the ownership is clear," Barry said. "And we're sorry for your loss, but I do believe we can make you a deal that will set you and your sister up for quite a while." Barry stopped talking and looked around the space again, pointing to a back corner where the juke box sat. "Good place for the barrels there."

Bill nodded. "Yes, there seems to be plenty of space here to do what we need. A good college crowd, good downtown location." Both men looked at Sierra, and the energy shifted.

"This business is a staple of the community, but imagine your parents' legacy magnified through an upscale dining experience," Barry said. "Brothers & Barrels isn't just a restaurant chain—it's a national treasure, a destination, a comfortable experience where no matter where you go, you know what you're getting."

Then the other brother, Bill, leaned forward and added, "We are offering stability, consistency, an opportunity for your people to keep working here, and even though the name may change, this place will continue to thrive under our leadership."

Sierra felt her hands get clammy, and chills ran up her spine. These were professional restaurant chain owners who were much better suited for running businesses like this than she was, and definitely better than her sister could ever be. Why did she feel something tugging at the back of her mind, though? A doubt? A hesitation? No. She ignored the nudging and kept smiling at the men.

"I like what I'm hearing, gentlemen," Sierra said.

Both men leaned back and clapped their hands. "Great," Bill said.

"Wonderful," said Barry. Then, he added, "We will get our people started on the offer, and we'll see you in a couple of months at signing."

All four stood up, they shook hands, and the brothers from Brothers & Barrels left.

"We should celebrate," Regan said. "Champagne?"

"It's still early," Sierra said, with a coy smile. "Mimosas?"

"Even better."

Sierra got them drinks, and they sat back down at the table. Zadie was side-eyeing them, so Sierra resolved to tell Zadie later that the brothers had offered to retain the existing staff. She was sure there'd be some downtime for them to do a little bit of remodeling, but it had been a generous offer that she would pass on to Zadie and the others—although she hoped that after graduating from college, Zadie would go find a real job and not keep working a split shift. She could not believe this was what Savannah wanted to do for the rest of her life. One day, her sister would thank her for pushing her out into the real world to find a real career and life.

The women clinked their champagne flutes together, congratulating each other before taking their first sips. The bubbles immediately relaxed Sierra. She was feeling optimistic about everything except… Savannah.

"You look worried," Regan said. "Don't be. The brothers will take care of everything. They will pull an appraisal, they will do the market analysis, pull property records to verify ownership, run inspections, etc. They may need to review profit and loss statements to do a cash flow analysis, but other than providing those records, you won't need to lift a finger until it's time to sign on the dotted line."

"It's not that," Sierra said. "I'm worried about my sister not wanting to sell this place."

"What do you mean?" For the first time ever, Regan's brow furrowed in concern—and maybe worry. The woman's body language shifted from a cozy celebration into high alert.

Sierra looked around and took a sip of her mimosa, which was more champagne than orange juice. "Savannah wants to stay and run the place."

"Oh no," Regan said, leaning back into her chair as if trying to escape what she'd just heard.

"Oh yes," Sierra confirmed. "But she's a total flake. She never finished college, even though she was only there for a liberal arts degree, so that would have been useless. She's been working here since she was fourteen, and then working at bars in Seattle, and now back here. Savannah has zero ambition, but now, all of a sudden, she thinks she wants to stay and run this place."

Sierra took another drink and shook her head. Anger started bubbling up. "If she tried to actually run this place, it would go bankrupt in a month, and we'd lose everything. She might resent me, but selling this place is the best thing for us. Right?"

This is the type of conversation Sierra would have had with her mother, Deborah, or with her New York friends, but instead, she was looking across the table into the dark eyes of a woman who sold legacies for a living.

"Absolutely, this is the right thing," Regan agreed. The words didn't make Sierra feel any better, though. "And hey, we are having an open house this weekend for your parents' place, and I'm sure we'll get some movement there, too. This chapter is almost behind you, Sierra. You can go back to New York, your sister will go back to Seattle, and both of you with more money than you've ever had in your lives. You'll start fresh, start over, and maybe she'll even finish school. This is a good thing for both of you."

Sierra slumped lower into her chair. "But what if I can't convince her of that?"

"Like, you're afraid she won't show up at signing?" Regan clarified.

Sierra nodded.

"Then you'd need to get a lawyer," Regan said, pointedly. "Legally, we can't sell without both owners, both inheritors of the estate, signing in agreement to sell. We could try to deem her unfit to make that type of decision."

Sierra drained her glass, another thought occurring.

"My sister makes rash, emotional decisions," Sierra said. "I think I have one idea to try before we get a lawyer involved."

Regan finished her drink. "Well, good luck with that. I have another appointment to get to. Remember to be out of the house from 11 to 3 on Saturday."

Sierra nodded, not needing a reminder. Regan left, and Sierra went out to the parking lot to make a call she never in a million years thought she would make.

The late April air was clean and fresh, filled with the sweetness of new growth and new opportunities. Sierra was ready to leave it all behind to be back in New York, the concrete jungle, where she could see the world from her high-rise office building.

The phone rang three times.

"Hello?" asked a scruffy, sleepy voice.
"This is Sierra, Savannah's sister."
A pause on the other line, maybe from shock or surprise.
"Why the fuck are you calling me?" Jaxon asked.
"I want to make you an offer," Sierra said.

33 SIERRA

Summer in Lincoln

Sierra and Caleb were in her bed, her ceiling fan spinning above them, cooling them down after another mind-blowing encounter. Her head was on his chest, listening to his racing heart slowly starting to return to normal. In these moments with Caleb, she felt good, relaxed, wholly satisfied in every way. She didn't want to think about it all coming to an end. She didn't want to think about how she could love both New York City and Caleb Porter. She heard Smokey bark once at something in the backyard, and her heart ached.

The last two months were filled with Sierra worrying about the Montgomery brothers finding something deal-breaking in the inspection or deciding to buy another historic downtown business. The offer on both the café and the family that had put an offer on the house was so much money that Sierra thought she would faint upon hearing the numbers. She was so worried that everything would fall apart at the last minute and that the entire, stressful year that she endured would be for nothing.

She had tried to avoid her sister more than normal, not wanting to get into another discussion, hoping her sister would drop her fantasy about running the café and bar. Sierra had one last-minute trick up her sleeve to ensure that her sister would drop the notion entirely by signing day.

"Is it almost time?" Caleb asked, and she knew what he was asking. Not was it time to get out of bed, time to go for a walk, time to make dinner? She closed her eyes tight and took in the smell of him, locking the memory of him into her mind.

"Signing is at the café tomorrow afternoon, yes," Sierra said. "Then at the title company for this place."

"Two closings on the same day," Caleb said. "What are the odds?"

"Everything worked out," Sierra said, trying to convince herself that it was true, it was meant to be, the sisters were meant to sell the house, meant to sell Sweetwater Café and Bar, and leave Lincoln for good.

"And your sister is going to sell?" Caleb asked, knowing about Savannah's hesitation.

"I put a plan into motion that will hopefully play out tomorrow before signing and help convince my sister that going back to Seattle is the best thing for her, so I'm pretty confident. Besides, she's never been good under pressure. At the end of the day, she always makes emotional decisions."

Sierra started to get up, but Caleb pulled her back down to his chest. "I'm not ready to let you go," he said, his words so quiet, so soft, so full of meaning. He gently grabbed her chin and turned it up toward his mouth, and she lost herself in his desperate kiss.

It was another hour before they left the bed. They dressed, took Smokey for a walk, sticking to the shaded sides of the streets, then returned to the staged home to make a simple dinner. Once she signed away the house, she'd only have two days to move out. Regan would have the staging company take all the furniture away, and Sierra would ship some things back to the apartment in New York, spending one final night with Caleb before catching a flight back home.

Home. That word had changed a lot for her over the last year. This house had started to feel like home again, even with different furniture. Caleb and Smokey had started to feel like home. There was no drama in their relationship, even knowing that it would come to an end. She was surprised by how long the relationship, sexuationship, situationship, or whatever it was, had lasted. Everything with Caleb had been so easy. Even knowing that her sister was upstairs, sleeping above the café while she worked the early shift, had become as familiar as breathing. There was a sense of security in knowing where her sister was. A small regret tugged at her heart, but she had to convince her sister to go back to Seattle. She had to make sure Savannah let go of the café and the crazy idea that she could run it herself.

I'm ready to let it go, Sierra told herself, repeating the words like a mantra or just a reminder. *Let it go, let it go, let it go.* She had other goals to achieve. She had a career to build. She had a wealthy New York City tycoon to find and marry. Sierra had plenty of time to redefine home.

"Good luck tomorrow," Caleb said, kissing her goodbye for the night.

At the last second before he turned to walk to his truck, she grabbed his wrist. "Will you come?"

"To the closing?" he asked, clarifying.

Sierra nodded.

"Sure, I think I can get away. You said it's at 3?"

Sierra nodded again, too embarrassed by her desperate need to have him with her as she sold off her parents' legacy, not knowing how she would handle Savannah if her sister refused.

"Alright, I'll see you there," Caleb agreed and then kissed her again.

Sierra stood on the front porch, watching the evergreen trees her mother had planted year after year swaying in the light June breeze. One year ago, she was in New York with her friends, working a job she loved, and living her life. One year ago, she received a call from Caleb telling her that her parents had died. And Sierra had handled it. She'd come back to Lincoln, run the business for a year with her derelict sister, managed the house, coordinated the realtor, navigated the sales, and it would all be over tomorrow. She could then get back to handling her life exactly how she wanted to… just without Caleb.

Caleb being in Lincoln wasn't a problem she could solve. At least, not until she replaced him with someone in New York. She wasn't ready for a serious relationship anyway, so maybe they could continue their fling by meeting up during weekend trips until one of them found something more serious.

An unwelcome image of Caleb kissing someone more serious popped into her mind. The girl was young with bouncy blond curls, a mouth covered in bright red lipstick, and large breasts. Argh, Sierra hated that imaginary person immediately. Hated the idea of Caleb ever kissing anybody else. Crumbled at the thought of Smokey snuggling on the couch with another woman.

"Dammit," she said out loud to the June night air. "I've gotta let this go. All of it. The man. The dog. The house. The café. My parents." She looked out at the trees one last time. She was certain that the next owner would take care of them. As she walked back into the house, she knew there was one more thing she needed to let go of in order to truly move on with her life. Savannah.

The next morning, Sierra got up and headed into her last shift, driving the truck she would end up donating before flying out, or maybe just leaving it in the café parking lot with the keys still in it.

Sierra was honestly surprised that Zadie and Mario were still there, still working, still holding out hope that the place wouldn't sell and close. Of course, she'd told them and the two busboys that they could stay and work for Brothers & Barrels, but she wasn't sure what they had decided. It was really between them and their new employer.

A sign outside announced that the café would be closing for a remodel and then reopen under new ownership on July 1st. The morning was so slow that she probably could have run the entire thing herself. Zadie and Mario used the morning to clean up and prepare to hand the café over. Nobody spoke, and Sierra seemed to be the only one not in a completely dismal mood. She was feeling accomplished and optimistic, relieved that this year of entrapment was almost over. She was looking forward to returning to the big city and picking up her life from where she'd left it. She'd tried to compartmentalize her relationship with Caleb, moving it back to a file of 'fling' and long-distance rendezvous from time to time. She convinced herself that her sister would return to Seattle and that things would go back to how they'd been before their parents died. She tried to shove the nervous energy down, blaming it on too much coffee.

Sierra had scheduled the signing for 3:00, knowing that her sister would be coming down to start her shift. It was Sierra's way of ensuring that Savannah would be at the signing no matter what. It was also good timing because the café would be dead. Regan arrived first, hugging Sierra and congratulating her. The girls arranged a table, pulling two four-tops together to ensure enough space for the brothers to sit on one side and the sisters on the other, papers spread between them, with Regan and the notary on either end.

Caleb came in then, dressed in jeans and a T-shirt. He looked handsome in anything he wore, and she was glad she'd get one more night with him before flying out. Regan raised her eyebrows at Sierra, who went to kiss him in greeting.

She introduced them, mixed them cocktails, and made small talk. Sierra expected Barry and Bill to show up right at 3, along with a notary and whoever they brought to the signings. Savannah came out to pour herself coffee at 2:15. She was dressed in a long, flowery dress that Sierra hadn't seen her wear before. Her wavy hair, dirty blond roots reaching her ears, with faded black hair touching her shoulders, was somewhat tamed. With a coffee mug in hand, Savannah walked to the table and looked at Sierra.

"I'm not signing," Savannah said, her voice shaky despite trying to appear confident.

"We've been through this," Sierra said, a nervous feeling tingling up her spine. Her sister seemed so matter-of-fact and not her usual mousy timidness. She squared up her shoulders, the epitome of eldest daughter authority. "The plan was always to sell and go back to New York and Seattle. You can't run this place."

"I can and I will," Savannah said. "This is as much my place as yours, and I don't have to sell it if I don't want to. You can't make me. I don't want to go back to Seattle. This is my home. And I don't think we should sell Mom and Dad's house, either. One of us may want to raise a family there someday. We're only in our early twenties. We shouldn't be making this decision to let everything go and start over. We *need* this place. We *need* our parents. I *need* our home. I'm not leaving."

The café door opened, and everyone turned to look. Nobody expected the Montgomery brothers to show up this early, but Sierra knew it wasn't the brothers. She knew exactly who it was.

In walked Jaxon Steele.

34 SAVANNAH

Jaxon sauntered in like a movie star on the red carpet, expecting photos and autographs. He wore a brown leather jacket over a white shirt, even though the afternoon had been warm. His jeans were ripped to the point where shorts would have made more sense, and he carried a leather bag that Savannah knew to be his overnight bag. If he'd come to win her back, he had high expectations on how quickly that would happen.

"Savvy, baby," he started as soon as he saw her standing in the café. "Savannah," he corrected himself, lowering his voice and saying her name as if he was craving her. Jaxon dropped his bag and opened his arms wide, walking slowly and dramatically toward her.

Savannah's heart pounded in her chest. Despite all his faults, this was the rock star who'd stolen her heart with his charm, his voice, and his music. She had dedicated two years of her life waiting for him to look at her with the same intensity that she looked at him with: an admiring obsession for a beautiful and impressive thing. She had wanted him to desire her deeper than sex; to look in her eyes and see the Milky Way, stars that guided his destiny, that told him secrets of the universe and what forever meant. Savannah had spent many nights falling asleep worrying and wondering about whether or not Jaxon loved her. Savannah had considered that maybe she could do things, say things, ask things, feign things, or change herself in ways that would help Jaxon love her.

She had waited for phone calls and reread text messages, reading their meaning like tea leaves in a storm. But Savannah wasn't a psychic. She could hear Laurel, though, in her mind. Laurel would say, why now? Why, after all this time of you pining for him, has he finally shown up with arms literally wide open? Why was Jaxon showing up on the day she'd resolved to stay in Lincoln?

Savannah was finally finding the courage to stand up to her sister because today was the day they signed away their parents' legacy if she didn't. Today was about more than Savannah and her insecurities or fears when it came to standing up to her older sister. Today was about walking away with a pile of money, throwing away everything their parents had built, or doing something that scared the shit out of her.

If she were being honest with herself, Savannah knew that the easy road would be the one where she signed the papers on the lines where her sister and the realtor told her to sign. Money would be deposited into her account, and she would go back to her apartment in Seattle with Jaxon. Maybe they'd have a good enough life together, but she'd always be chasing him: his fame, his love, his affection, his acceptance. In his mind, she'd always be the woman who followed him, like a groupie, like a dreamer, like someone who didn't stand up for something she believed in when she had the chance.

The money would buy them luxuries. They could have their own room together on tour. They could have the great sex that worked with or without an emotional connection. She could see areas of the world she'd never seen before. Savannah would have fun, get drunk, stay up late, have sex, pass out, and do it all again the next day with a man who said he loved her, sometimes. And maybe the words would come less frequently over time, as they had. Maybe the words would stop coming. Maybe the feeling wouldn't be there, or the passion would fade. And maybe that would be OK in some relationships.

Savannah looked at the man standing in front of her, waiting with his arms open, but she did not go to him. There was a hesitation that she felt deep in her soul, like a message from the universe, and it told her that there was a man out there who would see his destiny when he looked into her eyes. Love shouldn't be something you beg for or hope for, or gain hundreds of thousands of dollars in inheritance for. Love shouldn't be something you chase and doubt and question.

"Jaxon, stop," Savannah said, putting her hand out. She was just as shocked by her words and movement as he was, the smile slipping slightly from his lips. Savannah was not a forceful person and had never spoken to Jaxon in that tone. "What are you doing here?"

Part of her hoped he was about to beg her to reconsider their engagement—the insecure part. She tried to shove that small voice back as she remembered the early days of their romance. He had charmed her with his words, showered her with compliments, accepting her for every flaw as if she'd been built by Zeus, carved into flesh by Michelangelo like some Goddess who had stolen his heart. He acted like a man willing to give up immortality for one night with her, and he'd gotten his prize. For two years, she'd withered away in an apartment, her only source of happiness being listening to live bands at the venue where she worked nights. The Drowned Note, Savannah remembered fondly. Then, looking around the café where she stood, she could see it. She could see how she would bring more local, small bands into the space, converting the café into a music venue at night and during special events in the summer. It was never Jaxon that she was so attracted to; it was the music. She knew she could bring the music here on her own.

Jaxon looked around the room too, making eye contact with Sierra first and then Regan. He didn't acknowledge that Caleb was there. Zadie and Mario came in from the kitchen, and all of a sudden, Jaxon had an audience. Something in his stance shifted to one of even more arrogant confidence. He was about to perform, she realized.

"*Baby,*" Jaxon started to sing.

"I see you there, glass in hand, laughing like you don't give a damn. But I know the way you fake that smile, like you ain't been hurting all this while.

We were wildfire, burning bright, never cared who saw the light. Now you're standing just out of reach, and all I can do is plead—

Come back to me, Savannah, like the tide returns to shore. Come back to me, darlin', like we ain't broken anymore. I was wrong, I was blind, but I swear if you give me time— I'll make you believe in us again.

Your name still lingers in my mouth, like whiskey that I can't wash down. Every song's got your ghost in the chords. And I can't fight it anymore.

Maybe it's too late— Maybe you've locked that door. But if there's still a key, Baby, it's right here in my voice.

Come back to me, Savannah, like the tide returns to shore. Come back to me, darlin', like we ain't broken anymore. I was wrong, I was blind, but I swear if you give me time— I'll make you believe in us again."

He'd inched closer and closer to her as he'd sung the song he'd clearly written just for her. It's every girlfriend's dream to have your rocker boyfriend write you a song, but it was a song she'd been waiting to hear for a long time. A song she should have had from him years before, not as a desperate last chance, not after she'd ended the relationship.

"Jaxon, why are you here?" Savannah asked her question again, as if he hadn't just sung her a song begging for her to take him back. Her arms were crossed so tightly across her chest that her fingers started to go numb. Nothing was going to break the barricade around her heart. Her eyes were narrowed, as if daring him to respond.

He looked around, a befuddled expression on his face. He met Sierra's eyes, but she just shrugged. Savannah's brow furrowed, wondering what their nonverbal exchange was about.

Zadie walked out from behind the bar and over to the jukebox behind them. After a few seconds, Taylor Swift's song, "We Are Never Ever Getting Back Together," started to play. Savannah tried not to smile.

"Savvy, I want you to come back to Seattle with me," Jaxon said, taking another step toward her. "I want us to be together again, like we were, out there. You'll get some money from this place, so you won't have to work as much. You can come to my shows, or go on tour with us. We can spend more time together. This is my big romantic gesture. You women love that shit."

Zadie scoffed loudly, and Regan mumbled, "Oh geez," under her breath. Millie came in through the back door carrying the briefcase Savannah knew held her parents' Will and the papers that proved they owned this place. The executor froze and looked around. "What did I miss?" Millie asked.

Savannah looked to Sierra and then back at her ex-boyfriend.

"My sister told you to try to win me back, didn't she?" Savannah asked, things suddenly clicking. Sierra had seemed so confident in Savannah changing her mind.

Sierra turned her head sharply to Savannah, but didn't deny it. Jaxon looked nervously from one woman to the other.

"Listen, babe," Jaxon started to say. "I really do love you. I want you to come back home with me. Let's get married. Let's travel the world."

It felt like the café was spinning around her. Savannah had spent her life as an easygoing person. She followed her older sister around like a puppy, doing whatever Sierra commanded in order to win her acceptance and affection. Climb a tree to pull down a stuck kite? Steal a piece of cake so they could eat it in the pantry? Once her parents got too busy with the business, Savannah followed her sister around even more, looking up to her, hoping to be like her. The gravity of the realization that she would never be like Sierra was crushing. And then her sister was just gone, off to NYC and leaving Savannah stuck alone at the business.

And then Jaxon had come along. Had he only seen a lost, lonely, insecure girl without direction? Had he seen a girl who could be easily brought along like a tote bag on adventures, keeping him company, being agreeable? Was he only trying so desperately to hold onto her now because he missed having the tote bag?

Oh God, Savannah realized. *Maybe I am just a groupie to him.* This wasn't a man finally realizing her value. This wasn't a man chasing her. This was a man who didn't want to lose.

It was true that Savannah had hoped for this day to come—the day Jaxon professed his love in a song, but now that it was here, now that she was starting to understand more about what she wanted to do with her life, and who she wanted to be, the less attractive his entire proposal felt.

"How can you turn down a man who shows up with a song?" Sierra asked, her voice high-pitched and breaking through Savannah's emotions like a fist on an ice-covered pond.

Savannah turned to her sister. "Did you put him up to this?" she asked, simply, directly, and with more confidence than she'd felt maybe ever.

Sierra rolled her eyes. "Oh my god, Savannah. Just look at the poor guy, missing you, pining over you. Let's just get this all over with so you can go back with him to Seattle." Sierra took a step toward Savannah and put her hands on her shoulders, like a big, older, wiser, protective sister would do. "You have done such a great job here, but Jaxon loves you. You have jobs and an apartment and friends and a whole life out there in Seattle. I'm going back to New York, and we can get together for visits. But you and I know that neither of us belongs here. Our parents belonged here, and now they're gone. We left for a reason, and now, we don't have a reason to ever come back. We say goodbye, and we head back to our lives. OK?"

Savannah blinked silently, processing the feeling of her sister's hands pressing down on her shoulders. There were flashbacks to her childhood. This was the same girl who had told on her when she'd taken a toy or stolen a treat. This was the same girl who had climbed onto her mother when she'd already been there, pushing Savannah aside because she was jealous of the attention. This was the same girl who had cheered her on when she'd learned how to ride a bike. This was the same girl who had pulled her out of the pool when she'd slipped off the last step and gone under the water. This was the same girl who had kissed her knee when she'd scraped it on the sidewalk. This was the same girl who had held her hand standing in line to go into elementary school for the first time. This was the same girl who had helped her pack a lunch and taken her to school after their parents had opened the café and had stopped being available. This was the same girl who had moved away, leaving her alone in Lincoln, to pursue her dreams in New York. Through good times and bad, thick and thin, love and loss, they were sisters. Sierra thought she was doing the right thing, Savannah realized. But we all make mistakes. Savannah had let others run her life for too long, but not anymore.

"I want to stay here," Savannah said. She didn't look at Jaxon. He didn't matter. She looked straight into Sierra's eyes, the mirror-image brown hazel eyes that shimmered yellow in sunlight.

Savannah had grown up with those eyes: in her own reflection, looking into her mother's eyes, and at her sister. She had always both feared and trusted those eyes, which caused her to feel lost within every hard decision she ever had to make. Would she be judged, admired, appreciated, loved, or filled with doubt?

This time, for once in her life, Savannah knew what she wanted. Her feet started to feel like concrete, sinking into the ancient hardwoods beneath them as her energy flowed, grounding into the roots of the woods she stood on. Like the trees her mother had planted in the front yard over the years, she could feel the space around her as a living thing. The floors, walls, ceilings all breathed with her, anxious but now confident and aware. She was the café. The café was alive in her. Her parents were there, begging her to stay. But something else…

Savannah wanted to run this business. She wanted to try to do something that scared the ever-living shit out of her. She'd never balanced a checkbook, let alone managed inventory or payroll. But if it kept Mario and Zadie here. If it held a space for Laurel and all of the regulars. If Waylon came back…

"This is too much for you, Savannah," Sierra said. "I think it's sweet that you want to keep this place alive for our parents, but this was their dream, not ours."

"You're wrong," Savannah said. "I didn't really have a dream like you did. I didn't know what I wanted to do with my life, but this last year has felt so amazing. I feel like I'm home. I feel happier than I have in a long time. This feels right, and I want to learn how to do this for the rest of my life. I can do this, Sierra. I want to do this."

Sierra's nostrils flared in frustration. "You can't run a business, Savannah. I'm sorry, but you can't. You are a bartender. You don't have a degree. You have no ambition. You make irrational, emotional decisions." Sierra pointed to Jaxon as an example, and the man stood there dumbfounded and clearly as scared of Sierra as Savannah was. "You can't do something like this." Sierra swept her arms around, indicating the entire business.

Savannah felt something she'd maybe never felt before. It was an emotion so unfamiliar that she could not have named it as it surged beneath her skin, burning like a sunburn. A rush of adrenaline flooded her heart and brain, and the sound of her soul beat in her eardrums at a deafening volume.

"Fuck you, Sierra!" Savannah yelled. "This is my café, and I will not let you sell it. Not now, not ever. I can run this place. I can do just as good a job as you and as our parents. I will not let you sell this to anyone."

"Yeah, we ain't selling to a couple of old white men!" Zadie yelled from out of nowhere. Clearly, she'd been thinking about that for a while.

Everybody looked to see Barry and Bill Montgomery standing inside the front doors. They were wearing sharp navy business suits with different shirts and ties. Savannah watched them look at one another, nod, like brothers on some silent wavelength, then turn and walk out.

"Wait!" Sierra and Regan yelled, running after them.

35 SIERRA

Sierra chased Barry and Bill through the front door. "Wait! Please!" she called to them. Both men stopped on the sidewalk, standing in front of a very nice black car illegally parked, and turned toward her with scowls on their faces.

"I am so sorry for my sister," Sierra started, her hands outstretched in a non-threatening but pleading motion. "She's young and has a crazy notion that she could run this place on her own. Perhaps we could arrange where she can continue working here after the transaction? She lives above the bar, in the apartment, so she's worried about having to move. You know how it is, right? Could you come back inside, and we can talk about how to make a deal that ensures Savannah doesn't end up homeless and jobless?"

The brothers looked at one another, having a silent conversation, as only two siblings who had worked together successfully for decades could. Barry, the oldest brother, stepped forward and placed a hand on Sierra's shoulder. He looked at her and then at the people she guessed were standing behind her in the doorway. His eyes back on hers, he said, "Listen, I understand how hard it can be to have to consider someone else in the decisions you make. I've been doing it my entire life. First, with my brother, and then we both had to consider our wives and children in each and every decision. It is not easy, and I don't blame you for being frustrated. We have other businesses lined up here, so we are not locked into this place."

Barry motioned to the building with his free hand. Sierra's heart sank with every word she heard. She knew they'd decided to move on from buying the café, and it gutted her. She felt the panic of anxiety begin to fill her chest.

"But you," Barry continued, squeezing her shoulder to emphasize the recipient of his unsolicited advice, "you and your sister are connected to this place and connected to each other because of this place. Even though you are both young, and even though you may not think you and your sister are ready to own and run a place like this, it's in your blood, in your history, in your parents, and is now your legacy. You've been given an opportunity here that a lot of young people, new adults, would kill to have. Unfortunately, it came at the tragic loss of your parents, but they had faith that you two young women could work together here and be successful. And you have been. Regardless of your hesitation, this has been a good year for you both."

"How do you know that?" Sierra asked, feeling a little stalked.

"We investigate our potential acquisitions thoroughly," Barry answered. "My brother and I are not surprised by what we walked into this afternoon. You two will be fine. Remember that your parents trusted you both with this business."

Then Barry released her shoulder, and the two men prepared to climb into their car, which was already running, with a man dressed in all black sitting behind the wheel.

Worry and doubt flooded Sierra's mind. Savannah wasn't ready to run a business. She wasn't ready to process payroll, manage inventory, keep books, or pay taxes. "She's not ready!" Sierra shouted at the men.

It was Bill, who was on the passenger side of the car, who turned back to her to respond. "Nobody ever is," he said. Then they both climbed into the back of the car and were gone. There was another hand on her shoulder now, and she knew it was Caleb. Half of her wanted to curl up into his arms and cry. The other half wanted to push him away, storm back into the café, and yell at her sister until she crumbled and gave up and sold the damn café. Instead, she stood frozen in shock and indecision.

"You OK?" Caleb asked, his voice quiet and calm.

"No," she answered honestly.

One hand still on her shoulder, he slid that hand down to the small of her back and softly ushered her over to one of the patio chairs at a small bistro table out front. The day was starting to feel almost too warm, but in the shade of the canopy, a light breeze made it tolerable. Mainly working mornings and afternoons, she missed seeing this patio alive in the late evenings. People would smoke, drink, laugh, and even sing under the warm patio lights that cast a romantic glow, almost magical, over the patrons. Joy. That's what she always felt this patio created.

Sierra sat down, and Caleb sat beside her, reaching his hands across the table just in case she needed to touch him and anchor herself in him. He was so thoughtful and patient, she knew. Sierra worried that going back to New York City meant never finding a man like this. He just looked at her, watching her process through her thoughts and anxious energy.

Sierra finally put her hands on his, and he curled his palms over to protectively encapsulate hers. A feeling of calm comfort washed over her. She reflected for a moment on how wonderful and strange that was: touching someone, causing a shift in her own energy. "I don't know what to do now," she admitted, feeling vulnerable. She was used to being able to control most situations, but her sister… that wild creature was one thing Sierra thought she had tamed. "Savannah not signing the papers completely messes up my plans."

"The plans to go back to New York?" Caleb asked, clarifying.

"Yes, exactly," she said.

"How does her running the café change your plans? You can go back to New York now anytime. Maybe you don't have the money, as you'd hoped, but wouldn't you be going back to the same job, same apartment, just like the last year didn't happen?"

Caleb seemed to swallow something down, a lump in his throat? He squeezed her hands. She understood. If last year didn't happen, it meant that this relationship didn't happen, or at least, didn't mean anything to her. But this relationship did mean something to Sierra. It was almost too much to think about the next step of flying back to New York City now without this man. He'd become a constant, a comfort, and she thought she could even…

No, she shook her head. Sierra was not going to admit to herself that she had fallen for this man. He was a small-town fireman, and she was a big-city, high-fashion, future executive.

"You wouldn't be going back to the same apartment?" Caleb asked, responding to her shaking her head at him without explanation.

"No, I mean, yes, I would," Sierra clarified. "You're right that I'd go back to the same job, same apartment, same friends—but this year *did* happen, and it *did* mean something to me. I met you. I've loved being with you, and I don't want to think about what leaving you means. I know I'm only twenty-five, but I've never felt this good. I've never felt this safe with someone who wasn't my mom or my sister." The admission kicked hard in her gut, and she pulled her hands to her face, hiding her tears behind them.

Caleb touched her fingers gently and pulled her hands back down, looking into her eyes with deep concern and affection.

"Sierra, I need you to know that because of you, my life will never be the same," Caleb said. "I've fallen completely in love with you, but I would never ask you to stay. I'm proud of how committed you are to accomplishing your goals, and I want to be by your side as you do, but if this is it for us, I'll say goodbye, but I just thought you should know that I do love you. I am so grateful that I was able to love you for the time that we had together."

A sob came out of her chest, surprising her. It was followed by another one until she was barreled over in Caleb's lap, completely lost in his words and the overwhelming emotions. She didn't know how long she cried, but Caleb held her without impatience. She knew he would have held her there for hours, forever, if she needed it. Was she really ready to walk away from a man like this? But she couldn't give up her dreams either, not for anybody.

Sierra's sobs finally died down, air flowing back in and out of her lungs in a regular pattern. "Come with me to New York," she said, shocking herself again. The words were a faint whisper, but they were out.

"What?" Caleb asked. He gently helped guide her back up to sitting, looking each other in the eyes.

"Come with me," she repeated. And she knew she was serious. "Move with me back to New York City. I don't want to lose you and Smokey," she admitted to him and to herself for the first time.

"You're sure?" he asked, his eyebrows lowering tightly over his eyes.

She nodded. She was sure. Sierra had judged Savannah for following Jaxon to Seattle. Her sister had no goals, no dreams, no objective other than chasing the stars in her eyes. But Sierra loved this man. This was the first man she'd ever loved, and the realization that she could lose him forever hit her with desperation.

"I love you," Sierra said. He cupped her face into his hands and searched her eyes, as if trying to confirm that she was serious about the words, the offer, them, everything. And then he closed the space between them and kissed her hard.

She wasn't sure how long they sat outside, but she knew there was still more to take care of.

"I have to talk to Savannah," Sierra told Caleb.

"Do you really not trust her to run this place?" he asked.

"She's just always been so flaky and irresponsible. Messy. Complicated."

"We are all a little bit of those things," Caleb said, raising an accusatory eyebrow. "Maybe a year wasn't enough time. Maybe you could help coach her, teach her how to run the business from New York. Nobody comes into a new job knowing how to do everything. Well, maybe you do, but regular people need training."

He smiled, and she shoved him, lightly. Something had shifted. She felt happier, less stressed, knowing that she could go back to New York City and that this man would figure out a way to come with her.

"In the last year, have you seen your sister fail at anything here?" Caleb asked.

"Other than agreeing to marry Jaxon? No. I guess not. Oh God, he's still in there, and it's all my fault. He might be in there lecturing her on all the reasons she should marry him, sell the place, and go back to Seattle." Sierra dropped her head into her hands, ashamed. She was the one who had called Jaxon and convinced him to come to Lincoln and beg Savannah to go back to Seattle with him. Sierra figured that if her sister had a good enough reason to leave, that she'd sign the papers and sell the properties. She was trying to force her sister onto a man she knew Savannah no longer loved. "This is my fault."

"Then go in there and make it right," Caleb said. "Just know before you do that, I love you, and I'm going to come with you because you want me to.

Smokey and I will leave all this behind for you. Your love is worth that. What is your sister's love worth to you?"

Sierra hated how emotional she'd been in the last hour or maybe twenty minutes. But Caleb was right. She did love her sister, and she wanted Savannah to be happy and successful. She took a deep breath, stood up, and with Caleb at her side, walked back into Sweetwater Café and Bar.

Savannah was hysterical and seemingly inconsolable. She was pacing back and forth, tears streaming down her face, and wringing her hands. Zadie and Millie were trying to talk to her, trying to calm her down. Jaxon was looking lost and overwhelmed, his arms in the air, hands pressed against either side of his face. Regan sat at the table, nonchalantly flipping through the paperwork that started this mess in the first place.

Sierra walked right up to Savannah and grabbed the young woman by her arms, holding her still. "Hey," Sierra said, "let's talk."

Savannah looked shocked and maybe a little scared, but nodded through her tears.

"Come on," Sierra commanded, pulling her sister back behind the bar. Although Savannah had seemingly won the day, Sierra knew her sister. She was still emotionally reeling from standing up for herself, fear of losing the place despite her efforts, frustration with Jaxon's presence, and probably angry with her.

Sierra pulled down two glasses, dropped in ice, then poured them two giant servings of Irish whiskey. Savannah stood and watched until the glass was in her hand. Then Sierra clinked her glass to her sister's, and they both drank. The cool liquid warmed them from the inside out, sending a wave of calm through them. Savannah's tears finally stopped spilling.

"I'm sorry, Savannah."

Savannah blinked, her face squinting into confusion. "What?"

"I want to go back to New York City," Sierra said, nothing surprising there. "And yes, the money from the sale of these properties would really help me get a bigger, nicer place. It would make our lives easier, but it would be running away. Staying in Lincoln was never part of my plan, and when you went to Seattle, I thought maybe it wasn't part of your plan either. I was wrong. If you want to stay. If you want to keep running this place, live in Lincoln, I think that's great for you. I shouldn't tell you what to do with your life, who to love, or anything, really. We're adults. Young adults, but still. We can figure all of this out."

Sierra motioned to the café around them. And for the first time, she was starting to believe it. She could help her sister run this place from New York. Sierra would manage her career, Caleb would get a job as a firefighter in the city, and maybe they'd figure out how to get a place together.

"We can rent out our parents' house, if you want to stay here," Sierra said, agreeing to Savannah's idea. If she were getting some rental income from Lincoln, it could help her pay toward a new place with Caleb in New York. Then Savannah could keep the money she made at the café.

"Wait, wait, wait," Savannah said, shaking her head and holding up her hands. "You aren't going to fight me on this?" Savannah looked hesitantly at the front door. "Those two men aren't going to come back in here and force me to sign or threaten legal action?"

"No," Sierra admitted. "It's over. I can't force you to sign. I clearly can't trick you into signing." Sierra waved a hand loosely toward Jaxon, who was taking a verbal beating from Zadie.

"Hey," Regan said, stepping up to the sisters. "I'm going to remove the listings, but I can convert the house to a rental listing. I know a couple of local management companies if you don't want to run that yourselves. Just let me know."

"Thanks, Regan," Sierra said. "Sorry this didn't go as expected."

"Money comes and goes," Regan said. "It's a lesson I've learned in this business. "Family will always be more important." Then the woman smiled and headed out.

"I still can't believe you aren't going to fight me or yell at me, at least," Savannah said, wiping away the last of her tears before taking a sip of whiskey.

Guilt washed over Sierra, a feeling she wasn't familiar with, but identified it immediately. "I'm sorry I've been so hard on you. I was mad at Mom and Dad more than you. I was so focused on getting back to New York that I lost sight of… no, I just didn't care about what this whole thing meant to you." She felt a tear start to sting behind her eye, but before she could blink it back, Savannah threw her arms around Sierra. Their drinks spilled, but neither girl dropped her glasses. They were getting stronger at holding on.

36 SIERRA

Regan was disappointed at losing the potential commission on properties valued at nearly one million dollars, but she pivoted into property manager, willing to take a smaller commission on finding a nice family to rent the Sweetwater family home and keep things up and running and well-maintained. The house had only been listed as a rental for a few weeks, but was already receiving healthy interest.

Sierra was sweating in the muggy July heat, carrying a box of mementos to place into the trailer that Caleb had rented to tow behind his truck. They were packing the last of their things before driving to their new, small apartment in New York City.

Claire had worked her real estate connections to find something clean and affordable, a task she assured Sierra would be impossible for someone without connections. Claire also told Sierra that the girl who had been sub-leasing her small room had fit in wonderfully with all the young women. They'd asked her to be a permanent roommate, so Sierra didn't have to feel guilty about not returning to take back over her lease.

Caleb had easily obtained a firefighter position at one of the many NYC firehouses. He would be starting his new position as soon as they arrived and unpacked after the four-day drive.

Sierra's manager at Fytté was excited to have her back to take a large project off her plate. Things had fallen into place during the rest of June, and Sierra was ready to say goodbye to her childhood home, Sweetwater Café and Bar, and to her hometown for *now,* instead of goodbye *forever.*

"That it, babe?" Caleb asked. His calves looked sexy beneath the ends of his khaki shorts, and his muscles bulged from the tank top he wore.

"Yeah, I think that's it," she said. "I'm ready when you are."

Sierra locked up the house, depositing the key into the lockbox. Caleb opened the passenger side door to his truck for her, and Smokey jumped into the back to make room for her. Sierra was now a girlfriend and a dog mom. A year ago, she'd come to Lincoln knowing exactly what boxes to check to accomplish a task, but she was leaving her hometown as a completely new person. One she hadn't expected to become at all.

She climbed up, turned around to rub Smokey's head, then buckled in. They pulled out of the driveway and onto the street. Sierra watched the 'for rent' sign get smaller until it disappeared behind the decades of trees her mother had planted and nurtured. She was surprised at how relieved she felt that this wouldn't be the last time she'd ever see her childhood home.

Caleb pulled the truck and trailer up to the café, parking along the curb in the front. "Five minutes," Sierra said as she jumped down and ran inside.

Savannah was on the other side of the bar, leaning onto the counter. It was mid-afternoon, so there were only a couple of people eating late lunches or enjoying an early happy hour before the college kid rush. Since Savannah had taken over, she had hired additional employees and taken lessons from Sierra on how to run payroll and inventory. Millie had also stepped up to help train Savannah in accounting basics for free.

When Sierra walked in, Savannah's eyes lit up, and she came around the bar. Both sisters embraced in a hug that felt more and more healing. Pulling back, Sierra felt immense pride for her little sister, who had not only finally stood up for herself but also found joy and purpose. Maybe Sierra had been wrong all along. Maybe her sister was always meant to carry on their parents' legacy of serving their community. What Sierra only saw as coffee and whiskey, Savannah and their parents had seen something else. They'd seen the people, the regulars, the new visitors, the conversations, the tears, the dancing, and the memories.

"You're leaving?" Savannah asked.

"Yes," Sierra said. "We're all packed up, and aside from stopping for gas and snacks, we're on our way."

"I'm so excited for you," Savannah said, smiling from ear-to-ear.

"I'm excited too," Sierra admitted. "This is all new for me, but it feels good. Leaving Lincoln isn't new. Going to NYC isn't new. But going with a man? A boyfriend?" Sierra chuckled as if she couldn't believe she had actually committed to a man. "But being with Caleb feels right, and Smokey… he's like my child now."

Both women laughed and hugged again.

"How long is the drive?" Savannah asked.

"Leaving today, we'll drive about five hours a day," Sierra said. "I've plotted out a schedule of hotel stops that allow dogs. It will take us about four days, twenty hours of driving, so I want to make sure we have plenty of rest breaks."

"Gross," Savannah teased.

"I know. But we'll take it slow and stop at a few places along the way. We will want to let Smokey get his zoomies out."

"Aw," Savannah said, her face sincere. "You really are a dog mom now. Keep me updated on your trip. Be safe."

"We will."

The sisters embraced again, Sierra holding on to her little sister tightly. They had lost their parents, and even though the year hadn't gone at all according to Sierra's plan, Sierra was glad she wouldn't be losing her sister, too. If Savannah had gone back to Seattle, married that loser, signed everything away, she may never have forgiven Sierra. She was actually grateful now that they wouldn't lose what their parents had built for them, and they wouldn't lose where they'd come from.

They said their goodbyes, and Sierra took one last look around at the old tables, the wood floors and beams, and the juke box, before heading outside to climb back into Caleb's truck. As they rolled out of town, Smokey's head hung out of the window behind her, and Sierra said a quiet, temporary farewell. She felt good knowing she could come back to this place. She'd be back to visit her sister, Lincoln, her childhood home, and Sweetwater Café and Bar, just as her parents had intended.

37 SAVANNAH

Savannah wiped away tears watching her sister leave the café. Although she was sad to see Sierra leave, she had never felt happier. In just a few weeks, she'd taken over the business activities with ease. Her years spent working at this place and others, actually made her perfectly equipped to handle it. Sierra and Millie had both contributed valuable lessons in accounting, hiring, payroll, taxes, inventory, and more.

Savannah hired part-time help for the peak hours, and she started looking for Zadie's replacement. Zadie had graduated, and as her mother had hoped, had already gotten a job offer at a local credit union as a personal banker. Luckily, the credit union was downtown, and so Zadie would be able to stop in for coffee and lunch regularly. Although Savannah would miss having Zadie by her side, she was proud that the young woman had found something she was interested in.

The café was dead this late in the afternoon, but with the July 4th holiday coming up that weekend, she expected it to pick up sooner than later. Savannah looked around from the wood floors to the wood beams and felt proud of herself, too. This place was hers, and she was running it. She could stay here and live in the apartment upstairs for as long as she wanted. She could keep an eye on her childhood home, reconnect with childhood friends, be a part of Zadie's life, and be truly happy. There was only one thing missing, but she knew it was only a matter of time before the small-town rumor mill did its work.

The door chimed as it opened, and a tall man walked in. He was silhouetted by the sun behind him, but the wide brim of his cowboy hat was unmistakable. Savannah knew him by the way he moved, the way he walked toward her with a wide-leg saunter of a hard-working man who had grown up riding horses.

She tilted her head back, looking higher and higher the closer he came, a smile spreading across her face like wildfire.

"I heard you decided to stay and run this place," Waylon said. His voice was deep and sent a feeling like thunder rumbling throughout her body. Her heart beat so hard in her chest she could hear it in her ears.

Savannah was so nervous, she couldn't speak, although she'd thought about this moment a thousand times. After the Christmas Party, when they'd taken all the decorations down, she had pocketed the sprig of mistletoe the two of them had stood under right before Jaxon had stormed into the café. She'd pressed the mistletoe between the pages of one of her dad's old books in the apartment upstairs, and then, after taking over the café and bar, she'd slipped the sprig beneath the counter into a shot glass. She'd told everyone it was there for a reason and not to move it. The reason was tall, handsome, and watching her expectantly.

Savannah reached down and pulled the shot glass up, setting it onto the counter, the sprig of dried mistletoe nestled inside. Waylon looked down at it, confused, but then a look of recognition spread across his face.

"What's this?" he asked, a smile curling up his lips.

"Mistletoe," she said, remembering how they'd almost kissed beneath it. "*The* mistletoe." She dreamed about the kiss that hadn't happened, wished for it every night since. Even the nights when she was with her ex-fiancé, it was always Waylon's face dipped toward hers, mistletoe hanging above their heads, that came flashing back over and over.

"I kept it just in case you want another *shot*," Savannah explained, playing on the pun of the sprig in the shot glass. "Just in case you—."

Waylon flew around the bar, lifted her chin, and bent down, closing the distance between them as fast as lightning touching the ground in a storm. She had a whole speech planned, but he kissed her before she could say another word about wanting to be his usual from now on, and hopefully, forever.

The End.

Dear Reader,

Thank you for reading my women's fiction novel. If you enjoyed it, please consider leaving me a review on Amazon or Goodreads. Every review helps me continue spreading the message of female empowerment, strength, and overcoming trauma.

Find me on Goodreads:
https://www.goodreads.com/author/show/19938302.Tiffany_Nicole_Terry

And follow me on Amazon:
https://www.amazon.com/author/tiffanynicoleterry

Thank you,
Tiffany Nicole Terry (a.k.a. TNT)
TNTauthor.com

www.ingramcontent.com/pod-product-compliance
Lightning Source LLC
LaVergne TN
LVHW010857110826
845149LV00005B/1417

* 9 7 9 8 9 9 4 6 5 6 2 0 4 *